Glamour *in*
Glass

TOR BOOKS BY MARY ROBINETTE KOWAL

Shades of Milk and Honey
Glamour in Glass

Glamour *in* Glass

Mary Robinette Kowal

A Tom Doherty Associates Book
New York

GLAMOUR IN GLASS

Copyright © 2012 by Mary Robinette Kowal

Reading Group Guide copyright © 2012 by Tor Books

A Tor Book
Published by Tom Doherty Associates, LLC
175 Fifth Avenue
New York, NY 10010

www.tor-forge.com

Tor® is a registered trademark of Tom Doherty Associates, LLC.

ISBN 978-0-7653-2557-0

First Edition: April 2012

Printed in the United States of America

0 9 8 7 6 5 4 3 2 1

For Mom and Dad

If not for you, I would not be a writer, nor

have the courage to submit.

Thank you for teaching me that the arts

are important.

Mary wished to say something very

sensible, but knew not how.

—Jane Austen, *Pride and Prejudice*

Glamour *in* Glass

One

Dinner Conversation

Finding oneself a guest of honour only increases the presentiment of anxiety, should one be disposed to such feelings. Jane Vincent could not help but feel some measure of alarm upon hearing her name called by the Prince Regent, for though she fully expected to be escorted into dinner by someone other than her husband, she had not expected to accompany His Royal Highness and to be seated at his right hand. Though this was but an intimate dinner party of eighteen, by the order of precedence her place should be at the rear of the line. Yet one could hardly express such doubts to His Royal Highness The Prince of Wales, Regent of the United Kingdom of Great Britain, Faerie, and Ireland.

The only title Jane could claim on her own was that of Mrs. David Vincent, and her entire claim for being invited at all lay in her marriage to the Prince Regent's favourite glamourist. As they exited Carlton House through a tented hall, Jane felt all the eyes of those assembled fall upon her, and under their gaze the unequal nature of her station magnified. The dove silk which had seemed so fine when she had commissioned it last summer now seemed dingy by comparison to gowns such as Lady Hertford's rich claret velvet, which had long sleeves slashed to allow glimpses of a cloth of silver. Her mother had wanted to buy her a new gown, but Jane had resisted. She was an artisan now, and had no intention of pretending to be part of the fashionable set . . . and yet, being escorted by the Prince Regent made that choice seem less easy now.

But all that worry fell away upon entering the Polygon Ballroom, which glittered and dripped with diaphanous folds of glamour hung to create the illusion of a water folly filled with mermaids and sea-horses. She and Vincent had laboured for the past three months on the spectacle and they could justly be proud of the effect, though she would have to retouch the anemones when she had a chance. The colour was off when compared to the palette of this winter's fashions.

The Prince Regent stopped with her on the threshold of the temporary structure and inhaled with pleasure.

They had taken the Polygon Ballroom, designed by Mr. John Nash for the fête honouring the defeat of Napoleon, and transformed it for the coming New Year's Eve celebration by refashioning it into the home of a sea king. Elaborate swathes of glamour masked the walls so that they appeared to be in the midst of a coral palace with views onto an under-sea world. Past the casements of the illusory walls, brilliant tropical fish schooled in waves of shimmering colour. Light seemed to filter down through clear blue water to lay dappled on the smooth white tablecloths.

The Prince Regent smiled and patted her hand where it lay on the dark blue cloth of his sleeve. "My dear Mrs. Vincent. I have long been an admirer of your husband's work, but you have led him to new heights of glory."

"You honour me, far more than I think I deserve."

"I honour you as much as *I* think you deserve, and you must grant that my wishes are the law in this land."

Jane let him lead her swiftly across the vast ballroom to the head of the table and place her by the chair on his right hand. Only then did Jane understand the true gift the Prince Regent offered her. They had far outpaced the guests immediately behind them, who paused on the threshold, apparently overcome by the room. As the line forced them forward, they proceeded toward the table, but slowly, with eyes fixed in wonder on the illusion. Stationed as she was, Jane stood in a perfect place to witness the guests' approbation over and over again as even the most jaded halted to gasp upon the threshold.

Their faces shone with wonder at the work she and Vincent had created.

As the last couple approached, His Royal Highness leaned over and whispered in her ear. "Now watch."

Her husband stood on the threshold, escorting Lady Hertford. The Prince Regent began to applaud, and, as one, his guests joined him in honouring Mr. Vincent. Jane did not know whether to applaud with them out of her own deep admiration for her husband, or if she should remain silent, since she had borne half the burden of the work about them. She settled for folding her hands at her breast and letting forth an unfettered smile.

Vincent paused, clearly taken unawares by this open show of approbation. He inclined his head gravely, then, straightening, led Lady Hertford to the foot of the table and her place at his right hand. Never comfortable in company, the sternness of his face hid what Jane knew to be very real feeling.

The Prince Regent reached for his glass and raised it. "To Mr. Vincent and to his bride, who shows us that he is no longer a glamourist without peer."

Jane blushed at the attention as every head turned to her. She could see them recalculating her worth and now understanding why the Prince Regent had led such an unhandsome woman into dinner. Under the weight of their stares, her gaze fell to the table, taking refuge among the plate and crystal assembled there. Her relief when the Prince pulled her chair out and seated her could scarcely be imagined.

Accustomed as she was to the more retiring life on her father's country estate, Jane had not looked for any honours when she married Mr. Vincent. The few months of their marriage had been filled with work and the joy of learning to shape their lives together. This commission had seemed honour enough when it had come, almost as if it were a wedding gift from the Prince Regent.

Around them, the footmen began bringing out the first course, a turtle soup. Jane was glad to have the activity distract attention from her. She took advantage of the respite to gather herself so that when the Prince Regent next addressed her, she was better prepared for conversation.

The initial topics were of such amicable and unforced weight as the weather, and if she thought it might snow on the morrow. She did not and said so.

This relieved his royal highness, as the press of carriages expected for the New Year's Eve festivities would be immense. By the time the soup was cleared, Jane felt somewhat more at ease and was able to engage the Prince Regent in a conversation about music, a topic on which they shared some common ground.

"You must allow that Rossini is far superior to the froth that Spohr is passing off as composition. It confounds me that the Italian fellow is not better known." The Prince Regent selected an oyster from the array of dishes the footman laid upon the table with the next course.

"I have not had the privilege of hearing his music performed in earnest, so I am not a good judge, I am afraid."

He huffed. "You only have to examine the page to see the difference between them. One's music flows with the inevitability of a stream, the other staggers from theme to theme like a drunken beggar." He lifted his glass and nodded over it to the gentleman on her left. "Am I not right, Skiffy?"

On her left, Sir Lumley St. George Skeffington abandoned the conversation with his dinner partner to answer. "Of course you are right. When are you ever not? But what is it that you are right about this time?"

"I suggest that Rossini is superior to Spohr."

"Oh." Sir Lumley waved his hand in dismissal. "I do not follow such things. Ask me about a tailor, and I might honour you with an opinion."

The Prince Regent smiled, and glanced sidelong at Jane. "Then pray, tell me what you think of Monsieur Lecomte?"

"Oh! Horrid. Horrid, I tell you. I have never seen a man with less understanding of the nature of cloth than he displays. Why, did you know that I went in on the recommendation of a friend, whose advice I shall not favour henceforth, and M. Lecomte had the temerity to suggest superfine cloth? To me?" He took out a perfumed handkerchief and patted his forehead. "I turned on my heel and left without another sign. It was clear he was not *current.*"

Smiling, the Prince Regent adjusted the sleeve of his coat, which was, Jane was startled to note, cut from superfine cloth. "So, you see, Mrs. Vincent, he does not always agree with me."

Sir Lumley leaned back in his chair in a show of mock horror. "Now, Prinny, you do not mean to tell me that you have honoured M. Lecomte with your business?"

"I was, I confess, curious to see how a man who claimed to have worked for Napoleon might measure against our good English tailors."

Jane smiled in polite interest. When the silence seemed to indicate that it was her turn to speak, she ventured to ask, "How did you find him sir?"

The Prince considered for a moment and then offered a single word. "Foppish."

"And yet you wear the coat he made for you?" Jane studied the coat. It was cut along French lines, but she had begun to grow used to that as the fashionable set raced to catch up with the other side of the Channel. "Might I inquire as to why?"

"It amuses me."

Jane was uncertain if that amusement stemmed from the tailor or from the near apoplexy he had brought on in Sir Lumley. Her attention was distracted from this question, for, in examining the Prince's coat, she happened to spy the glamural beyond him. She could barely stifle an "Oh!" at what she beheld and kept her countenance placid only with some difficulty.

Behind a window in the coral, they had placed a school of iridescent fish, swimming past at intervals. The effect had been achieved by measuring out a long spool of thin glamour, which contained no illusion save for occasional bubbles, and then looping it around to tie to the fish. Though Jane had used such threads of empty space before, she had worked with none so long as this. It had required her to stand in one place to control the thread for exactly as long as she had wanted the interval to be. Her husband had but recently showed her his technique of braiding seemingly similar threads together at somewhat different lengths to create the appearance of random intervals. Jane had created the fish thrice, one that came at three minutes, one at five, and one at eight. It created the illusion of but one school of fish, swimming past at random moments.

And yet, as she watched, two schools of fish went by hard on the tails of one another.

"Do you not think so, Mrs. Vincent?" His royal highness leaned close to her, smiling.

Jane straightened in her seat, alarmed that she had lost track of the conversation. "I could hardly dare to venture an opinion."

"You do your husband wrong, if you should not vouch for him."

She would do her husband more wrong if her fears about the fish were correct, and yet to admit that she had been ignoring the Prince would not do. Jane sought for some answer that would serve. "But you see, sir as his wife I am over-partial to him and cannot be trusted to give an unbiased opinion. I must bow to yours."

"Then I will make it so, and trust that it give you some pleasure as well." The Prince Regent lifted the asparagus tongs and offered her a few delicate spears.

Jane nodded her assent, without having the least idea of what he would make so, while darting glances at the window where the fish appeared. If she unfocused her attention on the tangible world and let her vision slip into that realm of ether where the folds of glamour lay, she could study the thread as it flowed past. From watching others, she knew that such distraction gave her countenance a somewhat insipid expression which might be appealing on certain beauties, but not on her own unassuming plainness. It was too at odds with the sharpness of her features to be pleasing.

The knot went past. It had, as Jane suspected, slipped. What alarmed her more was that it showed every sign that it was on the verge of coming untied altogether. She tried to remember what she had fixed that thread of glamour around.

"And have you been to the Continent before, Mrs. Vincent?"

The question brought Jane's attention back to the table. "I have not sir."

"Then I suggest avoiding the north of France when you go, though I cannot remember where Mr. Vincent said his colleague lived. Still, I counsel against it, as well as parts of Spain and Italy. While Napoleon has abdicated, there are still factions that would seek to put his son on the throne. I think it shall be calmed by the time you travel, but you must let me make some arrangements for your tour."

Jane was all astonishment. To the best of her knowledge, neither she nor Vincent had spoken of going abroad, and yet the Prince Regent spoke as if it were a certainty that they would go. "Sir—"

He held up his hand. "Mrs. Vincent, you must do me the favour of not using my honorific with every sentence. It does wear on one. In an intimate setting such as this, I would rather be reminded that I dine with friends than that I am Prince. I shall have enough of that tomorrow, and while it does have its merits, one enjoys it only for a time."

He referred, of course, to the grand opening of the ballroom to the public, in which he would dine in great state. Once the ballroom was open, there would be no opportunity for repairs. Jane would have to attend to the fish as soon as dinner had completed, lest they unravel farther.

"Of course . . . and yet, one must call you something."

"Oh, as to that"—Lord Lumley again disregarded his duties to his dinner partner to drawl—"we all call him 'Prinny.' I dare say he would like you to do the same."

"Oh yes, would you do me that kindness?"

"And you shall call me Skiffy." Lord Lumley leaned in close. "We are all terribly fond of you, for your husband's sake."

Not for her own, but this could hardly surprise Jane. She attempted a smile while trying to recall where the thread of glamour went. "Thank you for the honour. And have you known each other long?" In this manner, she hoped to distract the gentlemen to talk between themselves. No matter how rude that might make Lord Lum—Skiffy to his dinner partner, it would grant her some brief span in which to puzzle out the fish. While Vincent had created glamurals this elaborate before, if perhaps on a smaller scale, it was the most intricate work which Jane had yet attempted, and the sheer number of threads, folds, weaves, and braids of glamour overwhelmed her memory.

"Prinny had come down to Eaton for a fête back when your husband was still a Hamil—" Skiffy cleared his throat, just avoiding pronouncing the name that Vincent had renounced. "Even in those days Vincent had the reputation of being a curmudgeon. Though we were all terribly fond of him."

Jane's attention was now split in two. On the one hand, she worried about the fish, for, if on their first commission together, she introduced a flaw into their work, it would not bode well for their future projects. And yet, Vincent so rarely talked about his life before giving up his family name to pursue his art that her curiosity was piqued beyond all else.

"Your husband had glamoured the clock tower so it showed the time backwards!" The Prince—Prinny— threw his head back and laughed.

Skiffy resumed the tale. "Oh, the deans were furious at that one, because he had managed to tie the glamour off so it did not show in the least. In any case, they could not conceive of how someone might have climbed the clock tower to weave one. Which showed your husband's cleverness, for he did not ascend the tower at all."

"No? How did he do it then?" Jane's interest in her question faltered almost at once as she finally traced the thread of glamour to its source. The fish's trailing line was wrapped around the support for the coral reef comprising the wall opposite her. She had thought herself exceedingly clever for finding a way to contain it thus without having to loop the thread into the earth for stability, but the trouble she now faced was that if the knot came undone all at once, it might snag and cause an unravelling in the wall as well.

Prinny chuckled again. "Your husband created it from the base of the tower."

Jane choked on her turbot at this and had to hold her serviette to her lips to stifle her coughing. The Prince patted her on the back, and passed her a glass of water.

"Thank you." She cleared her throat, conscious of once again attracting more attention from the table than she might have wished.

At the foot of the table, Vincent studied her, his brows raised in concern. She gave him the smallest shake of her head to let him know that she did not require his aid, though she desperately wished that she were seated near him. One of the distinct disadvantages of being married was that one never sat with one's spouse when dining in company.

Giving the Prince Regent her attention, Jane kept her composure smooth. "Though I above all should be partial to my husband's talents, still I find my credulity stretched by this."

Even with her deep admiration for her husband's skills, Jane could scarcely imagine the sheer strength it would take to work glamour from such a distance. As with a small stone, in the hand it might seem to weigh nothing, but if one held it at the end of a pole, it became increasingly difficult to manage. Though glamour borrowed the language of textiles to describe it, there were ways in which the manipulation of glamour also resembled water. One might direct a jet across a fountain, but it always wanted to return to the ground, widening into a mist as it curved downward. So too, with glamour: a glamourist could hold a strand of light pulled from the ether and direct it across a room, only to see it bend and lose its resolution. A skilled glamourist learned to adjust the ways in which the strand left his hands to compensate for its propensity to return to the ether, but it took much greater effort than producing a glamour at close range. To create a glamour from the base of a clock tower would have required great strength and steadiness of hand.

"Oh, it is quite true." Skiffy leaned in again, so that she could see the powder on his cheeks. "They all thought that something had gone wrong with the mechanism, and were after the clock-keeper's head. The poor fellow was up to his arms in the gears when Hami—when Vincent relented and withdrew the glamour. It happened right as the fellow pulled out a gear that truly broke the clock. Do you know what your husband did then? The great curmudgeon proved that it was all an act, for he stood beneath the clock tower and retied his glamour so that it showed the clock running the correct direction. He saved the clock-keeper's job by that, and I think it very handsome of him."

Jane could not be surprised by the generosity her husband had shown, but her attention was drawn again to that detail of distance in Skiffy's telling. If Vincent were able to create a clock illusion from so great a distance, perhaps he could retie the knot in the fish without drawing unwelcome attention to himself. Jane would have to stand and walk over to the section of the wall, which, besides the attention it would draw to her, would be rude to his royal highness . . . *Prinny*, that is.

At the foot of the table, Vincent was now engaged in

conversation with Lady Hertford. He did not spare a glance in her direction. Her attempt to reassure him had, it seemed, been too successful.

Perhaps her fears were amplified by the company she kept, and yet Jane could not help thinking of the courses yet to come and estimating the time which remained for the dinner. Would the knot continue to slip, or might it hold through the meal? She pushed the asparagus on her plate, unable to think of anything else. While the question of a few fish might seem but a trifle, to Jane, placed as she was in a position above her rank merely on the merits of the work around them, the thought of having the glamour *fail* at this moment was a thing of horror. To be sure, knots did sometimes come undone, but the Prince Regent, for all that he styled himself Prinny, had not paid them for inferior work. Left to its own, it would come undone before the end of dinner, and it would likely damage the coral with it. The work they would have before them to have it repaired in time for the official opening of the ballroom tomorrow would be immense.

Jane bit the inside of her mouth. No. No matter how honoured they were by this small dinner, the simple fact was that her role in life had shifted from guest to artisan, and, as such, her duties were clear. She set her knife and fork on the table and lifted the serviette out of her lap.

The Prince stopped in mid-sentence, and Jane realized that she had again lost track of his conversation. "Are you unwell, Mrs. Vincent?"

"I am quite well, thank you." She could not bring herself to call him Prinny. "Only I have noticed a spot in the glamour to which I must attend."

"Now? During dinner? Surely you have worked hard enough to have some rest." The Prince shook his head in wonder. "I see why Mr. Vincent finds you so appealing. You have the same focus on work that he does."

"And yet, not his skills. I am afraid that if the knot I have noticed comes undone it will require more effort to fix later. It will be but a moment, and then I shall be better able to focus on enjoying the evening."

Pushing his chair back, the Prince Regent said, "I know the artist's temperament too well to attempt to dissuade you again."

For that, at least, Jane was grateful. But when he arose to pull out her chair, conversation in the room stopped and all the guests attempted to rise themselves, unable to remain seated while their prince stood. Vincent rose as well, his face filled with alarm. The Prince Regent waved them back to their seats before resuming his own seat.

Jane smiled with as little concern as she could muster, though her heart raced as if she had already begun to work the glamour. "Please ignore me. I do not wish to disturb."

Keeping her head down, Jane walked across the ballroom floor as quickly as she could.

In moments, Vincent was by her side. "Jane, are you well?" His low voice grumbled in his chest, but the hand he pressed against her elbow spoke of deep concern.

"Embarrassed, rather. This school of fish is coming untied." She stopped in front of the window in the coral and reached out to grasp the line of glamour that the fish twined around. "Please sit down. There is no sense in both of us standing here. It will be some moments before it comes round again, and as this is one of my illusions, the error is entirely my fault." Letting the thread trail loosely in her fingers, she waited for the knot to reappear.

Vincent did not move from her side, and she could feel the warmth of him even through the heavy material of his coat. It was Bath coating, not the superfine which "Skiffy" so abhorred. Jane took a strange and momentary pleasure in that before she chided herself. They were not fashionable members of society who had to worry about these things, and being in such people's company would seduce her into wanting pretty clothes which she did not need. Still, she thought that her husband cut a fine picture, and that there was no harm in thinking so.

"Will you not sit?" She turned to find him staring at her with an endearing smile.

"Because you ask, I shall. Muse." He leaned forward as if to kiss her, and then gave a side-glance at the company, who had *all* turned in their seats to watch them. Straightening, he offered her the most correct of courtesies from husband to wife, and returned to his seat.

Jane set her back to the rest of the ballroom, grateful for that pretence of privacy. When the knot came under her fingers, she tightened her grasp to stop the fish. Carefully, she inched the two schools toward the proper relation to one another and then tied the knot with a triple hitch. It was less elegant than the *nœud marin* she had used before, but was unlikely to come undone.

Letting her attention return to the room, she stepped back from her work and was pleased to note that the diners had stopped paying her any heed. In truth, even the most astute observer would have noted only a woman standing with her back to the room, because the adjustments she had to make to the glamour were too subtle to be noticed. Only Vincent watched her, and offered her one of his rare and radiant smiles. Flushed more than the small amount of glamour merited, Jane returned to her seat, managing to slip into it with the aid of a footman before the Prince Regent noticed that she had rejoined the table.

She was thus prepared to enjoy the rest of the meal . . . until the table turned, and "Skiffy" claimed her attention.

Two

Art and Talent

Jane's perturbation was not due to any unkindness on the part of Lord Lumley. He was everything that is agreeable in a dinner conversationist: witty without being cruel, well-informed without being showy, and a gracious listener. But this very solicitude was what caused her some discomfort, for what Skiffy was most interested in hearing about was her impending trip to Europe, a trip of which Jane had no knowledge.

Indeed, the war had so recently ended that Jane was not yet accustomed to thinking of the Continent as a place to which one might go. In her mother's day, a tour abroad was quite the thing, but they had been at war with France since Jane was a child.

Concerns of unrest seemed trivial to Skiffy's

view of the Continent. "I am so excited that you are going abroad. Travel is so improving to one's character, do you not agree? I find that the most interesting people come from the Continent. Of course, one might be biased in that it is possible all the interesting people come here and leave only the dull ones there, but it is very much to be hoped that is not the case. In any case, I have so many friends who have gone to Brussels, some of them on the 'economical plan,' if you take my meaning. Financial difficulties would not be your reason for going, of course, and I am certain that with Prinny's patronage you can gain entrée into all the best houses there."

"That would be most generous of him."

"When do you set out? I must know so I can write to my friends and tell them to look for you."

Jane looked again to the end of the table where Vincent sat, wishing she knew whence this belief in their going to the Continent had sprung, but her husband's attention was occupied by the lady on his left, who was speaking with some animation. "We have hardly set our plans. I would hesitate to venture a guess which might cause you to lead your friends astray."

"Well then, I shall tell them they must look for you whenever you arrive."

"But indeed, we might not go to Brussels at all."

"Surely not Paris? Oh, that would be heaven. M. Lecomte aside, the French have quite the head for fashion. Everything is in the best taste there. I am so glad you are going to Paris."

Across the table, Lord Chesterford snorted, saving her a reply. "All this sallying forth to the Continent is in bad taste, if you ask my opinion. We defeated those cursed frenchies, and it was deuced hard to do—begging your pardon, ladies. Why the devil—pardon—anyone would go fawn at their feet in the name of Fashion now is beyond me."

"Oh, Fordy, you really must control yourself. The war is over. What more is there to say?"

"Over?" His moustache fairly quivered with indignation. "My brother left an arm there, and you speak to me of 'over'? Mark me: those frogs will be no end of trouble. Giving the Corsican Ogre leave to continue to rule is a travesty, after what we went through."

From farther down the table, Lord Fairchild abandoned his dinner partner to say, "Napoleon is 'ruling'—if you can call it that—the tiniest of islands. I scarcely think he can mount an invasion from there."

"But his followers might." Lord Chesterford huffed through his moustache. "Mark me: those cursed Bonapartists will use the youth of the Ogre's son as an excuse to place a regent on the throne."

The gentlemen conversed across the table in increasingly heated tones until the Prince cleared his throat. "This is hardly a topic of conversation suitable for the ladies. I think it is time for us to allow them to withdraw."

With that, the party broke up, and the ladies retreated to the Blue Room.

The moment they set foot outside the grand ballroom, the men began their conversation anew. Jane could not help but feel sorry to be shooed out, because the topic had been of some interest to her.

After the overt glamour of the ballroom, the Blue Room seemed positively staid, though it was appointed in the best manner. The walls were covered in blue damask which matched the upholstery. Gilt frames bordered the walls, with cleverly rendered oysters on the half shell in each corner. By the very absence of glamour, the Prince Regent displayed his taste and means here as much as in the ballroom, because everything from the elaborate carpet to the massive crystal chandelier was *real*.

Real gold gilded the arms of the chairs. Real candles stood in the sconces instead of fairy lights, so rather than the faint glow of glamoured light, the room truly was bright and airy.

The only glamour in the room adorned the ceiling, which had a glamural of sky and clouds drifting in a simple repeating pattern. The clouds circled the chandelier so that the crystals would not catch and diffract their glamoured folds. The effect seemed one part dance, one part storm—very like life at court itself.

The ladies echoed the movements of the clouds, drifting together in small knots. Jane found herself in a circle of five women who were comparing the merits of the gentlemen who had attended dinner. The topics ranged from the cut of their coats to their hairdressers to what subjects the ladies had been forced to endure during dinner. More than one had learned countless details about the pointer that her dinner companion favoured. Then the conversation drifted—as it tended to in these circumstances—to those who were not present, with shockingly cutting comments directed at Lady so-and-so's gown or Miss someone's latest conquest.

Jane had been introduced to these ladies before dinner, but otherwise had no acquaintance with them, so she tried to find it perfectly natural that they should speak so of their supposed friends. And yet they drew closer to each other as they chattered, gradually leaving her standing outside their group. Ill at ease, she wandered to the walls of the drawing room to study the portraits there.

As she worked her way slowly around the room, one portrait in an older style quite took her. It depicted a young boy mounted on a pony. He held a sabre over his head and looked as if he would charge into battle at any moment, for all the roundness of his cheeks and the becoming smile on his lips. His face possessed such an open friendliness that she felt herself steadier, even if her company were only a painting.

After a few moments, Jane sensed that someone had joined her. At her side now stood the inimitable Lady Hertford, who also gazed at the painting. This celebrated beauty's very presence lent the room an additional elegance. Her claret velvet dress might have been chosen as a deliberate complement to the blue walls. The line of her neck would have been a welcome subject for any artist. Without breaking her attention to the painting they both looked at, Lady Hertford said, "I think that Prinny still has the same smile, on his good days."

"Is it his highness?"

"Painted by Ramsey, when Prinny was seven. He has told me how he hated sitting still for it, but he was promised he could keep the sword if he did. He still has it, you know."

"I did not. Have you known his highness long?"

"We have been in the same set since our parents were children, but only became familiar these last few years." Lady Hertford took Jane's arm and steered her down the long gallery of the Blue Room. With a contemptuous glance over her shoulder, she said, "Please do not let them bother you. They cannot cause any true harm, but most of them are too silly to know how to deal with anything of substance. Faced with a woman who can actually *do* things, such as yourself, they simply do not know what to talk about."

At once relieved that she had not imagined being cut out of the conversation and disheartened that it had *not* been her imagination, Jane tried to brush off their rudeness. "But it is only natural that they should talk of acquaintances that they know. I shall be gone tomorrow."

"Ah, but I sought you out because you will be gone tomorrow. A pleasure that is fleeting must be seized when it is present. I am such an admirer of your work. I wish I could do glamour as you can."

"I am certain you could. It is only a matter of practice, as with any of the arts."

Lady Hertford laughed, a silver, gay laugh that tinkled like bells and put Jane in mind of her sister, Melody. "That is lovely of you to say, my dear, but I rather suspect that glamour comes so easily for you that you do not recognise how difficult it is for others."

"I do not deny that it is difficult, only put forth the argument that with perseverance anyone can overcome those difficulties. You saw this evening how I had to correct an error." Jane faltered, wondering if she should perhaps return to the ballroom to ascertain if her repair to the fish were holding. "It is an art that I am still learning, and it takes a great deal of effort."

"You see how you prove my point in an instant? I could not even see what it was you were doing, though your husband explained it to me when he returned to his seat. I watched you fixedly and try as I might, I could not see a flaw, nor what you were changing. I only knew that you had done something when Mr. Vincent grunted."

"I had not intended for him to abandon you. I should apologize on Vincent's account."

"Now see, that is something else I find perfectly charming about you: the way you use his surname like a man. It is *très moderne*. I think I might adopt it with my own husband, should I ever see him again."

Jane stifled the impulse to explain that Vincent was his given name but everyone in this group, save apparently Skiffy and Prinny, knew him as Mr. David Vincent, the glamourist, and not as Vincent Hamilton, third son of the Earl of Verbury. She wondered if she would rise in the other women's estimation if they knew, then dismissed the thought as unworthy. Vincent had offered to retake his given name and his place as his father's son when he married her, but she had refused, since it would mean giving up his art.

His art was his life, and hers as well.

"It is easier to refer to him by the same name our employer uses when working on a commission, lest they wonder who 'David' is, and eventually I fell into the habit of it." Jane stopped and turned to her companion. "I can teach you the basic principles of glamour, if you would like."

"That is too kind of you, but I cannot do glamour."

"Truly, you do yourself a disservice by believing so without making the attempt."

"Ah, I am unclear. My doctor advises me not to perform glamour." She let her hand rest on her stomach so briefly that Jane might have imagined it, but Lady Hertford's meaning was clear: she was increasing. Of course she could not work glamour in such a state, without risk to her unborn child.

"Perhaps after your confinement, then."

"I would delight in that."

"I congratulate you and your husband."

Lady Hertford offered another of her laughs. "I doubt that my husband is even aware, or that he would be pleased if he were."

"I am—I—" Jane stammered, recalling that Lady Hertford had just referred to her husband's absence. Indeed, he had not been at dinner. Suddenly half-remembered gossip combined with Lady Hertford's statement that she was a *familiar* acquaintance of the Prince Regent.

"I have shocked you."

The simplicity of her response made Jane aware of how tight her bearing had become. "Forgive my surprise. I have not been much in London, and am used to simpler ways."

"Do not let it worry you. I am past being offended. It is a subject of some confusion to me, why gentlemen are allowed their conquests and yet remain gentlemen, while a lady must bear the burden of the conquest all alone."

Jane could not offer an answer. As they turned the corner of the room, they again faced the small groups of women chatting amiably. It was hard to miss the disdainful glances cast their way as she promenaded up the length of the Blue Room with Lady Hertford. It came to Jane, all at once, the change in station she had experienced by becoming an artisan, for the only woman in the room who was willing to speak with her at length was the Prince Regent's mistress.

The confusion and dismay that filled her was extreme. Lady Hertford had been all kindness and interest . . . and yet, to have fallen into such a state. Jane hardly knew what to say or do. She could not approve of Lady Hertford's conduct, but neither was she willing to condemn a woman who had done her no ill. "It must be very hard for you."

"Well . . . it is not all difficulty. Prinny is a dear and is very good to me. These others,"—her tone might have been discussing cattle—"these others are friendly with me for his sake. Or rather, for their sake, because to cut me would be to cut their chances with him, and none have the strength of character to risk that by insisting on proprieties. And, my dear, you must understand that I chose this. I am not such a simpering fool as to not understand exactly what I was embarking on."

Just then, the door to the drawing room opened and saved Jane from answering. The gentlemen swaggered into the room with the masculine scent of cigars and brandy. Some had been more deeply in their cups than others, as was evidenced by their too-raucous laughter. The Prince Regent was one of these, and his voice carried over the others. "I tell you Vincent, I want them gasping tomorrow, and you will do that for me. You. You will. Yes. You." He had his arm around Vincent's neck as if they were chums, but Jane could see the muscle tightening at the base of her husband's jaw.

"If you will excuse me." She dropped Lady Hertford's arm with as much grace as she could muster and hurried across the drawing room to Vincent's side. His brown curls were tousled in the fashionable wind-swept look that so many men struggled to attain, but which came naturally to him. He swept his hands through his hair so much, knotting them in place while he thought, that it was permanently dishevelled.

"Of course, Prinny. I will make the changes tonight."

Jane stopped in front of them. "What changes shall we make?"

The Prince Regent dropped his arm from around Vincent's neck and took her hand. Raising it to his lips, he kissed it. "You shall do nothing. He works you too hard."

"Do not worry, Jane, it is a small thing. I shall attend to it now."

"You are a good man." Still holding her hand, the Prince Regent drew her away from Vincent. "He is a good man, your husband, with talent. A Genuine Talent."

Captured, Jane suffered herself be led away, while Vincent returned to the ballroom to work. Even as the Prince Regent did her the honour of making sure that the assembled crowd saw how highly he favoured her, Jane's mind was with her husband. The ballroom had been their collaboration. How could she be satisfied that Vincent was changing it without consulting with her? It must have been her error with the fish that prompted this. Rather than risk embarrassment, he was doing the work himself. What need did he have to consult her, when his skills were more than equal to the task?

Jane sat and smiled at the conversations twirling around her. But in her mind, she was tying knots.

Three

Flattery and Letters

As Jane waited for her husband at Carlton House, she eventually received word that she was to return to their apartments without him. The rest of the guests had long since departed, leaving her with only the company of Prinny and Lady Hertford. The gentlemen had been too much in their cups for conversation, and only Lady Hertford had made the hours tolerable.

Jane's concern that she had caused some major damage to the glamural gradually changed to discomfort that she was keeping their hosts up so late, then to annoyance with Vincent for placing her in such an unpleasant position. The Prince Regent had been beyond gracious, even in his inebriated state, and had arranged for her to be returned home in his own carriage. Under other circumstances, the use of the Prince's equipage would have been a matter of some excitement.

As it was, Jane returned home in a less than pleasant mood. Though she had every expectation of seeing her family on the morrow, as they had come to London for the express purpose of taking in the Vincents' glamural with the rest of the public, she wished very much for her sister's company. When she was home at Long Parkmead, Melody had long been her confidant, and understood Vincent the best out of Jane's family. But, as the hour was far too late to call upon her relations, Jane began a letter to Melody in an attempt to ease her mind.

She was on her third draft when Vincent returned to their rooms. His cheeks were drawn and his face had the unhealthy flush which so often marks the remnant of exertion. Jane abandoned her letter, alarm replacing her upset, and sprang from her chair. "Vincent?"

He sighed heavily. "I am quite well."

"I do not believe you for a moment." Jane took him by the arm, and, despite her smaller stature, led him easily to a wingback chair by the tall casement window. Despite his protestations, the memory of his brush with death from an over exertion of glamour remained strong in her mind. Leaving him for a moment, she flung open the window to let in the night air, and wove a simple glamour to help the breeze along, hoping that it would cool the fever evidenced by the ruddiness of his cheeks. So long as his art beckoned, Vincent would push himself too hard, like a racehorse, without a care for his health.

He dropped without complaint into the chair, and stretched his legs out in front of him, leaning his head against the chair back with a sigh. Jane stood behind him and leaned over to tug his cravat loose. Vincent caught her hand, bending his head to kiss the inside of her wrist.

The warmth of his fever seemed to pulse through her veins and, of a sudden, the room was too warm for her as well. "My love, you must not work yourself so."

"You have told me so before." He kissed her wrist again. "But this was entirely your fault."

Jane snatched her hand out of his grasp. "I am sorry. You may be certain it is not an error I will make again." As unaffected as he was, she had not expected him to be so blunt in his response.

"Jane, Jane . . ." Vincent was out of his chair in a moment and had her by both hands again. They trembled in his grasp, but Jane would not let herself cry when she had cause to be angry. "What are you going on about?"

"The—the knot that came untied on the fish." Her throat was raw with swallowed tears. "That is what you were correcting, is it not?"

"No! My love, no." Vincent pulled her closer despite her resistance and folded her into his arms. His voice rumbled against her cheek. "Prinny loved your fish. He wanted me to make more of them. If you have a fault, it is in being too clever."

She pushed herself out of his arms. "Then why did you do it alone instead of calling me?"

Vincent frowned, brows rising in confusion. "Prinny asked me. You were with the ladies."

"I had no choice in that!"

"Nor did I." Vincent rumpled his hair so that it looked as if he were a madman. "I could hardly call you back in. The room was filled with cigar smoke, and you witnessed the state of the Prince."

"Yes. I endured the state of the Prince for the next several hours. I am quite aware of it and would have been more than happy to have had some reason to leave the drawing room."

"But you must see that it was the simplest course. Prinny explained what he wanted to have added and it was not a task that required two glamourists."

"Since I created the fish, it should have fallen to me."

"I do not understand you."

All the upset she had felt transformed as it became clear that Vincent did not recognise how he had slighted her by altering her design without consultation. "I am—yes, I am vexed that you did not even do me the courtesy of telling me what the Prince Regent wanted. I might have lost your trust, but you could at least have told me so directly instead of leaving me like a bauble in the drawing room."

"My trust? I—I had no intention of slighting you. I just thought to spare you the effort. Indeed, it would have been more complicated to repeat his instructions. I could weave the fish with ease"

Her mind fixed on the word "ease." Of course, a task which took her hours of concentration was of no difficulty to *him*. Jane knew she was being unjust in guessing his intentions, and yet the upset she felt was no less real for it. The flush of anger heated her cheeks, and Jane railed against that fault of her complexion which so easily laid bare her emotions. She pinched her lips together and made some effort to slow her breathing.

"Jane . . ." Vincent's voice trailed away, at a loss. Hands held outward, half in entreaty, half in surrender, he said, "Tell me what I have done."

Jane resolved to make some effort to explain, but her words came out more clipped and forceful than she had intended. "The ballroom was our collaboration. To have you decide upon and make changes yourself makes me feel as though you have little regard for my skills or opinions. That the glamour you changed was one which I created makes . . ." She crossed her arms over her chest, suddenly cold. "I must assume that you have lost trust in me because the knot came untied."

"Knots do that!" He buried his hands in his hair, staring at her as if she were a perplexing strand of glamour. "I have not lost trust in you, and certainly not for something so small as that. For Heaven's sake, Jane, I corrected an error during dinner myself."

"You never left the table."

"Well. No." He had the grace to shift uncomfortably. "I have some practice at repairs from the dinner table."

The way he dug his toe into the carpet put her in mind of a schoolboy caught out, and it quite undid her. Jane glared at him with mock severity. "I heard from Lord Lumley about your exploit with the clock tower, so I do not know why I pretend surprise."

"Yes, well. Well. I was not a nice boy."

"I might vouch for that."

This prompted a hurt expression, so at odds with his usual gruffness that Jane softened and slipped her hand in his. "I did not mean it."

"No, you are correct. I should have spoken with you about the changes. I am used to working alone and have no practice at sharing responsibility." Shaking his head, Vincent returned to the chair, drawing Jane down to sit upon his knee. "I will amend that."

"Thank you." Jane kissed him on the forehead, which was still too warm for her liking. "You should always call me, if for no other reason than that I might stop you from overworking yourself."

Smiling, Vincent leaned back against the chair. "I work harder to try to match you than I do on my own."

"Stop." She tweaked his nose. "I will not listen to false flattery."

"It is true!"

"Hm." She did not believe him, for all that she was unwillingly pleased by his praise. "But how did you learn to work glamour from so far?"

He cleared his throat. "Remembering that I was not a nice boy, and bearing in mind that you love me now . . ." He paused to kiss her on the cheek. "You do love me now?"

"Very much." She leaned against his chest. "Now continue."

"When I was at home, my father forbade me to practice glamour, because it was a woman's art. So, I watched my sisters' lessons and learned what I could from them, simple as they were. But what I delighted in was to learn by *unstitching* glamours, so that I could get at their parts. I would take them apart and then slowly learn to put them back together again, not always with success."

"That must have brought you into terrible trouble."

"It did." He grew quiet for a moment and carressed her hair, lost in a memory. "I taught myself to work glamour from a distance so that I could unstitch things while my sisters were standing near them. If I were stealthy, one of them would get the blame."

Jane pushed herself up and stared at him in astonishment. "You did not."

"I told you I was not a nice boy."

"You did not say you were wicked."

His voice roughened. "I would have thought you had learned that by now."

"Rogue."

"Muse."

They were occupied for some minutes, then, with duties marital. To disturb their privacy would be indecorous. Suffice to say: the Vincents were a healthy couple, and with their differences settled, they were happily matched in temperament.

* * *

Some time later, Jane nestled her head in the space between her husband's neck and shoulder, that tender region usually shielded from view by high starched collars and cravats. "Vincent. At dinner, the Prince Regent seemed quite convinced we were going to the Continent. Had you said something to him?"

His hand, which had been stroking her hair, stilled. "I might have. The Continent is all the conversation allows, these days." Resuming his motion, he traced her hair where it lay unbound across her shoulders. "Would you like to go?"

"I hardly know. I have not given it any thought until tonight. I suppose we could, as I am not certain what we shall do with ourselves now that this commission is over." Though she had no real hope that her next gambit would work, she kissed his cheek. "You recall that Papa invited us to return to Long Parkmead with them."

As she suspected, Vincent grunted, but did not otherwise answer. A natural hermit, the confines of her home and the constant society which her mother pressed upon him sometimes overwhelmed his senses. At court, in the role of the Prince Regent's glamourist, he was given leave to be taciturn, and it was deemed an eccentricity. At Long Parkmead, in his role as son-in-law, that same silence caused her mother to think that Vincent did not like her. It was a difficult boundary for him to walk.

"Did you *want* to go to the Continent?" she asked him.

He shifted in the bed and resettled with his arm around her back. "I have a colleague, M. Chastain, whom I have not seen for years. We were both apprentices with Herr Scholes, but the war has kept us apart since then. With Napoleon abdicated, I will admit that I had entertained thoughts of visiting him. From our correspondence, he is doing interesting work with double-weaving glamours into something he is calling a jacquard."

"After the new looms? Has he found a way to mechanize glamour then?" Jane sat up on her elbow so she could see his face better. It would be a tremendous breakthrough if he had found a way to record glamour as M. Jacquard had used cards to record the patterns for weaving on looms.

"No. He merely had inspiration for the technique after seeing a demonstration of M. Jacquard's looms in Paris. From what he describes it is akin to a damask weave and creates variations based on one's prospect."

"What is the benefit to this method?" Jane sank back onto the bed, disappointed. Since the current trend in glamours dictated that they be created with full dimensions, walking around a tree of glamour had no difference from walking around one of wood.

"I am unclear in my description." He sat up and inclined his head toward his writing desk. "I had one of his letters this morning."

"Stay. I will get it for you." She hopped out of bed and fetched the small oak travel desk. When in transit, it folded neatly in half to present an unassuming box. Once opened, it contained a comfortable sloped surface, faced in red leather. Cunningly concealed within were compartments to store correspondence and writing supplies. The battered wooden sides attested to the constant travelling Vincent had done in his life as an itinerant glamourist.

While she was up, Jane also collected a clean handkerchief and the bottle of lavender water that her mother had sent up in case she was afflicted with "vapours." Handing Vincent the desk, Jane once more slipped into bed.

She dampened the handkerchief with a small amount of the lavender water, the scent immediately bringing back the memory of her mother and the countless ailments which plagued her. Jane patted Vincent's brow with the dampened handkerchief, wishing that he took a tenth of the care with his health that her mother did with her various nervous conditions.

He sighed in contentment, sinking into the pillows, his letter momentarily forgotten. The lines of fatigue eased and his breathing slowed. Jane continued to stroke his brow, commending his features to memory yet again. His face, when relaxed, always surprised her with its youth. When alert, his intelligent eyes flashed beneath a heavy, brooding brow. The guarded and constant thought which went into even the most casual of conversations made him seem older than his years. That very fact, that he did not utter phrases devoid of meaning just to fill the air with the sound of conversation, was one of the things Jane most loved about him.

He sighed again and opened his eyes, lifting the lid of his desk to rummage through it. Amid his other correspondence lay a letter written in French with another layer of tiny script crossed over it.

Holding it close to his eyes so he did not need to lift his head from Jane's ministrations, Vincent scanned the page. Marking his place with his index finger, he said, "Here. Chastain says, and forgive my translation, 'The effect of the double-weave is such that from one position in a room, the glamour appears to be, let us say, a tree, and from the other a woman. The transition from one to the other happens without a seam so that the tree seems to become the woman as the viewer walks about it. At the moment, these are but rough glamours. However, if I can perfect the technique, then one might have two glamours, complete in their own right, and merely by changing one's relationship with the illusion, one can completely change its nature.' He goes on with some unsatisfying descriptions of the weaves he is using, without enough exactness to duplicate." He peeked up through his eyelashes at Jane. "Does that remind you of anything?"

Jane shook her head. "I am afraid you have the better of me."

"My *Sphère Obscurcie*. On the exterior it bends the light around so that viewers believe they have an unobstructed view of whatever lies opposite, while masking that which lies in its interior. But the view to a person *within* the bubble is unobstructed."

Jane nodded, as she followed his train of thought. "The twist in the glamour creates, in essence, two layers of fabric like a damask, which keep the interior from being either a mirror or a dark sphere. And you think his jacquard would enhance the effect?"

"I do not know, but I am curious to see what it is that Chastain has created, and with the war against Napoleon there has been no opportunity before this." He traced a finger across her wedding band. "Besides. I have never given you a proper honeymoon."

Jane laughed and caught his hand. "Oh, love. Yes, let us go to the Continent. But you do not need to tempt me with any more reason than that there is a glamourist whom you wish to visit." She rubbed his temples, inducing him to shut his eyes once more. The Continent sounded like a grand adventure. The only cause for chagrin was that she had counted on visiting her family once their work here was finished. Her mother would be so distraught to hear that they were not coming.

"What is the matter?" Vincent lifted his head, seeking a better view of her.

"Pardon?"

"You sighed."

"I did? I have no recollection of that."

"Nevertheless, you sighed just now." He waited and Jane wished for a moment that he might not know her moods *quite* so well.

"I was only thinking about the difficulty of telling my parents. We should have them to dine with us on Monday."

He lowered his chin, and, with only the slightest compression of his lips, expressed his lack of enthusiasm for this suggestion. "Of course."

Jane sighed in earnest now. "Is it really that distasteful for you to visit my family?"

"It is not distasteful." Vincent worked his jaw, and then blew his breath out in a groan. "I esteem your family, but I will own that I am not comfortable with them. There is no place where I fit."

"You are my husband. My parents look on you as family."

"Yes, but . . . but your family has practice at being with one another." He picked a loose thread off the sheets, examining it rather than her. "I do not even have practice being with my *own* family."

Jane felt heartbreak for him. With all of her family's faults, Jane could not imagine a world in which she was not intimately connected to each of them, or doing without all the benefits of family, which only one who has been truly loved as a child can appreciate. Chief among her wishes was that Vincent might appreciate her family as she did, and likewise, that they would begin to see those qualities in him that she esteemed. "Perhaps rather than avoiding time spent with them we might practice together?"

"Of course."

Holding back another sigh, Jane stroked away the new furrow that had appeared in his brow. This was another type of knot to learn to tie.

Four

Family and Consideration

To contrast the dinner at the Vincents' home with that at Carlton House would be distinctly unfair, and yet the comparison was unavoidable in Jane's mind. With only her parents, her sister Melody, and Vincent present, they made an intimate company, which was fortunate, as the rooms they had let were insufficient for dining with more than eight. Though neatly furnished, it was with the dark wood that had been stylish in Jane's childhood, and lent a material weight to the rooms, which not even glamour and candles could quite dispel. The chief feature, and the reason they had chosen the rooms, was that they backed onto a park shared by Carlton House. The Prince Regent had offered to have them in residence, but the Vincents, being newly-weds, had chosen the modicum of privacy which separate rooms allowed.

Jane's family had arrived in London on the Thursday prior, but aside from one brief morning visit, there had not been sufficient time for company while engaged in preparations for the fête. Jane had briefly seen them among the press of guests, but her attention had been too distracted for her to do more than smile.

The first course of dinner was taken up with her mother exclaiming about the spectacle and pondering the worth of the plate on display. That accomplished, they began at once to catch her up on the news of the neighbourhood. The Dunkirks were not in residence, and rumour had it that Mr. Dunkirk planned on letting Robinsford Abbey. Banbree Manor had a tenant already, a general and his family, who were respectable but without any eligible sons.

During her mother's recital, Melody pushed her roast lamb across the plate, as if focusing on that could take her away from the table. Mr. Ellsworth watched her, rubbing his chin, and cleared his throat to change the subject. "That is all well and good, but I want to hear what Jane has been doing."

Jane's account of their work drew Melody's attention back to the room. Jane could now see that her sister was still paler than she ought to have been after the unfortunate events of the previous autumn. She made a note to take Melody aside and hear how she had fared while Jane was away.

"Well . . . you have seen the most of it. We do have

some important news, though." Jane looked to the foot of the table for support. Vincent smiled at her, but seemed more than willing to let her explain their plans. "We are going to a town near Brussels to spend time with a colleague of Vincent's. It is a tremendous opportunity."

"Oh!" Mrs. Ellsworth pressed her serviette to her mouth. "Oh! Jane, I do wish you would reconsider. I cannot understand what you could be thinking, to go off to France like that. It is too, too dangerous, and full of immoral characters. Why, just the other day, we heard the most appalling thing about dancers in Vienna with skirts cut above their knees."

"Mama, Vienna is in Austria, not France. And, in any case, I have told you that we are going to Brussels, which is in Belgium."

"But you have to travel *through* France, and that is every bit as bad as if you were choosing to remain there. And what if something becomes of me while you are gone? It is all very well for you to be sweeping off to London, but in France, how shall we contact you? How shall you hear from us?"

"I shall give our address to Mr. Ellsworth." Vincent inclined his head to Jane's father.

"There now, you see, Mama? We are staying with a colleague of Vincent's. He has letters from M. Chastain regularly, so I am certain it will not be a difficulty for you to write to us."

Melody tossed her head, honeyed ringlets swaying. "I think it is the most exciting thing. You must write to us and tell us all about the fashions. La! I am so enamoured of everything I see from the Continent, and simply beside myself that you are going abroad."

"Well . . . we will be in a village. I do not think fashions will be much the order of the day." Jane shook her head. "Besides, I imagine most of our time will be spent in the laboratory working glamour."

"Oh!" Mrs Ellsworth threw up her hands in dismay. "You will not still be working glamour, will you?"

"Well, yes, Mama." Jane stumbled in her recital. Her parents had just witnessed the glamural, so she could not take her mother's meaning. As glamour was widely considered a womanly art, it was far more unusual that Vincent should pursue it than she. "That is what we have set out to do, after all. The commission from the Prince Regent has served us quite handsomely so we can take some time to study."

"I only meant, that I am surprised that you are still *able* to work glamour. To think of you continuing . . . It is beyond my understanding."

Jane then saw the reason for her mother's surprise. Vincent had very nearly died from an over exertion of glamour the previous summer, and Mrs. Ellsworth's imagination had been overwrought since then imagining the same dire fate for Jane. "I am stronger than I was, in fact. Folds that once would have fatigued me seem quite easy. I attribute it to the consistency with which we were working."

"Really, Jane, it shocks me. I worry so about the risk. It is terrible, what you are doing. I wish you would not.

Indeed, I must insist that you do not take such a risk." Mrs. Ellsworth leaned back in her chair and fanned herself. "I do not wish to make any implications, but it shocks me, truly it does, that your dear husband would let you."

"It is not a matter of letting, madam. I should not wish to undertake the work without Jane at my side."

"We are careful to pace ourselves and do not court fatigue." Jane omitted any mention of the extra hours that Vincent would sometimes work, seeing no reason to bring her mother further alarm.

"My dear Vincent, I would not argue with you for the world, but I must differ with you. Yes, I must. You must see the risk this carries for Jane!" Mrs. Ellsworth wrung her hands. "Oh, I do wish you were no longer working glamour."

"But, Mama,"—Jane, concerned that every fear Vincent had about her parents was coming true, wished that the length of the table did not separate her from her husband—"you knew we were set on being glamourists. I do not see how I am to do that without performing glamour."

"La!" Melody laid her hand on Mrs. Ellsworth's arm. "You would save time, Mama, if you would simply say that you want a grandchild."

"Of course! That is what I have been saying these last fifteen minutes. How could you think I was saying anything else? My meaning was perfectly clear. I am certain that Jane understood me, but she is too obstinate to allow that she did."

A grandchild. Nothing could have been farther from

Jane's mind. She could not answer her mother. She had assumed that she and Vincent would have a family, but had not thought about what it entailed for the work they did together. If she had to stop working glamour for nine months, what would that mean for them? To be certain, Vincent had been working as a glamourist alone for far longer than they had worked together, but Jane so enjoyed the process of creation with her husband that she could hardly imagine taking any joy from being forced to stop.

And yet, was not the creation of a child the most important collaboration they could undertake? They had never spoken of children, and Jane realized that she did not know what Vincent's feelings were about them. Perhaps he had no wish to be a father. His face betrayed nothing, though his figure was tense. But that could be attributed to fatigue, or to the unwitting censure which her mother had heaped upon him.

"Well." Mr. Ellsworth tucked his fingers into his waistcoat. "I, for one, am glad that you are still performing glamour and hope that we might prevail upon you to favour us with some music tonight."

"Charles, she is too tired. Are you not too tired? I know I would be, if it were me."

"No, truly I am not." Grateful for an opportunity to silence her mother's conversation, Jane signalled their borrowed footman to clear the table. "Shall we adjourn to the drawing room?"

At one point, she had thought that the expense of renting

a pianoforte in London had been needless, as she had not had freedom to play it more than a few times toward the beginning of their stay here. Now, though, she silently blessed Vincent for insisting that she not give up her music.

Lifting the cover, Jane stroked a few random notes from the pianoforte to refamiliarize herself with the instrument. Vincent had brought her sheet music for an étude by Beethoven but she had yet to try it. Opening the music upon the stand, Jane followed the suggestions on the score to enhance the simple, pleasing tune with a fold of colour which hinted of birds flying amidst a whirl of blossoms. As she continued, Jane realized how long it had been since she had taken time to play or to create a glamour for pleasure rather than purpose. Her fingers were no longer as accustomed to the keyboard as she might wish, but she could not help but be pleased by how easily these simple glamours came. Jane wondered if she might create more elaborate images with her music with practice. How could she give that up to have a child?

Bringing the étude to a close, Jane was gratified by her family's approbation. "Wonderful!" "How we have missed that!" Even Mrs. Ellsworth seemed to have forgotten her objection to the glamour.

The rest of the evening passed in simple conversation, but Jane could never fully enjoy it. Her attention was split, noting Vincent's silence, and how he only ventured to speak if someone directed a comment at him.

Thankfully, her family seemed not to notice, but if the pattern continued, surely they would. The initial pleasure that Jane had felt at welcoming them to dinner transformed into relief that their visit would be so short.

The following morning, Jane rose with the intention of visiting her family before their mutual journeys separated them. Vincent declined the opportunity to accompany her, saying that he wanted to paint the Battersea Bridge and catch the morning light. After the fiasco of the previous evening, Jane could hardly blame him for wanting to escape under the thinnest pretence.

When Jane arrived at her family's hotel, her father was in the front parlour. She stopped in the doorway to admire the tranquil scene. Sunlight came in through the tall windows of the parlour and made the room gleam as though a coat of liquid glamour had gilded every surface. Mr. Ellsworth's silver hair became spun gold, and his rosy cheeks promised cheer. He held a newspaper off to the side, reading it as he sipped his tea.

Passing behind his chair, Jane bent down to kiss him on top of his head, noting that either his hair had thinned since she had last been home, or she had remembered a younger version of her father. He lowered his paper, beaming with delight. "Good morning. How did you sleep?"

"Well, thank you." Helping herself to a cup, Jane settled into the chair next to him.

"No Vincent?"

"He is out painting." Jane busied herself with doctoring her tea.

"Is he well? I noticed he was very quiet last night."

"We had been very busy these past few months. I think he is simply fatigued."

"I see."

Silence rested between them and Jane recognised the quality of it from her father. He was waiting for her to explain further. But what could she say that would not make everyone involved more self-conscious and uncomfortable? Her father, earnest as he was, would take it upon himself to engage Vincent, when that would do no more good than bringing a racehorse indoors and trying to teach it to dance. But perhaps she could explain that much. "He is . . . You must remember that he is an artist, and something of a hermit besides. Do not read too much into his silence."

"Your mother is concerned."

Jane almost dropped her cup. "Why?"

"Because you have not—that is to say, you and he . . ." He sighed and looked around the room to see if other guests had joined them. "The lack of grandchildren. It weighs on her."

Jane stared at him, vexed that he would bring up the topic again. "Papa. We have only been married these three months, and you must allow that we have been busy the whole while."

"Yes." He shifted in his chair and tugged at his waistcoat. "I think the fact that your mother was . . . we . . . well, her confinement began shortly after we were wed."

Jane frowned and tilted her head to the side, counting the difference between her birthday and their anniversary.

"But I was not born till you had been married some three years."

Her father studied his tea, stirring it with care, though there was no need. "She had some difficulties. You were her third confinement, and so she worries. She worries that you will also have difficulties, and worries the more that . . . that marriage might not be what you had expected."

To have this conversation with her father was almost more than she could bear, and yet she was thankful that it was not her mother, who would go on about her concerns and take no comfort in anything Jane had to say.

"There is nothing to worry about." Jane set her cup down, the taste bitter in the back of her throat.

"Jane, I—" Her father broke off as she stood.

"Yes, Papa?"

"He does love you?"

Cold and heat alternated in Jane's spine at the insinuation of the question. "Yes. And I love him. Good morning, sir."

Jane's first impulse was to find Vincent and lay before him the whole of the conversation so that he could join her in astonishment at the insensibility of her parents. But by the time she reached their rooms, she realized that would be one of the worst choices she could make. To bring these grievances to Vincent's attention could only make him less comfortable with her parents. Jane sat before her pianoforte and played until her head was somewhat cooler. As she did, she again found herself grateful that their visit was so constrained.

* * *

To her surprise, the rest of the visit passed without apparent upset. Vincent seemed to find a certain peace by attempting to be of some use to her mother. He busied himself with running errands, and in the evening entertained them with shadow-plays. Still, Jane felt that the conversation about grandchildren would resume at any moment, and the lack of them would be cited as a flaw in their marriage.

When it came time to leave London, Jane was nearly as anxious to be away as Vincent was.

So pleased had the Prince Regent been with their work that he had arranged for them to sail on HMS *Dolphin*, the only difficulty being that they would have to hurry to depart, as the ship was set to sail the Monday following. Jane could not say she begrudged the rush in the slightest, as it hastened the moment when she might escape her mother's examinations.

The January wind whipped off the coast and lifted sails and skirts alike. Despite the chill, Jane stood at the rail of the *Dolphin*, feeling as if a series of stays were releasing their laces with each length they moved away from the shore. Vincent stood at her back with one hand steadying her against the pitching of the boat. Like most professional glamourists, he eschewed gloves even in public. She could not regret this departure from fashion, though she had yet to embrace it herself. The warmth of his hand seemed to travel through her body, and she leaned into him, relishing the waves as an excuse for the public display of affection.

As they left the harbour for the deeper water of the Channel, several of the other passengers bent over the rail, emptying their breakfasts into the harbour, but Jane felt not the least bit of queasiness.

She inhaled the salty tang of the sea air and lifted her face to the sun, relishing the sense, if not the fact, of being alone with her husband. If she could wish away the other passengers and have only this quiet space with Vincent, she would. Still staring at the ocean, Jane sighed. "I wish a *Sphère Obscurcie* could work at sea."

"Why is that, muse?"

"So that I might kiss you here on the deck without shocking our neighbours."

Nodding his head toward a particularly unhappy traveller, who leaned over the rail as though worshipping Neptune, Vincent said, "I rather think that they are past being shocked. I wonder if I could work one." He drew his hand away from her back. Even before she faced him, Jane knew the expression she would find on his countenance. He stared at the horizon, concentrating on some equation in the middle distance. "I have been taught that glamour will not work on a moving ship, but have not had the opportunity to test it for myself. In theory . . . ."

"Do you ever stop theorizing?"

He brought his attention back and curled the corners of his lips in the small smile that was the most she had seen him give in public. "There are times, yes. You have been present at all of them."

As the ship swayed, it brought them closer together,

and Jane found she did not care what anyone on board thought. She could not recall the last time she had been with Vincent and had no obligations. Here, nothing could make claim upon their time. They had no social acquaintances aboard, nor work to prepare for.

Vincent tilted his head. "What are you smiling about?"

"Well." Jane took his hands. "You did say this was our honeymoon, and since we cannot work glamour, I thought perhaps there were other ways in which we might pass the time."

"Indeed there are. I brought my watercolours. Or, if you prefer, I have Herr Scholes's treatise on the reciprocation of light and shadow." His face kept a mien of utter seriousness except around the eyes, which wrinkled with amusement.

"A reciprocation, I think."

"As do I." Vincent took her hand and looked around the deck, his grip tightening for an instant before he released her. "May I help you?"

He addressed two young ladies—girls, really—who stood not far from them, staring quite openly. The one behind, younger and with a head of dark curls, nudged her sister forward. They were clearly sisters, with the same upturned nose and thick brows. "Pardon, but are you . . . that is to say . . . did you?" Her words seemed unable to form into sentences. She suddenly thrust a slender pamphlet at Vincent. "We saw you? In London?"

Vincent took the paper gently, his hand nearly twice the size of the girl's. "Ah. Yes. You did."

"I *told* you!" The younger girl nudged her sister again.

He showed it to Jane, steadying the paper against the stiff breeze. It fluttered so that the image on the cover seemed to move. It was an engraving, crude and hastily rendered, of their glamural at Carlton House, with the words "New Year's Souvenir" emblazoned in large type above it. The text below described the festivities in great detail, mentioning everything from the quantity of cake to the worth of the plate. Jane made a note to let her mother know the figure. Then her attention caught upon a sentence.

The glamural, created entirely by Mr. David Vincent, is one of the most complete . . .

There was no mention of her.

A penny publication did not signify much, yet Jane could not help but feel that her exclusion confirmed all that she had felt that last night at Carlton House. She was an unnecessary part of the weave of their glamour. Trying to put her sour feeling aside, Jane smiled at the girls. "Did you attend?"

Bouncing on her toes, the younger girl answered Jane's question, but directed her words at Vincent. She gazed at him with all the adoration a schoolgirl might bring to bear upon an older man. "It was wonderful! Oh! Sir! Mama says you are the best glamourist in England!"

Vincent coughed, his face reddening. "Your mother is very kind."

"Would you . . . that is, may I be so bold as to ask . . . ?" The elder girl twisted her fingers together and gazed at him so wistfully that she might have been before a prince in a bedtime story.

Her sister broke in. "Oh, please, sign it! That way we can prove that we met you!"

Her outbursts, which could only be rendered in justice with a superfluity of exclamation points, had begun to draw the attention of their fellow passengers. Vincent, who had no trouble conversing with the Prince Regent without seeming to note his rank, stammered and hemmed. Patting his coat pockets, he looked around helplessly.

Taking pity on him, Jane opened her reticule and produced a small pencil that she used for taking notes while they worked. Handing it to Vincent, she tried to find amusement in the embarrassment he so obviously felt at being singled out for attention. Of course, it was understandable that the pamphleteer would only mention the most famous personages in his accounting of the fête, and Jane was as yet an unknown. But though it was a prideful wish, she hoped someday to see the words *Mr. and Mrs. Vincent* appear with a notice of their work.

"Inscribe it to Miss Cornell and Miss Caroline Cornell!" Miss Caroline Cornell, the younger, bounced on her toes again. "That way our friends will be certain that *we* met you!"

"Of course." He penned his name on the page below the illustration and began to return it to them, then checked his motion. "Jane?" Vincent offered her the page.

"Oh, no." Finding herself the sudden object of the girls' curiosity did much to relieve Jane's sensation of being left out. She had no wish to be thrust into the public view, only to have her work recognised, and even that was vanity speaking.

"You did half the work." He pressed the pencil into her hand. Inclining his head to the Misses Cornell, he bowed slightly. "My wife is my creative partner, you see."

"But . . . what? That is . . . I mean . . . how? What did you do?"

"Did you see the anemones?" Jane asked.

This broke Miss Caroline's questionable reserve. She darted around her sister to bounce in front of Jane for a bit. "Truly! I loved those! They exactly matched my dress, you know!"

"I am glad to hear it." And glad too, that she had taken time to adjust their colour.

"Where did you learn to glamour so beautifully?" Miss Cornell managed to complete a question at last.

"Well . . . I learned from tutors when I was a girl, and the subject interested me, so I read books and practised quite a bit."

"Oh! We have a tutor too, but he is ever so dull!" Miss Caroline pouted. "I wish you could be my tutor!"

"Would you show us how you made them?"

Jane turned her palms out helplessly. "I wish I could, but the boat is moving too fast." Seeing the confusion in both girls' faces, Jane could not help but wonder what their tutor had taught them. "Glamour is attached between the ether and the earth. When we travel, the folds get pulled out of our hands too quickly to govern, so it is not possible to maintain a glamour and have it travel any distance without constant effort. At this speed, it would be too exhausting to be manageable or even safe." That inability to work glamour at sea was, in fact, one of the things which had kept Britain safe from Napoleon during the war. Any advantage the French might have had through their longer history with glamour was lost when approaching an island nation.

Miss Cornell tugged on her curls, thinking. "Is it like . . . I lost my pocket handkerchief to the wind. Is it like the wind?"

Jane hesitated, thinking the comparison through. "Somewhat. No metaphor is precise in describing glamour, any more than a metaphor can precisely describe light. We use a mixture of them to touch on the different aspects of glamour."

Miss Caroline stood on her toes, clapping her hands. "Oh! I always thought it was more like marionettes than fabric!"

Schooling her expression to hide her laughter, Jane asked simply, "How so?"

"Because! You move your hands here"—she waved her hands in front of her in a pattern that could not have produced any sensible expression of glamour—"to create something over here!" She hopped to the left, nearly toppling over with the movement of the ship.

Jane clapped her hands with understanding. "Just so. Yes, you see the difficulty. Embroidery is the closest one can come to describing creating a detailed glamour such my anemones, and yet one cannot embroider at a distance."

"Why can not people invent words for glamour instead

of borrowing from other things?" Miss Cornell screwed up her face.

"Some words are specific to glamour, but you will not find those until you have practised further."

Vincent had retreated a few steps away, the relief at having escaped obvious in the set of his shoulders. Not minding the girls' inquiries, Jane spent some time with them, explaining a few simple things about glamour that language sufficed to deliver until their parents called them away. Before going, the Misses Cornell pressed Jane to sign their pamphlet and swore their eternal devotion to her as well.

As soon as she was certain they would not see, Jane smiled and joined Vincent at the rail of the ship. "Oh, my dear. I have never seen the like of that."

He grunted. "This is why my father did not want me to use his surname. The spectacle."

Laying her hand on his, Jane rubbed her thumb against the fine hairs across its back. "Is it . . . is this normal for you?"

"Well . . . they were younger and more conspicuous in their enthusiasm, but yes, the part of a glamourist is often to be a curiosity. People assume that because my art is on display, I myself must also be an exhibit for their attention."

Jane remembered well their first meeting, and how he had given her his shoulder when she approached him. "I am sorry."

"Why?"

"Because I did the same when we met."

"Ah, Jane." He lay his other hand over hers, holding it with both hands. "I regret every moment I kept you at a distance." Leaning down, Vincent kissed her. Jane, in sight of the entire ship, returned the kiss with enthusiasm.

Five

Travel and a Little Napoleon

The prevailing winds were against their ship, and so the trip across the Channel took a full two days. Jane found that not even the rough weather could dampen her joy in their transit. The Prince Regent's favour had extended to arranging a private cabin for them. Though it was no larger than the linen closet at Long Parkmead, with Vincent's company the cabin seemed cosy rather than cramped.

Even so, she was glad to disembark in Calais and get her first taste of life on the Continent, but the port was quite filled with English travellers, so many of them that there were few places where she did not hear the accents of home. Jane consoled herself that once they left the city behind, she would find a more authentic experience of France en route to Belgium.

In truth though, the Vincents' travel from Calais to Binché was little different from any trip in a public carriage. It was too crowded for comfort, and the views out the windows—though of unfamiliar scenery—were only glimpsed by twisting one's neck.

The carriage exchanged passengers at inns, crossings, and stables so that they had an unending variety of new travel companions. Jane cared not at all. None of the other passengers took notice of them, and the freedom from responsibilities delighted her nearly as much as what little scenery she could glimpse.

For the first two days they travelled without concern, slowed only by a log across the road, which delayed their progress by some hours. As the carriage rolled through the country, Jane was enchanted by the differences between France and England. Not that she found France in any way superior, but the local garments, which changed with every region through which they passed, were endlessly charming. At one stop, the local women had red borders on their aprons. When they halted for a quick nuncheon at an inn in the north of France, the women wore heavy wooden clogs as they walked through the mud of the stable yard. In another region, white fichus were the order of the day.

But as the carriage bounced across the landscape, what Jane most wished for was more padding upon the seats. She was, therefore, delighted when the carriage slowed and then stopped, as this would offer a chance to escape its confines. Outside, she could hear a muffled conversation, but no coachman appeared to open the door. She hoped that it was not another log across the road, though even that might be welcome if it afforded them the opportunity to stretch their legs.

After a few minutes, one of the other travellers—an old matron whose black lace marked her as a widow—peered out the window and tutted loudly. She turned to the young girl travelling with her and said something disapproving in Flemish.

Jane sat on the other bench, by the door, with Vincent acting as a human shield between her and the German soldier who shared their bench. He would not have been objectionable as a companion were it not for his propensity to eat whole garlic cloves. Curious as to what the matron had seen, this soldier now leaned across the *diligence* to look out the small window in the door, though there was a window on his side of the carriage as well.

"We are in a field," he said in heavily scented English.

The door flew open and a man with a cravat wrapped around the lower part of his face looked in. He held a pistol.

Jane cringed against the side of the carriage, the shock of the gun combining with the strong memories of the last time she had beheld a gun at close range. Vincent sat forward, putting his arm in front of her as though that could shield her in some manner.

In French, the man said, "Out. All of you."

Vincent went first, though Jane would have held him back if she could. Within moments, she and the other passengers were standing beside the *diligence*. Three ragged men faced them, the one with the gun and two more with rusted sabres. A fourth held the horses, and a fifth stood atop the carriage with another pistol pointed at the coachman.

The German soldier said something in French, but his native tongue so coloured the language that Jane could scarcely understand him. She heard only the word, "Napoleon."

The ragged man with the pistol replied hotly. The others joined in, also shouting various imprecations at the German. She gathered they were Bonapartists set on taking the *diligence* for their cause and was not surprised that the German did not join his former allies.

Lowering his voice, Vincent said, "Dearest, do you remember your Beast?"

"Yes." She could not see what their ill-fated *tableau vivant* had to do with the current situation.

He then turned to the soldier and, to her surprise, spoke to him in German. This provoked a furious outburst from the rebel with the pistol, but a nod from the soldier.

The Flemish lady spoke up then, gesturing sharply with her fist at the ruffians who held them. "Napoleon? Feh!" She spat on the ground. Her young charge grabbed her arm and pulled her back all too late.

One of the sabre bearers advanced with his blade raised.

Vincent said, "Jane. Frighten the horses. *Jetzt!*" He and the German sprang to action in the same instant.

Startled, Jane could only stare for a moment, then she gathered herself and stripped off her gloves. With her hands bare, Jane threw the folds of the Beast around her, caring little about artistry in her haste. Raising the arms of the horrible creature, she menaced the horses.

The German clambered onto the top of the *diligence* while the rebel there struggled with his gun. His footing was upset as one of the horses reared, tearing its traces free. The postillion took advantage of this to urge the horses forward. His coachman helped the German subdue the gunman on the carriage while the Bonapartist holding the horses flung himself out of the way of their charge.

Jane dropped her folds of glamour and turned to Vincent in time to see him punch the ruffian with the gun in the nose. The man dropped to the ground. Scarcely had he fallen when Vincent turned to the man with the sabre who had threatened the old woman. Jane grabbed folds of glamour convulsively, as if she could weave some sensible illusion to help her husband from twenty paces.

The remaining sabre-bearer still threatened, so she could at the least remove the old woman and her charge from harm. Jane lifted her skirts and hurried to their side. She wove a *Sphère Obscurcie* to mask them from the rebels' view. The young girl was crying, but the matron seemed ready to take up a sabre herself. Jane put her finger to her lips. "They cannot see us," she whispered. They stared at her, uncomprehending, so she repeated it in French and Italian. When this did not quiet the girl, Jane glanced back to see how close the rebels were, and beheld something astonishing.

Vincent had somehow disarmed one of the sabre-bearers and was now fighting the other with the liberated sabre. While Jane had known that her husband was quite fit, she had not realized he had any skill with weapons. Yet Vincent wielded the weapon as though he were well used to it. Indeed, with his superior height and reach, it took but moments before he had reached past his opponent's guard to strike him in the upper arm. This drawing of first blood did nothing to ease Jane's fears.

When the carriage thundered back down the road, Jane nearly cheered, but stopped herself for fear of giving their position away. The German soldier jumped down and ran towards Vincent with the captured musket in hand.

The German shouted something, and the remaining rebel dropped his sabre. Vincent picked it up and gestured to the man to kneel. In short order, he bound the man's wrists with his cravat. Vincent stepped back and turned. "Jane?"

"Here, love." She dropped the fold which was hiding them and her husband heaved a sigh of relief.

"Cleverly done, Muse." He trotted across the field as the coachmen and the soldier secured the other rebels. A spot of blood flecked his sleeve.

"Are you hurt?" Jane hurried to meet him. Only now that the events were over did she have time to realize how very real the danger had been.

"Eh?" He stopped and noticed the blood for the first time. "No. It is the other fellow's. I am afraid it will be a bother to get out."

Jane pressed herself against him, trembling. "Never take such a risk again. You could have been shot."

"Nonsense." Vincent pulled her close and kissed the top of her head. "They were using ancient wheel-lock pistols. They take a few seconds to spark, and these guns displayed some rust, so it seemed unlikely they would spark on the first rotation. There was no danger of them getting a shot off. It was perfectly safe."

"How could you possibly know that?"

As he explained more about the mechanisms of guns, Jane shook her head and embraced him tighter. What she had really wanted to know was how her artist husband knew about weapons.

The *diligence* was delayed by a half day to deliver the captured rebels to the local authorities, so they did not cross into Belgium until very late on the second day. They arose with dawn the next morning and set off as the sun started to warm the winter fields. They arrived in Binché a few hours later as the village clock struck ten, bells chiming as if celebrating the Vincents' arrival. The sun painted the stucco walls of the village a pale red-gold that belied the chill of the season. Passing through into the town proper, the Vincents were charmed by the neat houses and tidy window box gardens which crowded the streets. The chaise set them down at the carriage post outside the A l'Aube d'un Hôtel near the centre of town. Mr. Vincent hired a boy to run to M. Chastain's to let him know that they had arrived. In short order, one of M. Chastain's students drove up with a wagon, and the Vincents were whisked—if bouncing over cobblestones can be called whisking—to the Chastain home.

The large front gates opened onto a courtyard faced on three sides by independent buildings. The grand staircase of the one at the back clearly marked it as the home proper, while the one to the right exuded the unambiguously ripe smell of a stable. A long single story building to the left with large windows and expansive skylights would have seemed well suited for an orangery if it had only been filled with trees. Instead, the windows exposed endless banks of disjointed glamour pressed against each other with neither rhyme nor reason. Young men and a few women toiled, faces tight with concentration, on these objects of curiosity.

No sooner had the Vincents alighted than a tall man with a full crop of iron-grey hair burst out of the laboratory. His aquiline nose bent as he beamed in delight, throwing his arms wide. "David! I am so happy to see you!"

Jane started. It had been so long since she had heard anyone call her husband by his assumed Christian name that she was quite unused to it. Her surprise at that was quickly supplanted by new astonishment as Vincent broke into a full smile.

"Bruno!" Her taciturn husband bounded across the yard and met M. Chastain with open arms. They pounded each other on the backs as if they were schoolboys, then parted and took the measure of each other. "You are old."

"You," M. Chastain poked a finger into Vincent's stomach, "are older. And rude. You must present me to your wife, you great lumbering fool."

Still smiling—no, *grinning*—Vincent brought him to Jane. "Jane, may I introduce Bruno Chastain. My wife, Jane Vincent."

"How do you do." Jane dropped a curtsey.

M. Chastain held out his arms, shaking his head. "We do not stand on ceremony here! You are family." He placed his hands on her shoulders and leaned close, kissing her on both cheeks before she could think of a response. "Welcome. David is like a brother to me, and you, a sister."

Jane had met Frenchmen before, but they had always belied their reputation for effusive displays, seeming only a little more enthusiastic than her native Britons. Jane sometimes wondered if that was because they had modified their behaviour to match that of her country.

From the door of the main house, a woman called, *"Bonjour, Bonjour, bienvenue! Je suis si heureuse de vous voir ici. Bruno, faites-les rentrer avant qu'ils ne prennent froid."* Then she hurried down the steps, delicate features glowing with welcome. Standing on her toes, she barely came up to Vincent's chest, but this did not stop her from clasping his face and pulling his head down to kiss him on both cheeks. Vincent did not appear to be surprised by this. *"Laissez-moi vous regarder. Oh, vous ressemblez en tous points à la description de Bruno. J'ai déjà l'impression de vous bien connaître."*

In this moment Jane learned that, though her written French was passable, she had almost no comprehension of the spoken language. She was fairly certain that the woman had just said that she had not met Vincent before, and yet that could not be the case, given how familiarly she had greeted him.

"Enchantée de faire votre connaissance." Vincent responded with French that sounded as fluent and easy as any of the natives. *"Bruno a fait votre éloge dans bien des lettres, Madame Chastain."*

"Oh, non, non, cela n'ira pas. Vous devez m'appeler Aliette." Without waiting for a response, Mme Chastain took Jane by the hands, quickly kissing her on both cheeks. *"Vous devez être Jane. Je suis si contente de vous voir ici."*

Flustered, Jane managed a *"Merci,"* which seemed to satisfy Mme Chastain.

"Je m'excuse de vous avoir fait attendre debout dans la cour. S'il vous plaît, suivez-moi à l'intérieur." Linking arms with Jane, Mme Chastain shouted at a pair of students who had emerged from the laboratory. Judging from the alacrity with which the action was taken, she had apparently asked them to bring in the Vincents' trunks. M. Chastain and Vincent followed, already talking about glamour and the work they would do in the laboratory. Though Jane longed to slow her pace and join the gentlemen, to do so would be intolerably rude to Mme Chastain, who kept up a running, though incomprehensible, commentary as they went up the stairs to the house. Jane gathered that the monologue was primarily concerned with fatigue and the perils of travel. She wondered if Vincent had told the Chastains of

their encounter on the road, or if Mme Chastain spoke in more general terms.

The inside of the Chastain home had broad halls with high ceilings that gave a feeling of spaciousness, but Jane could not be certain how much of that was real. Glamour hung on every surface, as if M. Chastain could not help himself, and must exercise his art at all times, defying even the most basic points of taste. Mme Chastain watched Jane's face and laughed as though she were quite used to this reaction. *"Oh, vous savez comment est mon mari."*

Understanding only the word "husband" and Mme Chastain's embarrassed tone, Jane took an entire volume from that sentence. M. Chastain must enjoy playing with glamour more than good taste allowed, and his wife indulged him in this.

Mme Chastain said something else in French, but it was too rapid for Jane to even hear the individual words. Colouring, Jane smiled an apology. *"Mon français est très mauvaise. Pourriez-vous parler plus lentement, s'il vous plaît?"* She had known French would be the language *de rigueur*, but until she arrived she had not realized how poorly she remembered it.

Patting her hand, Mme Chastain slowed down and spoke with such clarity that, though it was *en français*, Jane understood her perfectly. "Of course, my dear. You may have to remind me again. I only said that my husband allows his students to practice here. The whole will be refashioned by the end of the season."

They had a bare warning of squeals of laughter before a brace of children fairly tumbled down the main hall. Unaccompanied by a governess, they raced first to Mme Chastain, flinging their arms around her with such unfeigned affection that she nearly disappeared from view in their embrace. Joining in their laughter, she gently separated them, and presented each child in turn to the Vincents. Stilled in this manner, Jane could now discern that there were but three children. The eldest, Yves, was a boy of fifteen who already showed his father's height. His two siblings, Miette and Luc, were eight and six respectively, both appearing to be from the same mould as their more delicate mother. All gave very elegant greetings, with far more composure than Jane had expected based on their wild entrance.

As Luc executed an improbable bow, the toy sword in his waistband stuck up comically behind him. Yves's face blanched and he reached for the sword, with a furtive look at his father.

Though he spoke in French, M. Chastain's query was clear. "What is this?" He gestured at the sword, his brows lowering.

With no apparent self-consciousness, Luc pulled out the toy sword, made from two lengths of wood lashed together with twine, and held it above his head. Yves made an abortive movement to reach for the handmade sword, but stopped when Luc cried, "I am Napoleon!"

M. Chastain grabbed the boy's arm and wrenched the toy sword out of his hand, then used it to strike three swift blows across his son's bottom.

Mme Chastain, who had retaken Jane's arm, jumped as if *she* had been struck. Her hand tightened in a sudden convulsion.

In a very low voice, so unlike the laughter with which he had greeted them, M. Chastain said, "Not in my house." He handed the sword back to his son. "Go to your room, I will attend to you shortly."

The little boy bowed, his face pale, and walked up the stairs with stately dignity. When he was out of sight overhead, Jane heard one muffled sob, then his gait changed to a run, disappearing into another part of the house. Sighing, M. Chastain straightened his coat, adjusting the cuffs with care.

Yves cleared his throat. "Papa, the fault was mine. I made him the sword, and when he asked who the wickedest person in the world was, I told him it was Napoleon."

"Even in jest, I want nothing of that man in this house. You are old enough to understand why and to have known better. Pray go to your room as well, and wait for me there."

"Sir." Yves bowed and left with an apparent sense of dread, as if something worse awaited him.

Only Miette remained, standing on one foot, with her forefinger tucked in her mouth and her eyes wide. Through all of this, Mme Chastain gripped Jane's arm, only gradually relaxing her hold. "Bruno, I think we have left our guests on their feet long enough."

Spreading his arms wide, M. Chastain turned to them, his face lighting up suddenly. "Of course! Come, we have some excellent wine and cakes laid by. Unless you are tired and wish to take a rest until dinner?"

Seizing this opportunity, Jane made her apologies. The day had been long, she claimed, and the fatigue from the road made her only too grateful for an opportunity to recline. In truth, her nerves were shaken by what she witnessed. Never had her father struck her or Melody, and certainly not in front of company. She could not discard the very real expression of fear that all three children had borne or Mme Chastain's trembling.

They were led up the stairs and to their rooms, which were well appointed and lacking the extremities of glamoured ornamentation which overlay the ground floor. The suite afforded them a sitting room and a bedchamber, both with the large windows common to the rest of the house. When the door was at last shut and they were alone, Jane removed her bonnet and dropped with relief into the armchair by the fire.

"Muse, are you well?" Vincent knelt at her feet to help her off with her boots.

"Fatigued some, but more shocked—I know M. Chastain is your friend, but, truly Vincent, I am genuinely shocked by what I saw."

"The glamural in the front hall was something to behold." Chuckling, he set her right boot by the fire and settled his attention on the left.

Jane stared at the top of his head, thinking back. Had he not been in the hall when the incident with the sword had happened? No, no, he had been standing just beyond M. Chastain. She had attributed his composure to good breeding, but was it possible that he had not noticed? "I refer to his manner with his children."

Vincent raised his gaze from the laces of her boot, surprise writ large on his face. "His manner? How did it seem to you?"

"Overly harsh. There was no need to strike a child for so minor an offence, and Mme Chastain gripped my arm as if she were afraid he would do more."

"Ah." Vincent rocked back on his heels, still holding her boot. "Ah. And what does it say about me, I wonder, that I did not notice." He turned the boot over, running his thumbs along the sole as if measuring its thickness and weight. "My father would not have been so gentle."

Stilled by the reminder of how little she knew above her husband's life before he gave up his family name, Jane grieved at the volumes she learned from that single sentence. "But it cannot strike you as right. A father should be a source of comfort and a figure of respect."

He set the boot neatly by the other, aligning the two with painstaking care. "'Should' and 'are' rarely match. My father commanded respect, certainly, and if the respect seemed to him to be lacking, then he . . . corrected us. But, as I have mentioned, I was not a nice boy, so I cannot doubt that it was justified." Vincent stood, one knee popping audibly. Rubbing his head until his brown curls stood out in a mane, he paced a little away from her. "I think only my sisters could be said to find anything like comfort with him, but the expectations for girls are not so exacting."

"Different perhaps, but no less rigorous for that." Jane remembered the hours she spent walking the length of their hall with a glass of water in her hand, trying to develop the smooth and easy stride her mother wished her to have. To walk to the end of the hall without spilling a drop seemed such a simple task, but it was one Jane never fully perfected. Her sister Melody had been so graceful she could almost skip with the glass. "Still, I cannot believe that my father would have treated a son so."

"Well . . ." Vincent shook his head, cutting off the rest of his words. "Well, your father is an exemplary man, but I hope the comparison will not make you think ill of Bruno. Based on my friends' accounts of their childhood, he is the more common model of father."

Dismay crept by slow measure into Jane's heart. She tried once more. "Not a model, never an exemplar. You—that is, if we were to have children . . ."

"I would wish to follow your father's example." He adjusted a curtain to let more light into the room, his back carefully to her. "Interesting. Bruno has set his students to creating a group glamour in the yard. Or, no, I am mistaken. They are practising passing threads from person to person at speed. It appears to be part game and part exercise."

Swallowing her next question, Jane allowed him the change of topic. They had time enough to come to an understanding, and she was loath to push him into subjects about which he was so clearly uncomfortable, but at the same time, she desired nothing more than to know about every part of his life. Rising, she padded across the floor, thankful for the thick carpets that graced the room and protected her from the chill. Sliding her arms around his waist, Jane embraced Vincent from behind, trying to offer what apology she could for resurrecting painful memories. He placed his hands on hers, tracing the line of her fingers. Leaning her head to the side, Jane rested her cheek against his back and felt his breath through her body. She would be content if the world consisted of nothing but this connection between them.

His chest tightened with an inhalation. "Did you understand why Bruno was so angry?"

"In truth, no. Acting like a deposed monster seems a small infraction."

"In this region, the Bonapartists are still quite present, and want to put Napoleon's son on the throne. Bruno is his cousin on the distaff side, and has always loathed the little emperor."

The door to their room opened and a pretty serving maid entered, head bowed. *"Excusez-moi. Mme Chastain m'a envoyée pour vous aider."*

Releasing her hold on Vincent, Jane let him greet the girl, and soon understood that she was there to help to unpack their luggage. Despite his ease with the language, Vincent hovered in the background, more in the way than not, until Jane sent him down to watch the students and their exercise in the yard. Though she was wild with curiosity herself, she truly was fatigued from the journey, and the simple act of settling in would do much to soothe her.

Practising her uncertain French, Jane ventured to ask the girl's name, *"Comment vous appelez-vous?"*

"Anne-Marie, madame." She shook out Jane's dove grey dress and hung it on a peg in the wardrobe.

Jane put Vincent's writing desk on the table by the window, checking to make certain his ink-pot had not opened in transit. Feeling like a schoolgirl, she then asked, *"De quelle region êtes-vous?"*

"Paris, madame." Refolding each of Vincent's shirts with precise care, she placed them in the bureau.

"Avez-vous—" Jane stopped, trying to puzzle out if one asked "Have you lived here long?" or "How much time . . ." as she laid her watercolour supplies on the table next to Vincent's desk.

Anne-Marie pulled Vincent's blue coat out of the trunk, knocking the bandbox with his collars to the ground. The lid came off and the starched white collars rolled across the floor like snakes made of paper. "Oh! I am so sorry."

Crouching to help her collect them, Jane tried to reassure her. "No, not at all—" She stopped, nearly dropping a newly retrieved collar as she realized that the girl had apologized in English. "Anne-Marie, do you speak English?"

Blushing, Anne-Marie nodded. "You seemed as if you wanted to practice your French." She had only the faintest trace of a French accent, but her English was as good as if she were a native.

"But you said you were from Paris!"

"I am." She finished gathering the collars, then reached

for the one in Jane's hand. "But my mother is from London. She came as a lady's maid in 1788 and fell in love with a French student. When the family she worked for fled the Continent at the beginning of the Revolution, Mama stayed."

To choose to stay for love, Jane could understand, and yet she could not comprehend living through the Reign of Terror if another choice presented itself. "But that must have been horrible for you."

"Being born into it, I was too young to understand that the unrest was in any way out of the ordinary." She set the bandbox on a shelf in the wardrobe. "Mama made certain that I learned both French and English, as she thought it would be useful in helping me find work, and here I am." She shut the door and brushed her hand over the wood.

"And it is such a relief, I cannot tell you. I studied French as a girl, but have fallen out of the habit of speaking it. I find I can still read, but understanding is very difficult."

"Some of your difficulties are due to the dialect spoken here. You no doubt learned Parisian French and this has some Flemish mixed in with it." Anne-Marie brushed her apron out and surveyed the rest of the room. The trunks stood empty with their contents bestowed neatly in the vitrines and armoires of the room. "I think you are in order now. I will send someone to remove the trunks shortly. What time shall I return to help you dress for dinner?"

"It does not take me long to prepare. Six o'clock?"

Anne-Marie paused, biting her lip, before saying, "I believe . . . Mme Chastain traditionally sets the table at two."

"Oh." The time at which dinner was served in England varied widely from country to town, so it should hardly surprise Jane to find that there was a significant difference across the Channel, and yet she rather had the impression that the move to later dinner times came from the Continent. "I thank you. In that case, half past one should suffice."

Anne-Marie curtsied and asked for leave to depart, which Jane granted with some reluctance—not because she wished to keep the girl from her other duties, but because the opportunity to speak in her native language was already a relief.

At the door, Anne-Marie paused. "If it is not a presumption of me to make this offer, should you have any other questions or wish some help in understanding the local patois and customs, please do not hesitate to ask."

"I would not wish to keep you from your other duties."

"M. Chastain hired me for the purpose of attending to you and Mr. Vincent, because of my English. My other duties are light."

Taken unawares by this thoughtful act from a man Jane had begun to consider lacking in feeling, she took a moment before she could reply. "Thank you. Or rather, *merci*. If you would be so kind as to help me practice my French, I would be most grateful."

"Let me arrange for the trunks to be removed and then I will return, if you like."

"Merci, oui."

Anne-Marie smiled, *"Au revoir."*

She shut the door behind her, leaving Jane to ponder what could make a man so inconsiderate toward his own children and yet so kind to a stranger.

Six

Damask and Rainbows

The school that M. Chastain operated was
beyond Jane's imagining in scale and concept.
Seven young men and two young ladies studied
with him, learning far more than the basic elements of glamour the young ladies of England
were required to know as part of the womanly
arts. Aspects of glamour such as the principle of
attemperate cooling, which Jane had struggled
to acquire through books and experimentation,
these fortunate few were learning the way another student might learn the catechism: as if it
were a simple, solved, and knowable problem.
Her imagination was excited by the possibilities,
and she longed to have been a student there
herself and to have gained some of the formal

training of which she so often felt the lack when comparing her own skills to Vincent's.

In what used to be a carriage maker's showroom, the students each had their own working-place in which to practice and create glamurals. The two long walls of the building consisted of windows, one next to the other, and overhead, skylights afforded light enough to work late into the evening. One student, M. Archambault, had created a tableau *à la Chinoiserie*, which dripped with peonies and had a steaming dragon woven round a fountain. In sharp juxtaposition, an ice palace gave off a satisfactory chill to accompany the crystalline angles of its walls. Speaking in English for Jane's comfort, M. Chastain discussed his goals of providing a solid base of knowledge so that his students did not have to spend their time discovering the very simplest of principles that most apprentices would learn from their masters. With this pool of knowledge, they would be able to spend their efforts innovating new glamours rather than reweaving worn threads.

It was so noble a goal that Jane again found herself doubting that anything untoward had happened when they arrived. Certainly she had seen no further signs of unrest. She began to wonder if her nerves had been overrun from the rigours of the journey.

"Enough of this, old man. You dragged me across the Channel to see your jacquard." Vincent crossed his arms and lowered his chin as he did when he was displeased, but the corners of his eyes hinted at an incipient smile.

"Very well, vulture. Since you are swooping in to impose on me, I shall show you so you will leave me in peace." Barely concealing his pride with this teasing, M. Chastain led them across the floor to the end of the building, where a simple glamour of an oak tree appeared to cast shade over the floor. Entirely fixed, it was rendered with correctness, but to Jane's eye, it lacked a sense of life. He spun on his heel and gestured at the tree with an unambiguous expression of complacence. "Walk around it."

Keeping her attention fixed in the physical plane so she could experience the tree as art before she experienced it as craft, Jane followed Vincent around it, first noting that she was mistaken about motion, for the tree swayed gently in an unseen breeze. A few steps ahead of her, Vincent's breath huffed in a way she recognised as approbation, and a moment later, Jane understood why. What she had originally taken as movement was a transformation. As she continued around, the trunk shifted to become a dryad, and then the tree vanished entirely, leaving only a beautiful woman dressed in a short toga. None of the elements of the original tree were visible. Jane could no longer restrain her curiosity. She let her vision expand into the ether so she could see the threads of glamour that had been so deftly woven. The structure of the tree was visible in this light, but she could not yet tell how it had been arranged so that it was not revealed to the natural eye. Tracing one of the folds which created the pink glow of the woman's skin, Jane resumed her walk around the tree, wishing for Vincent's arm to steady her, as her sense of the physical world had been dampened. Moving with care, Jane followed the thread around until she found the twist which caused it to double back on itself. That twist was the marvel, for it had begun in green and now reflected only the pinks of the woman's skin. A twist, though, seemed insufficient to explain what she was seeing, since the structure of the threads appeared altered by the process. Jane stopped walking and let her cognizance drop as deeply into the glamour as she could, standing riveted for some moments before she located the element she was missing. The thread did not simply twist; it was twisted around another thread coming from the opposite direction. One conveyed the information about the woman, the other the information about the tree, and, bound together, they both supported and masked each other. Only at the sides could one see both sets of folds at once, which accounted for the sense of movement as different proportions of the folds became apparent. "Remarkable."

She let her cognizance return to the physical world, her breath coming a trifle quicker than the exertion merited, but entirely understandable given her excitement at the technique. Had the dryad merely been *behind* the tree with the spreading branches still visible, Jane would have thought nothing of the illusion, but to have it completely transform in this manner offered endless possibilities. "Truly, M. Chastain, this is wonderful. Yes, that is the right word, for I am full of wonder, not simply at the technique, but at the mind which created it. Am I correct that you are using complementary threads for—forgive me, I am not certain of terms—for the twisting in a double-weave?"

M. Chastain opened his mouth, then shut it again. Shaking his head, he snorted. "I had planned to next tell you how it was done, but I see that you have already discovered that."

Vincent clapped M. Chastain on the shoulder and gestured to Jane. "Allow me to introduce my wife, who—"

"Who is as perceptive as you said she would be." M. Chastain offered her a bow. "Forgive my astonishment. But I have several students who still cannot understand how this is done, and they have the benefit of having watched me develop the technique. I had begun to think I was clever."

"Oh!" Jane flushed. She must be seen as importuning, to come in and immediately pick his technique apart. It was a terrible, rude thing to do, but she had been so taken with it she forgot herself. "But you *are* clever. Recall that you wrote to Vincent about your new technique. I should never have thought of this idea on my own. Your invention is more clever by half than merely recognising that which one has been told about. Indeed, I believe that you give M. Jacquard too much credit by naming it after him and it should instead be called a Chastain Damask."

M. Chastain chuckled at this. "My students have said the same thing, but it seems immodest."

"But more accurate, perhaps?" Vincent inclined his head in a bow to his friend.

M. Chastain waved that away, but Jane silently resolved to give credit to the creator by calling the technique a Chastain Damask. He leaned toward her husband with a devilish gleam in his eyes. "And do you also see what I have done, David?"

Her husband shook his head slowly, gaze dulling as he let his perception shift. "I see the twist to which Jane refers, but had not yet recognised the pattern of opposites."

"The real challenge lies in finding an image which one can create from the pairs of opposing folds. I have yet to use it in a commissioned piece because it takes so much time to create, and clients rarely understand the intricacies or limits of glamour. I tell you, if I could ever find a way to create a glamour here and transport it, I should never leave Binché again. As it is, I must venture forth periodically and try to bring art to the uninformed savages."

"My husband and I disagree on this point, but I have often felt that an educated audience is a more appreciative audience."

"Appreciative, yes," Vincent inclined his head. "But I want to transport them, and whether they understand the craft of my work has little effect on that. All I want or care about is to know if I have taken them outside themselves, even for the briefest of moments. The effort to achieve that is well worth-while, even if they never comprehend my 'genius.'"

"Speaking of genius." M. Chastain bowed to Vincent, "I would like to see this *Sphère Obscurcie* of which you have written. I understand the theory, but not the technique."

Vincent returned Chastain's bow, then created the *Sphère* so quickly that it almost seemed to appear by itself. Because Jane had seen him perform this glamour many times before, she knew that he had taken a fold of glamour and twisted in his hand so the light in the room twined around itself. He then blew the bubble up into gossamer thinness, until it surrounded him and caused him to vanish from sight. She guessed that he performed it so quickly as a means of showing off to his friend. Other forms of masking glamours involved weaving a recreation of the scene minus the elements one wished to hide. Part of the genius of Vincent's technique was its simplicity and speed.

M. Chastain narrowed his eyes, stepped into the ball, and vanished. A moment later, Jane heard him say, "Again?"

Vincent dropped the folds and repeated the glamour, working slowly so that M. Chastain could follow his movements. On the third repetition, the Frenchman nodded. "I think I have it."

He pulled a fold of glamour from the ether and twisted it. Jane winced, seeing that he spun it in the wrong direction, but when she opened her mouth to speak, Vincent caught her eye and gave a tiny shake of his head. The *Sphère* would be invisible from the exterior but would not let light pass through. She held her tongue as M. Chastain expanded the bubble. In a moment, he harrumphed and popped it. "That was unexpected."

"Mirrored?"

"Yes. Most unpleasant to see oneself distorted upside down on a vast silver bubble. What did I do wrong?"

"Jane?" Vincent beckoned her to join them.

She hesitated, feeling as though she were intruding on a conversation of two colleagues. "You twisted the fold with the clock. It must go widdershins. If you do not twist at all, it is completely dark within."

"Fascinating." M. Chastain executed the glamour again, to perfection this time. "It only hides items which are completely within the *Sphère*, yes?"

"Correct." Vincent tucked his hands behind his back, in his lecturing posture. "I used a gossamer weight of glamour, which flows around objects that intersect it, leaving them visible. Had I used a heavier weight, it would have penetrated those items and shown their interior."

It was a clever solution, and Jane thought she could be justly proud of her husband for his invention.

"How did you come upon this, Vincent?"

"I was trying to find a way to record glamour at a distance and worked this out as an extension of that theory. You know how it goes."

They talked in this manner for some time, until M. Chastain was called away by M. Archambault with a question about temperature reduction. Vincent elected to accompany him, though Jane tried to hint that perhaps they had taken up enough of their host's time already. Excusing herself and hoping that Vincent would follow shortly, Jane made her way back to the main house.

Walking up the main stairs to their rooms, her mind was still half in the workshop, considering the ways in which she could improve on M. Chastain's creation, while chiding herself for the arrogance which had prompted the notion. Lost in thought like this, she nearly stumbled over Miette, who sat quietly on the stairs in a beam of light. She held a small crystal from a chandelier and was casting rainbows on the walls.

A radiant smile on her face, she held the prism up and spoke so simply that Jane had no trouble understanding her French. "I am making rainbows."

"I see. They are very pretty."

"I am working glamour like Papa." Miette moved the prism again. The rainbows danced on the marble stairs as the prism twisted in the sunbeam.

"What a good girl you are." Jane sat on the stairs by her, content for a moment to enjoy the simple pleasures of forming a connexion with a child.

Entirely trusting, Miette slid one of her small hands into Jane's and smiled up at her. "Mama says rainbows are *flèche lumineuse*. Is that true?"

Tripped by the words she did not know, Jane was forcibly reminded that she did not even have the vocabulary of a child, but her embarrassment was less acute than had she been speaking with an adult. "I am not certain. What does *flèche lumineuse* mean?"

Miette shrugged. "Decorations. Like at a birthday party."

"Oh, yes. That is what I have heard. When Zephyrus wed Iris they . . . made their wedding pretty with glamour. Rainbows."

"I like them!" Miette clapped her hand, forgetting the prism, which momentarily obscured the rainbows. She hummed a wedding march and stuck the prism back in the sunbeam, bobbing her head in time with her own music.

The rainbows dimmed as a cloud slid across the sun. Miette made a small sound of despair. "The party!"

Beyond the window, the sky had become quite dark, with the sort of heavy clouds which presage a snow-storm. Jane reached into the ether and pulled out a single fold, which she tied off into a strand of sunshine falling from floor to ceiling. With all the other glamours in the house it was barely noticeable, but for the bright patch it seemed to cast on the floor. She guided Miette's hand into the light. Though more faintly than before, rainbows still danced around them as the glamour bent on its path through the glass.

Jane cocked her head to the side, staring at the prism. All her life she had known what prisms did, and yet using one *with* glamour had never occurred to her. Doubting her memory of the glamour for rainbows, she grabbed another fold and divided it to match the colours Miette's crystal cast. To weave the rainbow, she split the glamour in exactly the way the prism split light. Jane let her vision expand into the ether, watching the sunbeam she had created for Miette and the way it neatly split itself inside the prism to emerge on the other side in a collection of dancing rainbows. The sole difference between Jane's glamoured rainbow and the prism's rainbow was that the glamoured one was fixed, unless Jane added additional folds and threads to make it dance.

Miette's prism took a simple glamoured sunbeam and scattered it into rainbows, which she was moving with no effort.

The glass, in effect, contained the pattern of a glamour *which could be moved.*

In a flash, Jane's head filled with the pattern of other glamours, and how each visual illusion was composed of the threads which might be described in the colours of a rainbow. The way they bent and twisted could—she was certain—be *recorded in glass*.

The epiphany was so strong that Jane was at the foot of the stairs before she realized she had decided to stand.

"Where are you going?" Miette called.

"To find my husband." Jane paused only long enough to say, "Thank you for the rainbows!"

Seven

Ensconced in Glamour

Jane matched intent with action and, gathering her skirts, dashed across the courtyard to the studio. Bursting inside, she tried to slow down to a semblance of reserve, but her excitement moved her through the space at a speed which only narrowly escaped being a trot. Jane spotted M. Chastain standing with M. Archambault, the student who had created the glamour *à la Chinoiserie*.

"Madame! What can I do for you?" Chastain left M. Archambault and met her half-way.

"Forgive me for troubling you, but I wanted a word with my husband." She looked past Chastain, expecting to see Vincent ensconced in the glamour.

"I am sorry your trip is for nothing. He left

shortly after you." He smiled. "Is there anything I can help you with instead?"

"No, thank you." Though Jane was bursting to talk of her idea, she wanted to share it with Vincent first. On reflection, she thought that it was probably prudent as well, for if there were a flaw in her scheme, he would spot it. "Did he say where he was going?"

"Back to the house, I believe."

Jane thanked him and returned at a slower pace to the house, wondering how she could have failed to see him, sitting as she was on the main stairs in the entrance. The wind had kicked up while she was indoors, and the first snowflakes, which had been predicted by the dark clouds drifted down, encouraging her to speed her way into the house. It was quite possible that he had entered during the very moment she had her epiphany, as her sight had been directed almost entirely inward.

The idea of catching a glamour in glass would not let her go, so she went to the parlour, hoping to find Vincent there. Mme Chastain sat sewing by the fire, and Jane had to endure some conversation with her as the snow coated the courtyard. Her thoughts ticked in time with the falling flakes as she spun through the possibilities opened by her discovery.

She had to constantly apply herself to keep her attention on Mme Chastain. They spoke of the children, the weather, and dinner parties to come, none of which held the slightest interest for Jane at that moment.

She resisted the urge to ask Mme Chastain for the addresses of glassblowers in town, though she wanted nothing more than to start experimenting right away. More than that, though, she wanted her husband.

As if someone had unstitched a pillow, the snow-storm wiped the courtyard from view in a wash of white. Miette and her brothers scampered into the room to seek their mother's permission to go out and play.

With this excuse, Jane made her escape and went up to her room. Though she could not see how it was possible to have missed Vincent on the stairs, she could still set her thoughts down on paper, which would give her some measure of peace. It might be that she would discover a flaw in her thinking as she did so.

And yet, Jane was certain that she would not. The theory was sound; the practice would be telling.

She opened the door to their rooms, anxious to begin at once, and stopped with her hand on the door. Vincent's coat, snow melting on its shoulders, hung on a chair by the fire and dripped upon the hearth. Her husband stood at the table by the window, his hair plastered against his skull and his high collar quite wilted by the damp. "I believe the snow is wetter in Belgium than in England." He dropped a paper into his writing desk and locked it.

"You are soaked through!"

"Believe me, I am well aware of that." Vincent undid the buttons at his cuffs.

Jane hurried to his side and began working at the buttons down the shirt's front. "Where have you been? I have been searching everywhere for you."

"The studio." He lifted his cuff to his mouth to pry a

stubborn button with his teeth. "Caught by the snow on my way back."

Jane pulled his arm away and undid the button herself. His hands were cold to the touch. "I was just there, and M. Chastain said you had returned to the house."

"I had planned to, but was delayed." He slid the shirt off, revealing his broad shoulders and the deep ribcage of a glamourist. "Why were you looking for me?"

Now that it was time to explain her idea, Jane's doubt in her own abilities came back with force. "I had an idea and wanted to share it with you to see if you thought it had worth."

He waited, prompting her to continue by his attentive silence. She explained. "I chanced upon Miette on the stairs, and she had a discarded crystal from a chandelier. She was using it to make rainbows on the wall." Jane smoothed the damp shirt and carried it to the fire, hanging it on the corner of the mantel, suddenly afraid that her idea was without merit. "It occurred to me that the prism bent the light in exactly the same pattern I use to create a glamoured rainbow. It seemed, looking at the prism and the rainbow, that one might craft a glass that could bend glamour in other ways, almost like a lens."

"Of course. Isaac Newton demonstrated this in his treatise on opticks. But splitting glamour into colours has no practical use other than giving us a greater understanding of how visible glamour relates to light." Vincent shook his head. "Besides, Newton's theories have been discredited by Thomas Young, who proved that glamour and light are not particles but related wave forms. The effect is interesting, but not useful."

Jane clenched her jaw, momentarily annoyed that he would assume that she had not read the latest works. Young's paper had been written in 1803, and she had read it eagerly. "Actually, it is Mr. Young's theories on the wave nature of glamour which led me to the realization that since glamour affects certain substances it might therefore be possible to record a glamour's pattern in glass. Such a record might stand in for a glamourist's hands, and create a path that the glamour is compelled to follow. The visual aspect, at any rate. I do not think it would work with other folds."

Vincent stood exactly as she had left him, feet spread wide and hair slicked against his skull. His eyes glazed over as he sketched a rainbow in the room. "My God." He raised his hands, tangling them in his wet curls. "My God, Jane. That might . . . I think." Abandoning words, he pressed her to his heart, the fine hairs of his chest tickling her cheek. His pulse thundered in her ear. Vincent squeezed her tightly, then lifted her off the ground, spinning in place with a laugh.

"You think it might work, then?"

Setting her down, he kissed her soundly. "Muse, we need to find a glassblower."

Eight

Language and Politics

By mutual consent, Jane and Vincent did not share their theory with M. Chastain, though each for different reasons. Jane feared that it would fail, and did not wish to appear the fool. Vincent, sure it would succeed, wanted to work out the technique and present it as fait accompli to his friend. Jane could not truly begrudge him this small professional competition, as it was not that far from her heart, either. This decision, though, hampered their ability to enlist his aid in a search for a local glassblower who had the requisite skills. Every event they had to attend, even those intended for pleasure, tried Jane's patience and seemed an insurmountable obstacle.

On the day following Jane's revelation, their attention was taken up by preparations for a dinner party that Mme Chastain was throwing in their honour. All the first families of Binché were to attend, and Chastain's students were pulled away from their studies to strip down the over-wrought glamour in the hall and replace it with a more decorous glamural.

Upon learning of the dinner, the first thought to come to Jane's mind was of how she could possibly survive an evening in which only French was spoken. When Anne-Marie came to help Jane dress, she confessed her fears to the maid and begged for her help. "I am only comfortable speaking with children, and that will hardly suffice to-night."

"Never fear. I have seen the seating plan. Mme Chastain has you paired with Colonel de Bodard, who speaks competent English, having been an émigré during the Revolution. He and M. Chastain should keep you tolerably occupied during dinner, though the conversation will tend toward war recollections." She opened the wardrobe. "What shall you wear tonight?"

"The primrose with the demi-train." Jane began pulling pins from the muslin frock she had on. "War talk is sure to be an improvement over hunters. At any rate, that is such a relief. I do dislike forcing others to speak in English for my benefit. My comprehension has improved in just the short span since our arrival, but I despair of my speech ever being fit for company."

Anne-Marie laid the dress on the bed and took a delicate bodiced petticoat from the bureau. "Madame, you do not need to fret. My mother never became fluent in her adopted language, and yet made herself well understood. No one will expect you to speak without error." Switching languages, she said, "And now, I will speak to you only in French. You must answer me so as well."

Choosing the easiest answer *en français,* Jane said, "Yes." After a moment, she added, "Thank you," and felt her vocabulary exhausted.

"Lift your arms, madame." Anne-Marie pulled the old petticoat off and slipped the new one on. Jane obeyed each instruction, sometimes gathering the intent from the actions rather than the words, but they managed to proceed with only the occasional bout of laughter born from misinterpretation. Through it all, Anne-Marie was unfailingly gentle of Jane's sensibilities, and yet firm in not allowing her to speak English.

Forced to use the language thus, even for simple tasks such as getting dressed, Jane began to realize that she knew more words than she had thought. Once dressed, Anne-Marie had her sit as she attended to Jane's hair. "I suggest that we play at conversation. I will pretend to be another guest and plague you with questions."

"That seems a good plan."

Heating an iron in the fire, Anne-Marie began the thankless task of attempting to force Jane's straight hair into fashionable curls. "I will begin with the most obvious questions. Where are you from?"

"I am from near Dorchester." She wrinkled her nose at the smell of heated hair.

Releasing the curl, Anne-Marie took up another section of hair. "Have you lived there always?"

"No. We lived in London these three months past."

"What did you do there?"

"We created a glamural for the Prince Regent." To her surprise, Jane realized that since so many of the common terms for glamour were French, she was suddenly possessed of a broader vocabulary than she had hitherto suspected. She chattered happily about the glamural as Anne-Marie worked her way through the rest of Jane's hair, leaving her with a respectable set of curls.

"All of that sounds lovely. I am consumed with jealousy that you got to see the Prince Regent." Anne-Marie took a tortoiseshell comb out of Jane's jewellery box and held it up to try the effect.

"It was on his recommendation that we came. I do not think we could have found passage at this time of year if it were not for his influence."

Shaking her head, Anne-Marie replaced the comb in the box. "That is a surprising kindness."

"Do you ever think about returning to England?"

"No." Anne-Marie's tone was short and took Jane by surprise. "I have never lived there, so I can hardly return. France is my home."

"Forgive me, that was thoughtlessly asked."

"It is nothing." Anne-Marie wrinkled her nose and selected a coral ornament, nodding with satisfaction as she pinned it to Jane's hair. "In truth, since Mama chose to stay here, I have always been given to understand that she found France preferable to England."

"I imagine your father had some influence on that."

Anne-Marie's face darkened for a moment. "Papa died in the Revolution. His ideals, I am afraid, were stronger than his judgement."

Sorry to have troubled her with a topic begun in innocence, Jane began to frame a more profuse apology, wishing to switch to English just for the moment. Instead, Anne-Marie held up a hand mirror to show the back of Jane's head. "There, Madam. Does that please you?"

It pleased Jane enormously. Dressing alone, she could never manage to tease her hair into anything so nicely arranged. "Anne-Marie! You are a treasure. I have always thought my hair unmanageable."

"I was at court for a time." Anne-Marie set the irons by the hearth to cool. "You would not believe the horrors I saw there, so please trust me when I say that your hair is lovely. One merely needs to know the trick of coaxing it."

Jane did not quite believe that mouse-brown could ever be lovely, but saw no need to press the point. When Vincent came in, she excused Anne-Marie and attended to tying his cravat for him.

Venturing to continue using French with her husband, Jane asked, "Have you had a pleasant afternoon?"

He did not seem to notice her efforts, instead slipping smoothly into the language. "Somewhat. No success in finding a glassblower yet." He lifted his chin to allow her easier access. "And you?"

"Anne-Marie has helped me practice French." She stepped back to admire the effect and decided that it would do. "Where did you learn to speak so fluently?"

"We had a tutor who was an émigré. Mistakes were not tolerated." This was one more reminder of his life as an earl's son, which he had abandoned for his art.

Together, they descended the stairs to wait in the parlour for the guests to arrive. Stomach twisting with dread, Jane managed to use her French to greet those to whom she was introduced, and learned to ignore the raised brows at her mispronunciations and mangled tenses. The purpose, she reminded herself, was to be understood, not to pass as a native. Even were she fluent, her dress would mark her as English, for the fashions had moved in different directions during Napoleon's reign, when communication between the two countries had been at a standstill. English waist-lines had begun to drop back to the natural waist, while French waists had remained high, and the decorations and embellishments here had a noted emphasis on lace, for which Belgium was justly famed. When Jane was introduced to Mme Meynard, she had a moment of coveting the belle's beautiful Pomona green gown with blond lace embellishments.

Jane soon realized that conversation was not so hard as she had thought it might be because at a party such as this one merely repeated the same topics again and again with different partners. How are you? Fine weather. Are you staying long?

She became more confident as the phrases loosened on her tongue, and by the time they went in for dinner, Jane had relaxed as much as was possible. As guests of honour, Jane and Vincent were led in by M. and Mme Chastain, but from that point forward, the dinner differed in nearly every regard from what Jane was accustomed to in England.

At home she was used to the dishes being placed upon the table in two great courses, and being confined to those closest to her. In France, though, the dishes were presented singly and carried round by servants to every guest.

Colonel de Bodard, far from regaling her with tales of battles as Anne-Marie had threatened, spoke instead of England, with an open fondness for his time there. He was the old style of chevalier, moderated somewhat by his time in England, and wore his greying hair pulled back in a tail. His coat was a pale green with some restrained embroidery confined to his waistcoat as the only nod to the more ornate fashions of his youth. He and Jane quickly established that they had acquaintances in common, and soon felt like the oldest of friends. He did her the favour of allowing her to struggle with her French, then offering correction in the gentlest manner.

As the table was cleared after dessert, the subject moved to politics, and a cross-table conversation began. Jane despaired of leaving the kind Colonel's side, but to her surprise, the ladies made no move to exit the table.

"I cannot like the formation of the United Kingdom of

the Netherlands, no matter how expedient the heads of state think it is." Mme Meynard, wife of the celebrated banker, accepted a glass of port from a footman. "Did not du Mezzier say, 'Blending wine must be done with care, else the character of both is lost'?"

Colonel de Bodard shook his hoary head. "You are mistaken to oppose it. Without a strong ruler, it is only a matter of time until the Bonapartists seek to reclaim what they regard as theirs."

Jane thought immediately of the brigands who had accosted them on the road from Calais to Binché. If those men were representative of the Bonapartists, Belgium had little to fear.

"Fie!" Mme Chastain shook her finger at him. "Napoleon is deposed and has no power here. I do not object to the new kingdom, but neither will I see support for it come from conjuring mitten-biters out of shadows."

Jane could hazard no guess as to what a mitten-biter was, but the conversation moved on before she could ask the Colonel.

"You do not oppose, but neither do you support!" M. Archambault pounced on Mme Chastain's statement with a vigour which surprised Jane. She still expected the party to separate at any moment, and yet there was no move resembling that.

The footmen distributed port to the gentlemen and ladies alike. Jane was at a loss as to whether propriety meant she should accept or decline.

Colonel de Bodard settled the matter by pouring a

generous glass for her. "Who could fully support it when they plan to put William VI on the throne? Him, I do not mind, but his son is as idle-headed a buffoon as ever lifted a sword, and I dread the day he inherits."

"Which is why"—Mme Meynard swirled her port in her glass—"it is worth attending to the Bonapartists. Napoleon might be deposed, but his son is still King of Rome. Might he not come to claim the land that belonged to his father?"

"With what soldiers? 'King of Rome' is a mere courtesy title with no power behind it." Vincent tilted his glass to her. "I hardly think that a threat, especially as Napoleon II is only three years old."

"What does it matter if the king is fit to rule if there is a strong regent? You British, of all people, should recognise that."

"I think," M. Chastain said, with enough force that his voice bounced off the far wall. Jane cringed, remembering anew his address to his son. "I think that I should like a cigar. Would anyone else care for one?"

With murmurs of "Very kind" and "Yes, thank you" cigars were distributed among the gentlemen. Then, to Jane's complete horror, Colonel de Bodard offered her one.

"No. Thank you."

"You English are so strait-laced." Mme Meynard blew a smoke ring. Jane was certain that her face utterly betrayed her, because Mme Meynard threw her head back and laughed directly at Jane's discomfiture.

"Come now, madame." Colonel de Bodard patted Jane's

hand. "You must not mind her. She only teases those she likes. I remember my own surprise at the differences between France and England."

"Long live the differences!" M. Archambault called across the table, pulling the lady to his right onto his lap.

Before Jane could rise from her chair to protest, the woman laughed and kissed him. "I say, long live the differences between men and women!"

"Hear, hear!" Many voices rose in approbation of the sentiment, and glasses were raised. Jane knew her face was red with shame for the woman, whom she could no longer consider a lady, yet she alone displayed any sense of consciousness of the indecorous behaviour. Even Vincent merely looked grave, which was not far from his natural expression under any circumstances.

Jane forced herself to stay in her seat, fighting her inclination to remove herself from a situation which she must, in England, find abhorrent. And yet, had she needed a firm reminder that she was abroad, nothing could suffice as well as the spectacle of a woman smoking a cigar and another being fondled upon the lap of a man whom Jane could only hope was her husband.

Not knowing where to look, Jane kept her attention focused on the glass of port, and how the light shone through the deep ruby liquid. She tried to think of how she would create that heavy shade and the faint greenish tinge where it touched the wall of the glass, but her attention was pulled—all unwillingly—back to the conversation.

"I see no reason to be upset by any of these changes in rulers, as we have been passed back and forth between France and the Netherlands for almost as many years as there have been people living here. As long as they leave us to our own devices, let the 'heads of state' play at ruling us. It makes no difference. We still have to pay taxes." Mme Meynard inhaled deeply on her cigar.

"But taxes to whom, and to what purpose, and how high?" M. Chastain drummed his fingers on the table. "All of these questions are dependent on who sits on the throne."

"Which, again, is why I find it curious that you are not more of a supporter of the Bonapartists than you are. Since Napoleon was such a great patron of the arts, it would seem natural for a glamourist to favour him."

"He was never a patron of mine." M. Chastain snubbed out his cigar. "Was he a 'patron' of yours?"

"It is possible," M. Archambault ventured, "to accept patronage from someone without agreeing with their politics."

"Only to your folly. You might begin by not agreeing, but time and habit will eventually cause you to mask your true feelings and, eventually, to forget them. Wiser to remove yourself from the influence of those with whom you cannot agree." M. Chastain slid his chair back. "Shall we adjourn and indulge in some shadow-play?"

The rest of the evening passed in a tolerable approximation of post-dinner hours in England, yet, to Jane's surprise, she did not find it as interesting as the dinner conversation. Shocking though the behaviour had been, she could not help but appreciate that the ladies' opinions appeared to have as much value as the gentlemen's.

Nine

Blowing Glass

A week after the party, the Vincents finally located a glass maker with the skills they thought they required for their experiment. M. La Pierre was accomplished in creating sheets of glass as well as blowing, cutting, and grinding lenses. More than that, though, he had a natural reclusiveness which left him little inclined to gossip.

Early on Wednesday, Jane and Vincent went to the workshop of M. La Pierre and laid forth the plans that they had for creating a glamour in glass. Across a scarred wood desk, the grizzled man chewed on his thumbnail while studying their drawings. The papers described the path a fold of glamour must travel in order to create a simple red cone, one of the first glamours a child might learn. They thought it was simple enough to be manageable and the finished prototype could serve as a building block from which they could create more complicated glamours. Their plan was to use the glass as a sort of lens, which would twist the light in the same manner as a glamourist's hands would. In this way they hoped to create a path for the glamour to follow once it entered the glass that would cause it to twist in such a way that it produced a red cone upon exiting.

M. La Pierre cleared his throat once and slid the papers back to them. "Don't know as that's possible."

"This seems to me to be a simple shape." Vincent traced a broad finger across the page. "I have seen glass blown with more complexity."

"Yes. But is the more complex glass blown with the specificiality you want? I can create a swan inside a glass ball, but ask me to make five swans and you will find none of them exactly alike. Glass is like water when you are working it."

"May we watch you blow glass?" Jane asked. "That might give us a better understanding of the process."

He rubbed his chin, his rough hand making a scratching noise against the stubble there. Nodding, he shoved himself back from his desk and led the way to the furnace. Pausing at the door, he took down heavy leather aprons from a hook and handed them to each. To Jane, he said, "You stay well back from the fire. Wouldn't want your finery to catch."

Past the door, the heat from the furnaces was nearly

overpowering, even with the chill of winter blanketing the town. Three furnaces, ranked in size, dominated the room. Vast skylights lit the workshop with warm winter sun, which made the glass sparkle brilliantly. M. La Pierre bade them stand some distance from the largest furnace and watch his apprentice work. Even with a heavy leather apron and gloves protecting him, the boy must have felt the heat terribly. In some ways, it was like watching glamour drawn in the physical world, as he worked a blob of molten glass into a refined and elegant shape. The red glow of the glass absorbed Jane, and she found herself possessed of a sort of jealousy that the apprentice was making something physical and of service. As much as she loved glamour, the illusions had few practical applications. Only the charms for cooling had any daily use, and those were limited by the amount of energy required to work them.

Though it was possible to create heat with glamour, governing folds at that end of the spectrum often led to poor health. As with all folds outside the range of visible light, it took such an inordinate amount of energy to manage them that it was far easier to make a fire with sulphur matches than to try to create one from glamour.

After they watched for a few minutes, M. La Pierre led them to the table of glasses his apprentice had already finished. The matched set had a delicate stem crowned by an elegant thin bowl. "Identical, yes?" He picked up two and held them out. "But look closely. See the bubbles? No two exactly the same. You need a simpler shape to put in-side it."

"The red cone is extraordinarily simple." Vincent pro-tested.

Snorting, M. La Pierre picked up the paper and pointed at it again. "You think introducing an inclusion to cause that bend is simple? I'd like to see you try."

"Your . . . good information is why we came to you, M. La Pierre." Jane tried to smooth over the man's ruffled feathers. To be sure, he was not the only glassblower in the area, but he was widely accounted the best. "Can you speak to what shapes are easier? Perhaps we can find a glamour that suits the medium."

He gestured with his chin at the boy blowing goblets. "Bubbles and tubes. That is what the glass wants to do." Setting the goblets down with deliberate care, he shook his head. "A fool's errand, if you ask me. If it were possi-ble, someone would have done it already."

Jane's stomach sank at that, for there was something to his argument. "But have the techniques for glassblowing not improved with time? Perhaps something is now pos-sible that was not before."

"Mayhap." He shrugged. "But it doesn't look so to me."

Vincent rubbed the back of his head. The furnace glowed with a visible heat, and beads of sweat crept down Jane's front, tickling as they went. The apprentice finished blow-ing the bowl and deftly drew a stem from the hot glass. His face was flushed from the heat, and sweat matted his reddish hair to his head. He did not break from his rhythm or let his attention waver from his business.

Jane marvelled at the regularity of his actions. "What causes the bubbles in the glass?"

M. La Pierre ticked off reasons on his fingers. "Air. Change in temperature. Impurities."

Vincent murmured to Jane. "I wonder . . . . If *any* impurity will show, might we control which ones do?"

"I would think so, to some degree, else they could not create glass paperweights containing swans or bubbles." She considered this as they watched the apprentice blow yet another in his seemingly endless stream of goblets. M. La Pierre seemed disinclined to say anything else. "What do you think would happen if we cast a glamour *inside* the glass as it is being blown?"

Vincent tucked his chin in, and his eyes narrowed in thought. "Intangible as the glamour is, I am not certain that it could have any effect. And yet, glamour changes when passing through the glass of a prism, so the two must have a connexion."

"I would be curious to see what happens."

The glass maker tutted and shook his head. "We will try it." Jane felt certain that he disapproved of the notion and was agreeing because of the funds they offered, but she hardly cared at this point.

M. La Pierre waited until his apprentice had finished with the last goblet and beckoned him over. "Mathieu, this gentleman and his lady want to try casting a glamour while glass is being blown. You will assist them until such a time as the task is beyond your skill. I want no repeats of your attempts to be an artist. Keep the craft clean and do the job." He cuffed the apprentice on the back of the head. The boy took the blow as if he were well used to this. "Understand me?"

"Yes, Father." Mathieu bobbed his head in assent.

Jane could not feel that it was truly necessary for M. La Pierre to discipline his son in front of them. She might resign herself to such casual disregard, but determined that she would never treat her own children with so little respect.

As La Pierre stalked away, Mathieu lifted his head and wet his lips, acting as though nothing untoward had happened. "May I see the drawings?"

Vincent pulled them out of his coat pocket and handed them to the young man, who drew off his heavy leather gloves to take the papers. His left arm had a healing burn that showed just below the cuff of his sleeve. Jane blanched at the thought of the molten glass touching his arm.

"Not glass. It was steam." Mathieu tugged his sleeve farther down in an effort to hide the burn. "Everyone asks. Glass would have taken the arm." He tapped the paper. "I can see why my father thinks this is not possible, at least not with the way we currently work. I have no idea what will happen when you try casting the glamour. Shall we find out?"

Mathieu led them to a different furnace and they began the process by having the young man blow a simple bubble. Since Vincent could work glamour at a distance, he stood back from the furnace, waiting for the ball of molten crystal to be lifted forth.

As Mathieu worked, Vincent deftly sketched the lines for the red cone they had first discussed. Almost immediately, he grimaced. Jane let her vision shift to see why.

Working at a distance as he did was difficult enough, but he was, in essence, aiming at a moving target. Though Mathieu was remarkably steady, the end of his pole was a good five feet away from him and shifted with even the slightest movement. Vincent was having problems aligning his glamour with the glass.

After some minutes of trying and failing, he shook his head and signalled Mathieu to leave off. He dipped the pole back into the furnace and let the crystal dissolve into the mass. Wiping his forehead, he stepped away. "How did that work?"

"Not well. The tip moves."

Mathieu laid his pole on an old table charred with evidence of previous work. "If I had a stand to keep the end still, that would help?"

"I believe so, yes."

He quickly found a stand with a Y yoke at the end. "We do not use it often, but it is handy when doing larger pieces."

Once again they took their stations, Vincent still staying well back. Jane watched, wishing that there were something she could add to the proceedings, but at this point there was nothing for her to do. The next hour passed in this manner, with Vincent repeatedly trying to simply get the glamour to pass through the glass while Mathieu attempted to hold the end of the pole steady. To the naked eye, it would seem they were succeeding, but each time, Vincent grimaced and shook his head.

Tugging at his cravat, Vincent pulled it free from his collar. "I am going to need to be closer. The end of the pole moves no matter how steadily Mathieu holds it, and my control is not specific enough at this distance."

"Shall I have a go at it?" Jane asked.

Mathieu shook his head. "Not in muslin, madame."

Chafing at the restraint, Jane could offer no reasonable argument against it, because the danger from the fire was, in fact, quite real. Still, she did not like having Vincent standing so close to the bulb of molten glass when Mathieu next pulled it out, either. The light from the bulb lit his face eerily, accenting the sweat pouring down his temples.

This attempt, however, resulted in greater success, for Vincent was able to create a red cone from glamour and align the pattern of the weaves with the bubble of glass. The glamour faded away as he released his hold and they all stepped back from the furnace to examine his efforts. Jane held her hands behind her back to fend off the urge to touch the still hot crystal.

Using tongs, Mathieu held it up to the light, gnawing the inside of his lip. "Do you see anything?"

Barely perceptible inclusions marred the otherwise un-flawed crystal, tracing a pattern which, when raw folds of glamour were applied, would result in a red cone. Vincent blew out his breath and wiped his hands on his apron. "Jane, do you want to do the honours?"

Almost trembling from the excitement that the glamour had created a physical impression, Jane pulled a pure fold out of the ether and directed it at the ball. The crystal seemed to radiate as if it were back in the furnace, but nothing further happened. She twisted the angle of the glamour, trying to find the entry path that Vincent had used when creating the red cone, aware as she did so that both Vincent and Mathieu held their breath. She could not achieve any effect beyond a luminescence of the entire sphere, and that had no red in it. As she was about to give up, Vincent shouted, causing her to drop the fold.

"Pardon." He winced. "For a moment, I thought I saw it."

Mathieu hesitated, squinting in thought. He lowered the ball of glass. "Maybe."

"It was very faint, and on the side opposite you, Jane." Vincent tucked his chin into his chest and rubbed his hair into a tangle. "What if . . . what if the faults need to be more pronounced? I felt as though the glamour wanted to fold, but did not quite know where to do so."

Jane considered, the only sound in the room the muted roaring of the furnaces. "If we laid another skein of glamour alongside the cone, say, one of cold, would that work, or would we merely have a recording of cold in glass?"

"Possibly . . ." Vincent stared into the furnace for a moment. "Mathieu, are you ready for another attempt?"

The boy asserted that he was.

"Shall I handle the cold, or shall you?" Jane asked.

"You tend to be more perceptive of the path of glamours than I. Let us say that I will hold the pattern for the cone and you can trace it."

Mathieu started at the suggestion. "Wait. The lady cannot go near the furnace. Not in those clothes."

Jane looked at the fire and she looked at her muslin dress and she looked at the sphere resting on the table. "Do you have some trousers I might borrow?"

Emerging from the storeroom in borrowed buckskin trousers, belted tightly at the waist to keep them from tumbling off, and a man's shirt with the sleeves rolled up to leave her hands free, Jane felt terribly exposed. To be certain, the same amount of material covered her form as before, and the buckskin was sterner stuff than her muslin, and yet for all that, Jane could only think about how her legs were in full view. She kept her back straight and her head high as she marched across the room and took her place by her husband.

He opened his mouth, and she silenced him with a glare of determination.

Mathieu seemed to find everything in the room more interesting than her, checking his tools and the end of the long pole very studiously.

Jane clapped her hands. "Shall we?"

For the next two hours, they did. Repeatedly, Vincent

cast the simple glamour of the cone and Jane traced it with the threads of cold. Though each attempt ended in failure, they felt that they edged closer to success as Jane learned the amount of cold she had to apply to create a response in the crystal.

The heat from the furnace weighed on her oppressively, magnifying the fatigue from the glamour. Each breath seemed harder to draw. Matching her line to Vincent's glamour, Jane adjusted the thread of cold, trying to make the place where the glamour should fold more apparent.

With a crack, the crystal shattered.

Yelling as one, they all flinched and ducked as pieces of crystal flew through the furnace room. Glass clattered to the ground. Only the roar of the furnace broke what silence remained.

Hoarse with tension, Vincent said, "Is everyone all right?"

"I am fine." Mathieu's voice cracked.

Jane straightened, the intensity of her emotion making her feel ill. "I am so sorry."

"But are you well?"

"Quite. Only mortified that I misjudged so."

"Jane." Vincent tilted her head up. "You are bleeding."

The room spun around her, but from long practice at keeping herself erect while doing glamour, Jane ignored the black specks that swarmed around her vision. "Not much, I presume, or you would be in more of a panic."

A single, very thin scratch, lay below her right eye. She would not let herself think on what might have happened if the shard had been an inch higher. Nor would she let Vincent do so. As he tried to fuss over her, Jane pressed a cloth to the scratch until she was satisfied that the bleeding had ceased. "Shall we begin again?"

"I think we are done for the day." Vincent stood, nodding to Mathieu.

"Nonsense. I know the bottom limit of cold now and will not cross it again. We are very close, my love." Jane lowered the cloth and folded it neatly into a square. "Mathieu are you willing to . . . hazard another attempt?"

"Yes, madam." He stood from the stool upon which he had been resting and went to his place by the furnace with remarkable steadiness.

"Jane, I cannot ask you to risk yourself in this way."

"You are not asking, I am choosing." Jane put her hands on her hips and spread her legs wide in a man's stance. "We have work to do, and I want to see the results through."

Vincent paused a moment and then shook his head. "All I ask is that you not tell your mother."

Jane could well imagine her mother's reaction. "I would not dream of it."

They began again and, attention focused by the previous events, found that their next effort produced a sample which they thought might serve. As soon as it was free from the pole, Vincent took a fold of glamour and passed it into the glass ball.

With her vision extended into the ether, Jane watched the glamour fold and then fragment. The pattern, simple though it was, had too many small errors in it to produce the red cone. But the beginning of the path showed promise.

Vincent sighed. "Well, that is hopeful at any rate. The theory is sound, but the practice will take some doing."

Mathieu narrowed his eyes, staring at the ball. "May I make a suggestion?"

"Of course." Jane's own head was worn out from trying to solve this riddle, and she was only too happy to hear someone else's thoughts.

"This cone . . . I have been watching as you worked, and I think the pattern goes off because the glass expands as I blow. What if you made a sphere instead of a cone, so the shapes match?"

"That"—Vincent rubbed his hands together—"is a very good idea."

"What about the *Sphère Obscurcie*?" Reinvigorated, Jane wondered how they had not thought of it before. Rather than start with beginning exercises, they should have sought folds that matched the medium. "It is a single fold, and designed to expand in a bubble."

Nodding, Vincent took his place, rising up on his toes with enthusiasm.

As Mathieu dipped his pole into the crystal and blew the beginning of a sphere, Vincent wrapped the *Sphère Obscurcie* in the glass, making both it and the end of the pole invisible. He expanded the glamour so it passed over the group, bringing them within its sphere of influence. Jane quickly matched Vincent's fold, twisting her cold threads around to add more definition to the channel in the glass. She nodded to him that it was complete.

Vincent released his hold on the glamour and Mathieu stepped away from them to remove the sphere from the pole. Jane gasped.

Despite the sunlight bathing the room, Mathieu was not visible. The glamour had lingered, leaving Mathieu invisible within the *Sphère*'s influence. Invisible while he was *walking*.

Jane clasped her hands, laughing in excitement. This was beyond what they had hoped, to have the glass work without glamour entering it. She and Vincent walked to the spot where they had last seen Mathieu.

As they passed within the *Sphère Obscurcie*, he popped into view, frowning as he tried to understand the excitement apparent on their faces. Of course, being in the centre of the *Sphère*, he had no way of knowing that for a few moments, he had been invisible. Vincent explained as best he could, and then Jane took Mathieu by the arm to lead him out of the *Sphère*.

When she turned him to face whence they had come, the boy's jaw dropped. He stood gaping like a fish.

"This is a wonderful thing you have helped us with, Mathieu La Pierre." Jane took him by the hands, and, in the French fashion, kissed him on both cheeks. "You have my undying gratitude."

"And mine as well." Vincent's disembodied voice expressed firm approbation.

"Madame, monsieur, the pleasure is mine." Mathieu

mopped his brow with a handkerchief already soaked with sweat, while staring in wonder at the place where Vincent had been. He walked back into the *Sphère* and disappeared. "I should put it in the tempering chamber, before it cools too much."

Jane, following, asked, "Why is that a danger?"

"If it is not tempered properly, it will be over-fragile, and chances are good it will crack from cooling too quickly."

Jane's hand went involuntarily to the scratch below her eye. "How long will this take?"

"Should be cool enough tomorrow or the next day." He jerked a finger at the windows. "On account of the cold, we have to be more careful about getting it cooled down far enough."

"I see." Vincent rubbed his chin. "I had hoped to demonstrate it to Bruno tonight, but we can wait. Possibly."

"Are you professing impatience?" Jane raised her eyebrows in a show of surprise.

Clearing his throat and pointedly ignoring her, Vincent arranged to have the crystal spheres packed for them to carry back to M. Chastain's on the day following, while Jane changed back into her street clothes. As she stood in the relative cool of the storeroom, she felt all the fatigue of the day wash over her at once. She sagged against the wall as the room swam around her, and wished Anne-Marie were there to help her dress. The amount and complexity of the glamour might have been small, but the heat made her feel as if she had been working glamour for a lifetime. Regardless of how ill she felt, the effort seemed well worth it every time Jane reminded herself that the *Sphère Obscur-cie* had worked.

Ten

Parade of Gilles

The effects from Jane's over exertion at the glass factory extended into the following day. She woke the next morning feeling as if she had an ague, though she tried to hide it from Vincent. For the first time since their arrival, she counted herself fortunate that the Chastains did not take breakfast in the English fashion, as Jane could not manage more than a slice of dry toast.

She had overdone glamour before, but never coupled with the heat of a glass furnace. Despite her attempts to behave normally, her head spun so severely that when Vincent pressed her to return to her bed, she did not argue with him. She did, however, make him promise to wake her the moment he had retrieved the glass *Sphère Obscurcie* from M. La Pierre's.

The sun was low in the sky when the sound of the apartment door awakened her. She pulled herself out of bed, feeling aches in every joint in her body. Her head throbbed yet, and even the low light pained her eyes. Still, Jane recognised the sound of Vincent's tread in the room beyond, and hoped that he had been out fetching the glass *Sphère*. Pulling on her dressing gown, she secured the ties as she went into the outer room.

Vincent sat at his desk, writing, with the ball of glass on the table beside him. Both Vincent and the *Sphère* were in plain view. Jane's heart sank for a moment before apprehending that it might be one of the balls that had failed. Vincent's forehead had deep furrows running across it, and his pen scratched furious lines across the surface of his page.

Not wishing to disturb him, Jane quietly took her place behind his chair and laid her hands on his shoulders to rub some of the tension away. Vincent gave a muffled cry and rose half out of his seat, spattering ink across the page. "Jane! You have surprised me."

"So I see." Laughing, she reached for the blotter, her illness momentarily forgotten.

Vincent snatched it from her, blotting the ink from the page quickly and tucking it into his writing desk before it could fairly be dry. "Are you feeling better?"

"Thank you, I am. To whom are you writing?"

He compressed his lips at that and locked the writing desk, pushing it away from him on the table. "I am making notes for myself, though it has occurred to me to write to Herr Scholes."

"One might almost think you were hiding something from me. You never locked your desk in London." He coloured at that, and Jane, surprised at his self-consciousness, tried to tease it away. She shook her finger at him. "Have you taken a mistress, in the manner of the French?"

He laughed at that. The unease Jane thought she had seen vanished, and his countenance was open once more. "Rather, a distrust of servants. In London, I had no fear of those with whom they might share my letters."

"And here?"

Vincent ran his hand through his hair and stopped with it tangled at the back of his head. "What do you see on my desk?"

Here at last was the chief source of her interest. "One of the glass balls we made yesterday."

Nodding, he picked it up. "Specifically, this is the *Sphère Obscurcie*."

And yet he and it had been perfectly in view when she entered the room. "Are you certain it was not exchanged for another?"

"The inclusions in the glass seem to be identical to those we created yesterday." He held it out to her. "I do not wish you to exert yourself, but I trust your eye in such things better than I do my own."

Pleased that he thought so highly of her discernment,

Jane took the ball. It had more weight to it than she had supposed, and seemed to retain some warmth from the fire. To both her naked eye and her expanded view, the patterns in the glass seemed to match exactly those they had created.

"Do you think it needs the heat?"

"I had the same thought, but taking it nearer the furnace produced no effect."

"Is that why it is warm?"

He nodded. Jane turned the glass over in her hand, the faint imperfections they had introduced catching the light. "Did you try glamour?"

"I did, but neither Mathieu nor I saw any result." He shrugged. "I cannot account for it."

She handed the ball back to him. "May I see?"

Walking a few steps away, Vincent folded a piece of glamour into the glass. It went in, swirled, and exited, but Vincent remained stubbornly in view. He might have faded a little, but it was nothing to what they had seen before.

She thought, though she was not certain, that the glamour was significantly diffused when it exited the sphere. Jane reached out to feel the folds on both sides of the glass, to ascertain by tactile sense the difference between the glamours.

A wave of nausea struck her within moments of touching the folds. She barely had time to withdraw her hand and stagger to the ash bin before she lost what little she had been able to eat that morning. Vincent tossed the glass ball on the wingback chair and hurried to her side, holding her shoulders till the worst violence of her illness had abated.

Jane's shame at this weakness was acute. "Forgive me."

"Forgive you? No, the fault is mine entire. I should know better than you the results of over-exertion." Vincent helped her to her feet with gentle solicitude. "Let me tend you as you tended me."

Jane laughed, but willingly leaned on him as he helped her back to bed. "If by that you mean that you will visit me but once and insult me while you are here, I think I might suggest a better course."

"You saved my life once, Muse." He tucked the counterpane around her and sat on the bed by her side. "Let me advise you to rest until you are recovered."

"Considering the alternative, I hardly think I have a choice." She lay her head back on the pillow, closing her eyes against the too-bright light. "Perhaps, given that the sphere worked while still glowing from the forge, it needs folds of light *and* heat."

"Hush." Vincent's hand stroked her brow, soothing the headache that plagued her. "We can think on it tomorrow, or the day after that. For now, I want you to rest."

Though Jane thought that her curiosity would outweigh her fatigue, she soon proved herself wrong and fell asleep.

The next day was not much better. As soon as Jane sat up, she felt as though she were on a heaving ship, though their crossing on the *Dolphin* had given her no such intimations of seasickness.

Vincent brought a cold compress to her. "This will help."

"I am perfectly well."

"And yet, I do not believe you." Vincent pressed a hand to her forehead, frowning. "I should have insisted that we leave the factory when I saw you were tired."

"It was a trifling amount of glamour." That very fact made her irritable, that she should so misjudge her strength. It was true that cold weaves were significantly more taxing than visual glamours, but it had been a single thin fold. "Truly, love, it was only the heat that undid me."

Despite her insistence that she was well, when she asked the following day to return to the glass factory, Vincent found himself occupied, and again on the day following. Somehow, he managed to fill a week with errands which he must perforce do on his own, leaving Jane to her rooms with nothing more to do than practice French with Anne-Marie. Jane suspected that these errands were all inventions to delay their return to the glass factory. She resented the coddling, but had to admit that the effects of the glamour still made themselves felt. What she most feared was that Vincent would take this episode too much to heart and hesitate to engage her assistance on future projects.

Nearly a week passed in this manner before Jane felt well enough to insist that she had recovered. "I should like to return to the glass factory today."

Vincent winced, which Jane felt as a reprobation.

"Forgive me, Muse. I promised Bruno that I would take a turn in the laboratory with his students. He and Mme Chastain have an excursion planned with the children."

"Shall I assist you?"

By his hesitation and the manner in which his shoulders rose toward his ears, Jane knew that he was going to say that he did not require any assistance, but not out of deference to her health. "Perhaps another day."

Before Jane could assert her health further, Anne-Marie arrived with a smile on her face. They were, by this point, conversing entirely in French, which did give Jane some measure of satisfaction. "Madame! Monsieur! You must quit these confines and allow me to take you on an excursion."

"An excursion?"

"Today is the annual Gilles parade. The entire town will be there. It should be great fun."

"I am afraid my time is committed already, but Jane, you should go." Vincent kissed her hand with such tenderness that she could not resent him. "The air will do you good."

Jane squeezed his hand in return. "Very well. But tomorrow, we return to the glass factory."

"If you are well."

"I am quite, *quite* well," Jane said, with more heat than she intended. "Thank you."

Anne-Marie cleared her throat. "Mme Chastain has already left with the children, but if we hurry, we may catch them."

Reluctantly agreeing, Jane followed Anne-Marie into the streets of Binché. The normally quiet village was filled with people walking toward the centre of town. Banners hung from windows in brilliant reds and yellows, with occasional tricolours marking a supporter of the Bonapartes.

As they neared the centre of town, Jane began to hear music of a jolly bouncing sort. They rounded a corner and the cross street at the end was lined with people, all staring to their right. Anne-Marie caught hold of Jane's hand and pulled her through the crowd to the front row.

Marching toward them came row upon row of men dressed in nearly identical costumes, bright yellow shirts and pantaloons, striped with red and green. Each man had an enormous collar of lace, and a padded hump and belly. They all wore wax masks with spectacles and curling moustaches.

Most remarkable though, were the dragons that hung in the air above them. The dragons themselves were simple folk constructions, rendered with broad strokes of glamour. What astonished Jane was that the dragons travelled with the parade of men.

She let her vision dissolve into the ether, focusing first on the Gilles, in an attempt to understand how they were managing the folds while marching. Upon examination, she traced the threads governing the dragons to the women who lined the street. They passed the folds one to the next, so that no woman had to maintain the folds for more than a minute or so. But letting her attention expand into the ether made Jane queasy, so she dropped her focus back to the physical plane, glad that Vincent was not there to witness her discomfort.

"What are Gilles?" She leaned over to Anne-Marie and had to fairly shout in her ear to be heard.

"I do not know, unfortunately. I only came to Binché last July. I think they ward off evil spirits, or some such thing. Whatever they do, my friend says they have been doing it for hundreds of years." Anne-Marie pointed as one of the Gilles threw an orange into the crowd. The dragon overhead made a show of snapping at it, and the orange passed ineffectually through its intangible jaws. The crowd screamed with laughter, jostling each other in their attempts to catch the fruit. As they marched, each Gilles threw oranges to the crowd from a seemingly endless supply.

When the Gilles passed in front of the spot where Jane and Anne-Marie stood, the crowd scrambled for the oranges and pressed the ladies forward. Jane struggled to keep her footing, seeing a similar alarm on Anne-Marie's face. An orange soared overhead and the crowd surged back as people reached up to catch the fruit.

Despite her earlier protestations, Jane felt not at all well. The press and the noise of the crowd brought back the unease in her stomach and made her head spin. "I think I should like to go now."

"Of course!" Anne-Marie's eyes widened in alarm. Jane could only assume that her countenance had turned as sickly as she felt.

Pressing her hand to her forehead, she sought a way out of the throng. The wall of people pressed toward the street, and would not give way with any ease to their efforts to move away from the parade. The day darkened around her, and, with no other warning, Jane fainted.

Though Jane was entirely insensible of her surroundings, what happened next was this: One of the Gilles, upon seeing Jane's distress, broke away from the parade and lifted her in his arms. With quick instructions from Anne-Marie, he made his way through the crowd, which gladly gave way to one of their folk heroes. Once clear, he carried Jane all the way back to the Chastain residence.

As they were entering the gates, one of M. Chastain's students spied them, and the household was raised in a state of general alarm. Neither the master nor the mistress of the house were in, so it fell to Anne-Marie to organise things. The Gilles, who would not remove his mask in accordance with tradition, handed Jane to one of the students and left without another word.

By the time Jane was deposited in her room, she was roused enough to be distressed by the fuss and bother she had created. "Forgive me." She tried to sit up, despite the grey spots which danced in front of her eyes.

Anne-Marie pressed her back into bed. "Nonsense, madame, the fault is mine for taking you out before you were ready. Now, please, be still until the doctor arrives."

"A doctor!" Her dismay increased. "No! I assure you that is unnecessary. I was only overcome for a moment."

"Nevertheless, I have called him, and he will arrive shortly."

Jane could not contain a groan. "Vincent will never let me hear the end of this."

Anne-Marie straightened the bedclothes but had a certain consciousness to her expression, which made Jane realize that Vincent must not know that she had taken ill. Relief rising, she grasped Anne-Marie's hand. "You have not told him yet?"

"No, madame." Anne-Marie rested her free hand on Jane's and kept her eyes low. "He was not in the laboratory, and none of the students know where he is."

"But he said . . ." her voice trailed away, unable to account for his absence. The relief that she had felt upon thinking that he would not discover her weakness became confusion and concern.

"It may be that he decided to join us at the parade after all, and we missed him in the crowd."

Before Jane could decide on the merits of this argument, voices and footsteps in the hall announced the arrival of the doctor, a tall, slender fellow, with a shock of dark hair. He was younger than she expected a doctor to be, but exuded such an air of confidence that Jane could not help but trust him. Settling himself on a chair at her bedside, he smiled. "What seems to be the trouble?"

"I am quite well. I was only overcome for a moment."

"I think that is true of every ailment." He produced a

pair of horn spectacles and slipped them over his ears. "It only overcomes our good health for a time. So, let us see if we can determine what has overcome you now."

Chastened, Jane submitted to reciting her history, pausing now and again when he asked questions. When she had done, he poked and prodded at her, checking the colour of her sclerotics, listening to her pulse, and other less pleasant acts.

When he finished examining her, the doctor wiped his hands on a cloth from his bag and settled back in the chair. "Well. You are in very good health."

"You see!" Jane felt every relief that you may imagine at this pronouncement. "I wish you would write a note to that effect for my husband. He has been quite stubborn in insisting that I not return to work."

"I am glad to hear it." The doctor took his spectacles off and polished them. "Mme Vincent, you are with child."

Jane stared at him, astonishment overcoming her powers of speech. All the French which she had so painfully learned fled her grasp, and Jane could not form the simplest question. She opened and closed her mouth, gaping like a fish, before she managed to ask. "Are you certain?"

"Oh, yes. Your history made me suspect it, but examination proves the fact. I congratulate you."

"Thank you." Far from feeling jubilant, a hollowness began to develop under Jane's breastbone. To have been restricted from working glamour for a week had been trial enough. Stopping for the length of her term seemed impossible. "My mother will be pleased."

"But not your husband?"

"Yes." Jane forced a smile, while in no way certain how Vincent would feel. "Of course. But my mother has been daily expecting grandchildren, so this news will please her no end."

"Madame, I must remind you that you are to undertake no glamour or other strenuous exercise until after your confinement. Plenty of fresh air, simple walks and hearty meals are my prescription for you. The nausea, I am afraid, may worsen before it improves, but you must try to eat anyway, for the sake of your child."

Jane listened to his instructions but could think of nothing other than the proscription against glamour. "No glamour at all?"

"None." On that he was quite firm and unsmiling, as if he knew what a temptation it would be for her.

Nodding and smiling by rote, Jane endured the rest of his call and thanked him for his aid, the whole while wondering how she would explain it to Vincent. Which led rapidly to wanting to know where he was. When the doctor left, Jane dismissed Anne-Marie as well, saying that she wished to take a nap. In truth, the moment the door closed and Jane was alone, she curled onto her side and clutched a pillow.

What was she to do? Her entire life, Jane had been a plain girl with nothing to make her stand out except for her skill at the "womanly" arts, and chief among those was her glamour. She could still paint, yes, and play music, to be certain, but always she had enhanced both of those with glamour. The art form had given her an unparalleled satisfaction.

And glamour was what had made Vincent fall in love with her.

Jane pressed her mouth to the pillow and squeezed her eyes shut. There was more to their marriage than glamour, but working together on it had comprised the majority of their time since wedding. She would love Vincent just as fiercely without glamour for the keenness of his mind, but—and this was where Jane nearly came undone—but she had nothing else to set her apart.

She was plain. Her nose was too long, her complexion too sallow. She had no grace in her carriage. Jane was clever, yes, but many women were clever. Her doubt in her own merits, the utter disbelief that any man could find her of interest, came back with full force.

And what if Vincent did not want a child?

What if, in one stroke, she had gone from a source of interest to a burden?

Even recognising the unlikeliness of the accusations she lay upon Vincent's shoulders, Jane had trouble wresting her thoughts away from the dark spiral she had embarked upon. She pushed the pillow away and rolled onto her back, staring at the canopy above her.

She was of two minds. In one, she wanted Vincent there to reassure her that he loved her. In the other, she was glad he was away, because it delayed the moment when she would have to know how he reacted to the news.

Sitting up, Jane swung her legs out of bed, steadying

herself against the quick wave of dizziness that washed over her. When it had passed, Jane went to her dressing table, took up the bottle of lavender water which her mother had sent her, and used it to wash her face.

Glancing at the mirror, Jane's pallor surprised even her. She pinched her cheeks to try to restore some bloom, then stopped. What was she doing? Primping as if a blush on her cheeks would make the difference between Vincent loving her or not?

Jane sat with her elbows on the table, hands cradling her head. This would not do. Until Vincent by some action or word gave her a reason to think that she had lost him, she dishonoured him by assuming the worst. She sat thus for some time, and was sitting there still when Vincent ran up the stairs and threw open the door to the room.

She jumped as it rebounded against the wall.

Vincent's face was red and his chest heaved as if he had run some distance. He strode across the room and knelt at her feet, taking her hands. "Muse, is it true?"

Incapable of words, she could only nod.

He rose to his knees, embracing her and pulling her tight. "And you are well?"

"The doctor says I am in excellent health." Her voice broke. "Only I am not to do glamour."

He shuddered. "Your mother was right to take me to task for letting you risk yourself." With her ear pressed to his chest, his voice vibrated through her. "If anything had . . . I should never have forgiven myself."

"But I wanted to. And neither of us knew." Timidly, she ventured. "You are not displeased?"

Vincent released her, sitting back on his heels in apparent shock. "No. Why would you think that?"

"Because I cannot help you with the glamour in glass any longer." She did not, would not, voice her deeper fears.

He caressed her face in one hand, tracing the line of the scratch under her eye with his thumb. "Muse, have you been crying?"

"Maybe a little," she whispered. "I so wanted to work with you, and now . . ." She bent her head, twisting her wedding band around on her finger. The sapphire caught the light and winked as though it held a glamour in its depths.

"I deeply regret that I was away and left you to these unhappy thoughts." He lifted her chin. "Jane, it is only for a few months. Less than a year. It will give us time to talk about the theory of our glamour in glass. And when your confinement is finished, we shall have a better start."

"We shall have a child then, Vincent. I am not certain what I will be capable of after." Jane had seen women broken by childbirth, and knew more than a few who had not survived their first laying in. But by her husband's open countenance, she could tell that these morbid thoughts had not occurred to him. Perhaps among men, such womanly concerns were never spoken of and he had no reason to know and to fear them.

"I have great faith in you." Vincent stood and pulled Jane to her feet. "I want only for you to be happy and well."

Jane leaned against him. "Then I will do my best at both."

Eleven

The Lamb Lies Down

The requisite letter was sent across the Channel to inform Jane's parents of the prospect of a grandchild. Vincent did not bother sending a similar letter to his father, but wasted no time in telling the entire Chastain household the happy news. Jane rather wished that he had not, for the whole of the house became deeply solicitous of her comfort to a degree that oppressed her. When she went to the parlour, she must have the best chair. At meals, the menu seemed clearly calculated to appeal to her uncertain appetite, for—as the doctor had predicted—her nausea grew worse and Jane spent a portion of each morning performing indelicate functions.

She was thoroughly unhappy.

Though Jane tried to find solace in music, the piano-forte seemed barren without the addition of colour and light. In some regards, needlework gave her greater comfort than anything else, because she did not notice the lack of glamour as keenly when she worked.

Into such comparative tranquillity, one of the servants entered with the mail borne on a silver tray. The majority of those letters went to M. Chastain, but one found its way to Vincent who grunted in some surprise.

"Jane." He held the letter closer, as if doubting the address. "Do you know a Mr. Gilman?"

Lowering her embroidery hoop, Jane considered her acquaintances, but could think of no one with that name. "I am afraid not."

"Well he sends you his particular compliments." In response to Jane's raised eyebrows, Vincent continued, "Mr. Gilman says, 'Even if your wife's famed wit and beauty were not enough, I would be remiss in not paying my respects based on what I have heard of her talents.'"

"Whoever Mr. Gilman is, he surely has proven himself unknown by *that*." Her "beauty" could at best be considered plain. "I cannot account for it."

Vincent shook his head with his small private smile, and continued reading the letter. "Ah. Here, buried in the body, is his reason for address. He is a friend of Skiffy's and proposes to commission us."

Jane resumed her embroidery then, stabbing the cloth with particular vengeance. "Does he. For what purpose?" All pleasure she might have felt at such a favour from her dinner partner turned to a sensation akin to bitterness that she would be unable to accept it.

"A drawing room. He has a house in Brussels." Folding the paper, he shook his head. "I will write to decline later."

Jane lowered her embroidery, gratified beyond expression that Vincent should understand the pain that a commission must cause her at this time. "Decline? Is that necessary, do you think?"

Tilting his head and frowning, Vincent hesitated. "It does seem as though it would be an imposition on our host to accept a commission which must otherwise fall to him as the foremost glamourist in the region."

Embarrassment heated Jane's face at the way in which she had exposed her thoughtlessness. M. Chastain, seated just to the other side of the drawing room, affected to be interested in his book, but Jane could not see how he might have failed to hear her gaffe. Putting all her attention on her embroidery, she tried to pretend that her next words had been her first thought. "I only meant that you could share the commission with M. Chastain. Since Mr. Gilman is British, the introduction might be desirable, as it would bring our host to the attention of different parties."

The doubt in Vincent's voice was clear in the slowness of his answer, but he did not betray her by pointing out her initial slight. "Ah. Yes, there is some sense in that." Rising, he crossed the room to M. Chastain and explained the scheme to him. Chastain, in turn, proved his worth as a friend by claiming he had no interest in a commission in Brussels, and not only insisted that Vincent take the commission, but offered the use of M. Archambault as an assistant.

As they talked and made arrangements for transportation to Brussels, Jane worked the only threads she could, trying with the tangible embroidery to distract herself from the conversation, of which she could have no part. Better that she become used to the restriction and leave Vincent to do the work, which he had done alone long before they met. It cannot be supposed that the embroidery was sufficient to keep her attention, and most of her mind was occupied in listening to their conversation. They spoke in French so rapid that Jane had difficulty following more than the tenor of it and realized in the process how much the household had slowed down to accommodate her own inferior understanding.

If it were possible to take ship and flee to England at that moment, Jane would have abandoned her trunks and gone. She had no place and no purpose for being in Belgium now, and worse, forced everyone to accommodate her simply by being in the room. Jane rose from her place by the fire and walked to the window, staring disconsolately out into the courtyard. Her breath fogged the glass, and a chill crept across to cool her cheeks.

Vincent approached, the heavy sound of his heel marking his stride as if each footstep were trying to press the world beneath him. "Are you not cold?"

"I was too warm by the fire."

"Then let me draw your chair farther away."

"No. Thank you." They stood silently and Jane reproached herself for being needlessly morose. She had that which other women craved, a loving husband with the prospect of a family in the not too distant future, and yet the discontent would not leave her. "When will you go?"

"Mr. Gilman asked me to wait on him tomorrow, but the carriage is engaged, so I shall ask him for another day."

"Could you not ride?"

"To be sure. But a horse would not suffice for you, I think."

"Me? Of what use could I be there?"

"I—do you not want to go? I had thought you would want to see the space, and be involved in the design."

Resigned, Jane faced her husband. "Vincent. I cannot do glamour. I cannot help you in this."

"But, the design. You can still think and paint." He wiped his hand down his face. "I want your help. Please?"

Touched by the earnestness of his plea, Jane acceded to his request, and a day was set to meet Mr. Gilman and his drawing room.

Mr. Gilman's residence commanded a view of Brussels Park, which anchored the town, and was nicely appointed without being ostentatious. The Vincents were greeted by the butler at the front door and shown into the drawing room in question, where Mr. Gilman greeted them. He was a slender, dashing young man with a nose that bent as if he might have taken a turn as a pugilist.

His surprise at seeing Jane could not be concealed, and

she began to wonder how Skiffy had described her to make Mr. Gilman expect a great beauty. "Well." He clapped his hands together and rubbed them briskly. "I suppose we should get to business. Mrs. Vincent, our front parlour has quite a lovely prospect, if you cared to take it in while we talk."

"Did you also intend to have us do the front parlour?"

"Er. No. I only thought that we might bore you." He gestured between the two gentlemen. "Business is so often trying to the ladies."

"Often does not equal always, and to all ladies." Jane offered him a smile to reduce the bite of her words. "I assure you that I am not one of those women who are put off by such things. My purpose here is entirely to focus on your commission. So." She clapped her hands together, in mimicry of him. "I suppose we should get to business."

Mr. Gilman straightened as though he were little accustomed to a woman who spoke so directly, and Jane coloured slightly. She had been long enough in Belgium that her manners had quite changed. But she had not said anything outside the bounds of propriety even to an Englishman, and his assumption that she must be feebleminded quite annoyed her.

Vincent held his hand over his mouth to hide a smile and affected to study the walls. He winked at Jane and walked a little away from where they were standing. "What did you have in mind?"

"My wife is coming over in the next month and . . . we are but newly wed, you see. I do not want her to be homesick, and she has a favourite window at her parents' home. In Yorkshire, with lambs gambolling."

Vincent turned entire, his spine straightening. "In Yorkshire? With lambs gambolling. How many lambs will you have, sir?"

"Three at this time, I believe." He glanced back at Jane, and offered a brief smile. "She likes lambs."

"I see." Jane walked the room, considering where they might place an additional window. "Did you have a spot in mind?"

"I had thought perhaps the front windows, so that she might have one room in which there was no reminder of Brussels."

Jane almost answered that this was not a possibility, given that those outside the house would see the same glamour as those within, which would make it appear that lambs gambolled upon the lawn of the house. Strangely rendered lambs at that, as they would be foreshortened to provide perspective for those viewing from within the house. Fortunately she remembered M. Chastain's new technique. "Vincent, do you think we could combine the Chastain Damask with the *Sphère Obscurcie* to create that? It might be possible for the illusion to be clear on the exterior and present from within."

"Hm?" He studied the window and rubbed the back of his head. "Interesting. Possible. Mr. Gilman, have you a picture of the view?"

"I do. My wife, you see, she often paints it." He directed their gaze to a watercolour hanging over the mantel. While not lacking in talent, it had that stiffness which so often characterizes the amateur artist. The lack of spontaneity and life betrayed a mind too cautious and a reserve too great to pass from technical skill into art. Still, it was a better rendering that Jane had hoped for when Mr. Gilman said his wife painted.

A hill swept up to a copse of trees. Cutting from left to right, a small stream meandered across the hill, lending a natural composition to the painting that brought the eye back in to the centre. On the slopes, a flock of lambs and their mothers dotted the grass. "Perhaps we should consider a small flock?"

"No. Three alone." Mr. Gilman hesitated. "I might ask for the number to change later, if circumstances warrant."

Jane studied the painting, wondering what circumstances those would be. They discussed the terms, which Jane left to Vincent, as she still had no sense of what one should charge for projects such as this. With things settled, Jane and Vincent returned to the carriage, and thence back to Binché, promising to come again the next day to begin work in earnest.

After they had been an hour on the journey, Vincent shifted in his seat. "Jane, I was thinking. This project will require no under-painting, and the design is done for us. I can see no real reason for you to make the trip tomorrow, aside from keeping me company."

"I do not mind. There is little for me to do at the Chastains'."

"But the rigours of travel." He gestured in the general

direction of her middle. "I do not wish to fatigue you un-necessarily."

"Two hours in a carriage hardly seems fatiguing."

"You are so often ill, though. Why add to that?"

"The illness will happen whether I am at home or in motion." She took his arm and nestled against him. "Besides which, we are supposed to be on honeymoon. This way I am at least assured of four hours without the distraction of others."

Vincent kissed the top of her head and rested his cheek against her. "Which raises another point. If you do not come, then I can take a horse, which is faster, or stay overnight. Either way, the project will proceed more quickly."

Jane traced her finger around his hands, feeling the strength that lay there. "Vincent." She slid her hand into his and squeezed. "If you do not want me to come, it might be easier to simply say so."

He was silent, and held very still. The creak of the carriage filled the space between them. Jane closed her eyes, regretting the impulse that had led her to speak. She had expected him to protest and proclaim that he needed her there, only feared for her, which would have let her tell him that he was being silly. Instead, there was only silence. Then he spoke. "I do not want you to come. Not every day. It seems senseless on such a simple project, especially when there is nothing which you can do. I would worry about you."

"Of course. I do not want to be a source of distraction while you are working."

"Jane, it is not that. You are not a distraction. It is only that this is a nothing job, and it would be a waste of effort for you." He lifted her hand and kissed it. "You said it would be easier to simply say so."

She felt the chastisement immediately. It was unjust of her to demand his honesty and then punish him for it. And if she were honest with herself, there was sense in what he was saying. "I am sorry. You are correct. But I should like to come sometimes. I do like to watch you work."

"Of course." Vincent rested his hand over hers. "You are my muse, and I would be lost without you. Even if I am only painting sheep."

The next day, sitting on a chair to the side of Mr. Gilman's window, Jane watched Vincent sketch a tree into being. He had already laid the ground for the slope and the stream using M. Chastain's technique, but rather than a transparency, he was endeavouring to have the exterior of the window show the drawing room. Very sensibly, they had both realized that it would be unpleasant to have someone viewing you if you could not see them.

Since Jane could not extend her senses into the ether, the tree Vincent worked on seemed to coalesce out of nothing, first as a rough shape, then with more detail as her husband refined the form. The bark seemed unpleasantly uniform to Jane, and she cleared her throat. "This might be a nice place to use an *ombré*. It is very easy to thin the—"

"In fact, I am." He did not break his attention from his work.

Jane shifted in her seat and opened her drawing-book to sketch him working. He stood in front of the window, hands dipping in and out of the ether as he stitched the threads he wanted into place. Legs spread wide, he had doffed his coat and had his shirt sleeves rolled up to his elbows. The line of his hands captivated her, the grace of his movements combined with the play of muscle in his forearms creating a quiet strength. She had begun to recognise the glamours he was working by the movement of his hands, even though she could see only their effect, not the folds he was managing.

He inhaled in a deep steady breath designed to pull as much air into his body as possible. Even so, beads of sweat stood out on his brow from the exertion of the morning. If she could do glamour, she would make a cooling breeze for him, but that was an impossibility.

Still, there were other ways of making a breeze. Jane tore a page out of her sketchbook, wincing at the noise the paper made as it ripped free. Folding it in even pleats, she made a crude fan and abandoned her chair. Standing by Vincent, she fanned the air, trying to cool him some. Beyond stirring his hair, it seemed to have little effect, and he scarcely seemed to notice her presence, so deep into the glamour was he.

Sweeping his hand back as he worked a Chastain Damask pattern, he caught her raised arm with his elbow.

Startled, Jane dropped her makeshift fan and he dropped the glamour. Part of the tree disappeared.

He wheeled on her. "What in God's name are you doing?"

"I—You looked hot."

"Yes. That happens. I am working glamour. Or rather, I am *trying* to work glamour." His face was far redder than it had been moments before.

"I am sorry. I only wanted to help."

"You cannot." He gave her his shoulder and focused again on the window. "Now excuse me while I rebuild this tree."

In agony, Jane took a step back to keep out of his way. "You could use your *Petite Répétition* technique to build it faster."

"If Mrs. Gilman did not, undoubtedly, know every tree in that painting better than her husband's face, that might be an option. But as it is, I must build each one individually." He tied off the thread of glamour he was stitching and faced her, gaze fully in the physical world, and burning her with the anger under his skin. "I *am* sorry you find this tedious, but I did warn you not to come."

"I thought that was because you were concerned for my health, not because I would be in the way."

"Well, had I anticipated it, I might have expressed that as a reason, too."

Jane stared aghast at her husband, trying to understand what had provoked him to this undeserved harshness. Often he could be brusque when he was distracted, but never cruel.

Mr. Gilman chose this inopportune moment to step into the room. Jane hardly knew whether to be thankful for his interruption or to wish him away. "Ah. Mr. Vincent. Might I impose on you for a small change to our plan?"

With an obvious struggle, Vincent calmed his features. "Yes?"

"There is to be only one lamb."

The colour faded from Vincent's face and the muscle in his jaw tightened. "Only one?"

"I am afraid so."

Jane tried to distract Mr. Gilman before he could notice Vincent's anger. "Of course, you know your wife better than I. But it does seem as though the effect of a single lamb gambolling is much different from the flocks which Mrs. Gilman has painted."

He shifted from one foot to the other. "Nevertheless. I find that one will suit my needs."

Not wishing to broach the subject of funds, Jane could not help but wonder if he thought that removing two lambs would reduce the cost. "Truly, it is barely more trouble to make three lambs than one."

"The difficulty hardly signifies, if Mr. Gilman only wishes one lamb." Vincent offered him a brief bow. "Of course we can do that. May I ask in what area you wish the lamb?"

Mr. Gilman strode to the window and waved his hand at the lower right portion. "About here, and moving along this line." He sketched a line across and up the hill in a direction that seemed designed to least serve the composition.

Rather than offering an alternative, as Jane expected,

Vincent nodded his head again and made a sketch in the glamour to mark the intent. His communication ended, Mr. Gilman took his leave, although not before passing an inquiring glance at the two of them.

When the door had closed and his footfalls faded, Jane shook her head. "How are you going to get around that?"

"Around what?" Vincent had already begun pulling folds into place to create the lamb, abandoning his work on the trees.

"His suggestion about the placement of the lamb. I can think of few places he could have asked for it to be which would be worse."

"I am going to place it where he requested it."

Astonished, Jane could only stare at her husband. He had long professed that his art was more important than his life, and she could not understand how he could now show so little care about accepting such an obviously poor suggestion. She had seen him lead the Prince Regent to a different understanding of what a composition required rather than refusing an unreasonable request outright. And yet here Vincent had made no such effort, despite his clear dislike for the prospect. "I confess I do not understand you."

Vincent lowered his head, hands still wrapped in glamour. When he spoke, it was to the floor. "What is there to understand? I am trying to complete this commission and satisfy *my* client." He put perhaps too great an emphasis on the word "my" and Jane had to bite back an angry retort. Spiteful though his words were, there was truth in them.

She had nothing to do with this project, and it had been a mistake for her to come. Taking her seat again, Jane pulled out Signor Defendini's book, *The Essentials of Glassblowing in Murano* and read until it was time for them to depart. Neither Vincent nor she had much to say to the other on the carriage ride back to Binché.

Twelve

Repeating the Coda

Jane tried to fill the days while Vincent was away in Brussels by focusing on those activities that she still had at her disposal. She went with Mme Chastain on her rounds, visiting the local ladies and learning enough about the village to engage in the common hobby of gossip. Mme Meynard's home in the centre of Binché was a frequent destination for their excursions. Fond of conviviality and more than twenty years younger than her husband, Mme Meynard had regular card parties to which she seemed to delight in inviting guests of different beliefs merely to watch the conflicts that ensued.

Having borne silent witness to several of these conversations which, while interesting to watch, must cause a strain upon the participants,

Jane was understandably apprehensive when Mme Meynard greeted her with enthusiasm at the door. "Mme Vincent! I am so glad to see you. There is someone here that you must particularly meet." Before Jane could utter a word, Mme Meynard took her by the arm and led her into the drawing room and across to a small knot of people. "Lieutenant Segal, a moment of your time."

Willingly, the young man turned from his conversation. His countenance was comely, with that openness of expression and lively gaze indicative of a strong understanding. Had Mme Meynard not named him a lieutenant, Jane would have known him for a French officer from the blue and white coat and the shako which lay on the side table, with a tricolour cockade rakishly pinned to the side of the hat. The pale blue of the coat set off his blond hair to advantage. Jane quickly realized that his audience consisted almost entirely of young women, all of whom gazed upon him, almost cooing their pleasure at being in his company.

Lieutenant Segal stood immediately and his eyes widened in surprise. "Madame, it is a pleasure to see you again."

Jane furrowed her brow, trying to place him. "I am afraid you have the better of me."

"Ah. Of course. You were unwell, and I? I was masked." He took Jane's hand and bowed very low, while raising her hand to his lips. He kissed it, never removing his gaze from her face. Even through the leather of her gloves, his lips were warm.

Jane felt the colour mount in her cheeks and she hardly

knew where to look. This then, was the mysterious Gilles who had carried her from the parade?

Mme Meynard threw back her head and laughed. She tapped Lieutenant Segal on the shoulder with her fan. "You must excuse Mme Vincent. She is English."

Though he did not drop her hand, Lieutenant Segal lowered it with remarkable speed. "Pardon, madame. I would never have trifled with you had I known."

"Is it trifling with a woman's affections to kiss her hand, in England?" Mme Meynard flirted her fan open. "I had always thought it was a mark of respect."

"No, no! Mme Meynard, the English are so chaste and pure that one cannot touch them without marring their virtue."

Jane would not allow herself to be baited by Lieutenant Segal, so she addressed herself to her hostess instead. "You misunderstand. To kiss a woman's hand is a sign of esteem, certainly, but you must acknowledge that it is impossible to esteem someone who is but newly met. Therefore, to do so upon meeting seems insincere at best."

Mme Meynard raised her eyebrows and gazed coquettishly over her fan at Lieutenant Segal. "I would say that the charge of insincerity is not far off the mark."

"I am wounded. I have been in your bedchamber, Mme Vincent, so you can hardly say that we have only met."

Outraged at his insinuation that their acquaintance was more intimate than it was, Jane tried to set the record straight. "While I thank you for your rescue when I fainted at the parade, this hardly counts as meeting."

Lieutenant Segal pressed his hand to his breast and widened his stance slightly to include his audience in his reply. "Perhaps, but I have kissed the hands of all of these ladies, and you must believe me sincere in the admiration of them all."

Several of the younger ladies giggled at that, lending credence to his protestation that his behaviour was within the bounds of delicacy.

"If you say you are sincere, then I must believe you and yet . . . you cannot base your admiration on the mind, for our first meeting did not have the pleasure of conversation. Indeed, I was entirely insensible." Jane fingered her own overlong nose. "I doubt that it is on the basis of physical appearance. May I inquire what forms your admiration?"

"Why, that the focus of my admiration is a lady. What can be more admirable than that?" Lieutenant Segal gestured at the small crowd surrounding them. "To a Frenchman, there is nothing so worthy of admiration than women in all their forms. The source of Napoleon's genius, some say, was his Joséphine."

"And not Queen Marie Louise?"

"I did say 'in all their forms.' Queen Marie Louise is the source of his happiness. Genius and happiness are both admirable." He bowed shortly. "But I am prepared to concede that perhaps it is only French women who are thus."

As she had seen at other of Mme Meynard's parties, a small group now surrounded them, listening to their conversation. Though Jane resented being made a spectacle and would rather excuse herself at once, she lingered. In part, because she was certain that Mme Meynard would derive great amusement from her departure, and though her conduct was reprehensible, she was a particular friend of Mme Chastain and Jane would not willingly slight her. Rather than acceding the field, Jane resolutely maintained her composure. "I see. I will not ask for your opinion of the women in Britain, but what of the women in Belgium?"

"Madame. They are French." Coming from a military man who had undoubtedly fought under Napoleon, his disregard of borders should not have surprised Jane, particularly in a nation that had so recently belonged to France. "Have you no defence to offer for your countrywomen?"

Jane opened her mouth to provide a list of arguments and then closed it again, remembering the dinner at the Prince Regent's which marked the last occasion on which she had spent any time with ladies of society. Save for Lady Hertford, none of the ladies had shown much in the way of sense, and she could not imagine putting forward the Prince Regent's mistress as model of English virtue. Turning her mind to her own family, she again faltered. Her mother was unlikely to provoke admiration, save for her sense of fashion and her concern for her daughters. In Binché, despite the impertinence with which Mme Meynard arranged these conversations, Jane had seen more sense displayed than in most of her companions at home. "No. They are, by and large, insipid and concerned only with fashion. This is, perhaps, why I suspected insincerity from you, though I owe you my gratitude."

"Then, madame,"—he offered her a bow and held out

his hand—"allow me to greet you again, and know that you have my full admiration for your wit and your honesty."

After a moment, Jane placed her hand in his. He kissed the back of it very gently, and Jane could not doubt his sincerity.

When she returned to the Chastains' home, Jane practised French with Anne-Marie, who was wild to hear about the French officers. Jane found it not at all surprising that she had already met young Lieutenant Segal and was quite in raptures about him. It seemed that he had been making the rounds of Binché society without regard for social distinctions. He was quite the favourite, and Jane was forced to admit that she could understand why, for his manners were appealing even if the content of his remarks was impertinent.

Her mind still troubled by their conversation and the way in which she had been unable to defend her countrywomen, Jane retreated to the drawing room and the pianoforte. In many ways, the solitary pursuit of music best suited her temperament, and Jane applied herself to it in an effort to make up for the deficiency of glamour accompanying it. She tried to see it as a blessing that she could focus on but one aspect of performance, but in truth she missed the glamour too much to be content with mere sound.

She finished playing an air by Rossini, one which she thought the Prince Regent might enjoy, recalling as she did his fondness for the composer. She then leafed through the pages toward the beginning, in search of a passage which had troubled her.

"That was very pretty." Vincent said from the door.

Jane turned, surprised at how much her heart sped at the sight of her husband. She could not help but compare him to Lieutenant Segal, who might have more elegance to his carriage, but had none of Vincent's strength. "How long have you been back?"

"Since the coda." He came in and sank into the chair closest to her, weariness evident in the sag of his shoulders. "Play it again?"

Jane did, letting her attention drift from the page to her husband's face. He listened with his eyes closed, brows drawn a little together in concentration. As she played, his tension slackened and slowly, slowly, his head tilted forward until his chin rested on his chest. Jane kept playing long after he had clearly fallen asleep and begun to snore. She could not suppress a smile at this. Her husband had the tiniest snore in the world, more like a small cat than a barrel-chested man. It pained her to see him so tired, but she had no way to relieve his fatigue if he insisted on making the ride to Brussels so often.

Bringing the music to a close, Jane let the notes fade from the room until the only sound was the faint wheeze of Vincent sleeping. It was impossible, seeing him so reduced by fatigue, to have anything but tenderness in her heart toward him. Her husband stirred and lifted his head, his eyelids still heavy. "That was lovely."

"Thank you." Jane did not point out that he had slept through the most of it. "Shall I ring for some dinner for you?"

"No, thank you. I have already eaten."

"Were you in Brussels today?" When she had woken, he was already gone from the house, as had been common these past few weeks.

"With Mr. Gilman."

"I take it he needed the sheep adjusted again?" It seemed as though once a week, Mr. Gilman sent a message asking for the number of lambs to go up or down.

"Yes. Well."

"Have you thought of suggesting a random braiding of lambs so that the number appears to rotate?"

"Even if—" Vincent rubbed the bridge of his nose, sighing. "That would not work with the Chastain Damask."

"Of course." She perused the pages of her music, pretending that ordering the score took more attention than it actually did. She was uncertain why she still felt the need to offer opinions on the subject when Vincent clearly had no interest in her thoughts.

"Forgive me." He pinched his eyes shut in a wince. "I am tired and irritable today."

"If you . . . if you wanted to stay the night in Brussels, I should not object. It would make me easier to know there was one less fatigue weighing on you."

"Thank you. But I needed to spend part of today in Binché, and likely will again this week." Vincent tugged at his cravat and Jane was fairly certain that only being in the public rooms rather than their apartments kept him from removing it altogether.

"Oh. I had not realized you had business in Binché." She paused, waiting for him to tell her what it was.

He stood instead. "Come upstairs and tell me about your day."

That he had changed the subject, and baldly, was apparent, but Jane could not account for why. This did not mark the first time he had done so, but the subjects he wished to avoid were so varied she could see no pattern in them. At times she thought he did not wish to speak to her at all, at others his pleasure in her company was so evident it seemed impossible that any coldness had ever existed.

Had he not been so evidently fatigued, she might have pushed him for an explanation. Indeed, she found herself tempted to take advantage of any lack of discretion which his weary state might lend. "I would rather hear about your day, if you do not mind. I see so little of you that I find myself quite hungry for even the smallest details."

He tucked his chin in as he did when he was thinking. "Would you humour me and allow me to forget about the day? I will confess that I am somewhat overweary."

"Of course." She accompanied him upstairs, taking his arm and feeling him lean some weight upon her rather than the reverse.

"That does not mean you should be silent." He squeezed her hand on his arm. "Distract me. Tell me what you did today."

"I went with Mme Chastain to the Meynard's home."
Jane tried to drag her mind away from wondering what could
leave Vincent so irritable and exhausted. "Mme Meynard is
charming enough, but the conversation is . . . challenging.
She delights in introducing people who are likely to disagree, so she might observe the resulting fireworks. Today
she had me paired with a French lieutenant."

"Are there troops in town?" Vincent opened the door
to their apartments and let her pass through.

"Only a small contingent. Some four or five officers. I
did not hear what their purpose was, only that they seem
determined to attach every young woman in town." Jane
helped Vincent off with his coat, making a note to send it
out to have the road dust removed. He had ridden so much
lately that the coat was more brown than blue. "According
to Anne-Marie, who has also seen the officers, Lieutenant
Segal is absolutely the most noble man she has ever seen."

He tugged off his cravat and dropped it over the back of
a chair. "This sounds much like your sister. Are all women
thus taken with dashing young soldiers?"

"Not quite all."

He bent down to kiss her cheek. "I am relieved to hear
this."

She smiled as his lips tickled her skin. "I confess that I
do not understand what it is about a red coat which makes
young women lose their minds, but it seems that a tricolour
cockade can do the same." Jane reached to undo his cuffs and
considered telling him about Lieutenant Segal's outrageous
flirtation, but Vincent moved away to the window.

"Tricolour cockade, eh? Interesting fashion choice. How long are these officers in town, do you know? I am certain that there must be a ball. It is impossible for officers to be in town without the young ladies demanding a ball."

"I little doubt that you are right, but I do not remember anyone noting their departure date, so perhaps they are to be here for long enough that time is not a concern, or perhaps they will be gone so soon that there is no time to plan a ball." She followed him to the window and wrapped her arms around his waist, leaning against his back. The difference was yet small, but already she could tell a change in the way they fit together. "Would I be able to persuade you to go to a ball?"

"Possibly." He stifled a yawn, poorly. "But at the moment, I need to write some letters before I fall asleep standing."

"Should you like me to rub your shoulders while you write?"

Vincent drew in a breath as if to speak, and let it out again unvoiced. Removing her hands gently from his waist, he turned and lifted them, kissing first one, then the other. "That will make me fall asleep all the faster. Go to bed, and I will join you shortly."

There was a stillness or a reserve in his face, which spoke volumes more than did his tender caresses. This distance between them, which came and went for reasons she could not penetrate, had returned. Jane only knew that he kept something from her. "What could be so urgent when you can barely keep your feet?"

"I owe Skiffy a letter." Vincent sat at his desk and rolled the glass *Sphère* under his palm. "If I wait until I am not tired, I shall never write it."

"And this is part of what concerns me. I do not like seeing you this exhausted, and have serious concerns about where it will lead. You must rest."

"Then let me write this letter in peace." He saw her chagrin and immediately softened. "I am sorry. I did not mean to snap. Only I am weary, and really must write this."

Jane nodded, having done her best to protest, and withdrew. She could not help but notice that, though he sat at the table and played with the ball of glass, Vincent did not unlock his writing desk while the door to their bedroom was still open.

Thirteen

Leaves and Embroidery

Jane woke after Vincent had departed, and took her breakfast in their apartment. The dry toast, bland though it was, turned her stomach, and she had to force herself to chew each mouthful and then swallow methodically. If she focused her attention on other matters, she could put much of the nausea out of her mind. It was fortunate, then, that her mind occupied itself so thoroughly with Vincent's odd behaviour.

She sat at the table under the window, and tried to ignore Vincent's writing desk, which sat upon it. Running her hand along the edge of the travel desk, Jane did not try the latch, but it was clear from the solidity of the connection that it was locked. She took another bite of toast and drummed her fingers on the wood surface of the writing desk. What would Vincent need to keep secret?

The only thing which Jane could summon to her mind was the glass glamour, although he left that sitting upon the desk freely enough. In truth, there was little need to hide it, since the experiment had failed. She sighed and pushed the toast away from her. It would lead to no good, worrying at a problem which had no basis in anything more than her own unease. Still, she could not keep her mind from wondering what Vincent would have cause to hide from her.

To escape the perambulations of her thoughts, which would insist upon treading paths she did not wish to visit, Jane took herself downstairs, intent on seeking Mme Chastain's company in the parlour. As she descended the grand stairs, Vincent came out of M. Chastain's office, his riding coat slung over his arm.

"Oh, I thought I had missed you already." Jane hurried down the last few stairs.

He raised his eyebrows in surprise and bent down to kiss her on the cheek. "I was in the studio, and only stepped in to see if the mail had come before I head out."

"Where are you off to today?"

"I have a few errands to run. Nothing terribly interesting."

"Shall I come with you, then? To keep you company?"

He shook his coat out and slipped one arm into it. "Thank you, but as much as I would enjoy your company, I must go on to Brussels today and will not have time for dallying."

Jane helped him with the other sleeve, trying to mask

her hurt. Of course, if he needed to go to Brussels then she would only slow him down. Of course, that was entirely sensible. And yet she felt that only part of the truth had been spoken. In each of these instances where she had the sense of omission, she could not name the elements which built her unease. That he had not looked at her when he had spoken could be no great reason for alarm, for what could be more natural than to look at one's coat while donning it?

And yet . . . and yet.

"Jane? What is the matter?" Vincent took her hand and rubbed his thumb across the back.

She concentrated on the blunt shape of his thumb, and the way the weather had reddened his knuckles. "I miss you."

"But I am here."

"Yes." She struggled out of her melancholy state and resolved to have this conversation with him in earnest when he returned that evening. The foyer was not the place for confessions. "And now you must be on your way. I should not want you to be any later in your travels than necessary."

He squeezed her hand. "Thank you." Vincent took a step away, and paused as if he wanted to say something more, then shook his head. "I will see you this evening."

As Vincent strode out the door, Jane took herself to the parlour. M. Archambault and M. Bertrand sat by the window, poring over a book, each with a steaming cup of coffee beside him. Their gestures and the snippets of conversation that burst from them from time to time indicated that they studied some obscure bit of glamour history.

Mme Chastain sat by the fire and smiled as Jane entered. "How are you, my dear?"

"Well enough, thank you." Jane pulled her chair closer and took up her work basket, rather wishing she could sit nearer to the students so she might overhear their conversation, unbecoming as eavesdropping might be.

Peering over the edge of her embroidery frame, Mme Chastain tutted. "I think you are not eating enough, am I right?"

"Perhaps." Jane shook her head. "Is it . . . do you enjoy being a mother?"

Mme Chastain took another few stitches in her tapestry. "I think there is only one acceptable answer to that question. But the truth of the matter is that there are days when I do and days when I wish that my life were somewhat more my own." She lowered the frame. "But to answer the question you did not ask, yes, it is worth every ache and pain and worry. For me. Not all women are the same, I think."

Jane bit her lip and bent her head to her embroidery once more. Her own mother had been so much the invalid while Jane was growing up that it had often fallen to Jane to act as mother to her younger sister. Her bond with her mother had been strained by the fact that Jane could not trust her as a source of comfort. She loved her mother, yes, but she had little respect for her beyond what was due by filial duty.

As Jane was pondering this, Mme Chastain caught her eye and nodded to the door. Yves stood there, his hands in his pockets and his head dipped in a modest manner. His left cheek was tucked in as though he were chewing upon it. Mme Chastain raised her eyebrows and cocked her head as if to say, "behold," then bent her head to her embroidery, ignoring her son's presence.

After some minutes spent thus, neither in nor out of the parlour, Yves fixed his shoulders and sauntered in, affecting nonchalance. "Good morning, Mama."

"And to you as well, my dear." She tilted her head to accept a kiss upon her cheek without appearing to take her attention from her embroidery, though Jane could not help but notice that her stitches had slowed.

Yves leaned over her chair, his brown hair tousled in the most stylish manner. "That is very pretty."

"Thank you. The window seat needs some attention, and I thought to replace the covering. It will have the view from the Roman walk when I finish." She smiled up at her son. "Do you approve?"

"Approve!" He clutched his hand to his breast. "Mama, you could doubt my approbation? Of course I approve. You are the cleverest of mothers."

Jane tucked her tongue into her cheek to keep from smiling at his excessive flattery. Mme Chastain had no such compunction. "And how many mothers have you with which to compare me?"

He lifted his hand and ticked off names. "There is Giroux's mother, who cannot embroider. And Mme Meynard, who has not seen her son in five y—"

"Hush." Mme Chastain narrowed her eyes at her son. "I will not have you speak ill of her. You know well why their son was sent away."

"You would have kept me though, would you not?" Yves sobered and put a hand on her shoulder. "No matter what."

She patted his hand, her face softening with such obvious devotion that Jane's heart ached to witness it. "Yes, my dear."

"And no matter how wicked I was, you would still love me?"

Her eyes narrowed and she glanced at Jane. "Why do I suspect that you will apprise me of some wickedness in a matter of moments?"

"It is not wickedness, Mama. Only . . ." He came around and knelt at her feet, taking both of her hands in his. His cheeks coloured prettily. "Only, I have run through my allowance and am somewhat embarrassed because it is my turn to treat the lads at Brinkmann's."

"I see." Mme Chastain pursed her lips. "Mme Vincent, what would you do in my position?"

Startled at being brought thus into the conversation, Jane felt a sudden rush of heat. She looked down and inhaled swiftly to gather her thoughts. "I suppose it depends on why he has run through his funds."

Yves flushed and stammered. "I do not know. Everything

is expensive, and it is hard to keep up when my allowance is so low."

"Perhaps you might retrench," Jane offered.

"But if I do that, what will the other fellows think?"

"It starts so young . . ." Mme Chastain shook her head and took up her embroidery hoop once more. "Have you spoken with your father about this?"

"No! That is. I mean—" Yves stood, and paced away from her. "I thought you might understand. The need for hospitality. And all."

"Hm. Well, draw up a list of your expenses and we shall discuss it this evening."

"But—"

"Yves." She snipped the slender skein of green silk close to the tapestry circle. "If you cannot account for your funds, why should we think that you would be responsible with a larger amount?"

The boy looked as though he would protest again, or offer some other rationale for his mother, but a servant entered with the morning mail. Mme Chastain smiled at her son as she accepted the tray. "It will not be as bad as all that." She sorted through the mail and held one elegant, hot-pressed envelope out to Jane. "Here is one for David. Would you prefer me to leave it here, or have it sent over to him?"

Jane spread out the hem of the gown on which she was working. "Who is it from?"

"Mr. Gilman. I thought it might affect whether or not David makes the trip to Brussels today."

"It might." She smoothed the linen, embarrassed to admit that she did not know where her husband was. "I am afraid I cannot offer the direction of his appointment today."

Mme Chastain tapped the letter on the tray. "M. Archambault? Do you recall where Mme Maçon lives?"

Jane twitched, driving the needle into her finger as she realized that Mme Chastain knew where Vincent was. Did he keep his actions only from *Jane*?

"She is on Ruelle à Cafou, but he is only there in the mornings, I think." He waited until M. Bertrand nodded to confirm this before continuing. "Would you like me to run the letter to him?"

"No, thank you." Jane fumbled in her work basket for a scrap to staunch the bleeding of her finger. M. Archambault and M. Bertrand also knew? "I have not taken my excursion today. This will be as good a destination as any, if you would but give me the direction."

Mme Chastain nudged Yves. "You have been there before, with M. Vincent, have you not? Would you show Mme. Vincent the way? And then when you return, I will help you with your accounting."

Yves bit his lower lip and then nodded. "I should be delighted."

With that settled, Jane took only long enough to put aside her work basket and—though she did not wish to delay for a moment—go upstairs to fetch a bonnet and wrap. If Vincent had related the particulars of his whereabouts to the rest of the household, then it must be that she had misread his silences due to her own anxiety. He had nothing improper to hide. Clearly he had taken on an additional commission and, given her frequent concerns for his fatigue, had elected to not tell her so as to keep her from worry. She would have words with him about this omission, which would not do. Jane paused as she tucked the letter into her reticule, struck by wondering if Vincent had taken on this other task because she was increasing. She had not considered that he might fear lacking the means to provide for their child.

Yves met her at the front door, very erect and with his brown hair carefully tousled in the current fashion. He bowed quite correctly. Jane had to stifle a smile at his transparent efforts to appear in the best light, perhaps in hopes that she would make a favourable report to his mother about his maturity.

The day had not yet grown warm, making Jane glad that she had brought a wrap with her. A light breeze carried the scent of the baking district toward them, and Jane was afflicted with the uneasy sensations of hunger and nausea. Some of the nausea she thought she could attribute to a nervous state, rather than her general condition.

The houses grew smaller and the streets narrowed as they directed their course into an older and poorer part of town than Jane had yet visited. On more than one occasion, refuse filled the gutters, and she found herself wishing for the crossing sweepers of London to clear the path.

Yves cleared his throat. "Mme Vincent, if you should wish me to deliver the letter for you, I would be glad to do so."

"Thank you, Yves. But Vincent is gone so much from the house that I confess that I would take a smaller excuse than this to see him for some few more moments."

"Ah." He nodded with a sagacity beyond his years. "Marriage."

"Indeed." They walked some blocks farther in silence.

Jane spied Anne-Marie standing outside a shop on a cross-street and thought for a moment that she might be able to release poor Yves from his duties. As she opened her mouth to suggest it, Lieutenant Segal stepped from the shop and pressed a small packet into Anne-Marie's hands. Jane's heart seized at the clear devotion in Anne-Marie's eyes, and the tender regard with which Lieutenant Segal beheld her. The ease in their manner reminded her too painfully of the distance which had grown between herself and Vincent since they had discovered she was with child.

Jane pulled her attention away, determined not to bother them. As a distraction, she searched for some topic on which one might converse with a young man. "How do your studies go?"

He shrugged. "They are well enough, I suppose."

"And do you study glamour as well?"

Scowling, Yves kicked a loose cobble and sent it skipping down the road. "It does not seem to be a skill I have. At least, not to hear my father tell it."

"There are other masters . . . if it is something you have an interest in."

"I shall have to find some other occupation. He will always be better than me, you see." He straightened his shoulders. "I had thought to join the army, but without a war on, there is no way to make your fortune, or any likelihood of rising through the ranks."

"But glamour is less dangerous."

He flashed her a smile. "Which means less of a chance for glory or distinction. No, I think I shall have to find something else."

"Is being distinguished so important to you?"

"It is to my father." He stopped in front a petite two-story home fronted by neat window boxes filled with purple tulips. "Here we are."

Vincent's horse was tied to the fence, and flicked its ear disinterestedly at their approach. Jane thanked Yves, and—though he offered to wait for her—the way his boots shifted on the cobblestones gave a clear indication that he wished to be on his way. After she assured him that she could make her way back, he trotted off in the direction whence he had come.

Jane knocked on the front door, thankful for the gloves which covered her suddenly sweating palms, though she had no reason to be nervous. As she waited, she took in the details of the house, noting that the tulips which graced the window boxes were crafted from glamour. At a distance they had the right shape, but on closer inspection they were crudely rendered, and clearly not her husband's work.

The door opened and a young woman answered, dressed in the simple local costume. She had curling flaxen locks, and clear grey eyes which greeted Jane with a twinkle. "May I help you?"

"Is this the home of Mme Maçon? I was told that Mr. Vincent would be here. I am his wife."

The young woman looked Jane up and down, taking notice of her English walking suit as though her accent alone were not enough to identify her. "Of course, madame. He is right this way, with my grandmother, Mme Maçon."

She led Jane down a narrow hall and into a tiny sitting room. An elderly woman, white hair thinned to a wisp, sat in a rocking chair by the fire. Vincent sat next to her, a notebook open on his knee and a pencil in his right hand. His left hand gestured under a floating glamour of a single green leaf.

As Jane entered, Vincent started visibly, dropping his notebook. It slapped to the floor, and as he grabbed for it, the green leaf trembled and scissored out of view. "Jane!"

Jane could not miss the sudden pallor of her husband's face, nor the flaring of his nostrils as he inhaled at the surprise of seeing her. More than mere surprise, though: in the widening of his pupils and the vein that leapt at his temple, she saw fear. Not wishing to record more of his alarm at her presence than she had already witnessed, Jane focused on the ribbon of her reticule.

The paper of the letter rattled as she drew it forth. "You received a letter, and I thought it might have been the one you were looking for this morning."

"Thank you. You did not need to bring it all this way." Vincent rose and took the letter from her outstretched hand.

"The doctor did encourage me to go for walks, and this provided me with a new route."

"I see." Vincent cleared his throat. Jane could not miss the glance he shot to the young woman who had greeted her. "Allow me to introduce you to Mme Maçon, who has been graciously taking time to show me her approach to glamour."

Now it was Jane's turn to lift her eyes in surprise. She made her courtesies to Mme Maçon and her granddaughter while her mind filled with wonder. Why in Heaven's name would Vincent be studying with a folk glamourist? She could only have the most primitive of techniques, beyond which he was far advanced.

The Maçons spoke small pleasantries and invited Jane to sit. The sofa, which appeared to be covered in deep green satin, creaked under her, and she could feel the loose threads which lay under the glamour on its surface. Jane suspected that Vincent had executed this one. The work was flawless, and did not match the other, more obvious, glamours which adorned the neat but worn room, such as the unabashed sprays of reds and blues surrounding a faded portrait of Napoleon, as if banners clung to the wall. A shaft of light illuminated a hair wreath over a side table, and seemed to cast a silhouette of a young man on the wall. Though the glamours had no finesse or delicacy in their execution, they were nevertheless charming.

When Mme Maçon's granddaughter pressed them to stay for tea, Vincent shook his head. "I am afraid I need to be on my way. Thank you, ladies. I will see you next week."

When they were outside, Vincent offered his arm. Jane found herself hesitating before taking it. She chided herself for . . . well, she was hardly sure how to categorize her thoughts or fears.

"You do not need to walk back with me. I know you must be on your way." She gestured to his horse, which lifted its head to greet them.

"I should be nothing more than a hardened blackguard if I let my wife walk out to deliver a letter and then did not escort her home."

"But it was not my intent to delay you."

Vincent sighed and untied his horse. "Jane, you have allowed me to leave Mme Maçon's earlier than I might otherwise have left, so the very small detour in seeing you home will do me no great harm. I am rather more worried about you." He offered his arm again. "You gave me quite the turn, appearing like that. I thought something had happened."

Blushing, Jane accepted his arm, understanding in a rush how it must have seemed to him. The fear she had seen on his face was not of being discovered, but fear for her. "I am sorry."

"There is nothing to apologize for. I am glad to see you, and glad to have a moment with you in the daylight. I have quite neglected you." He tucked her hand into the crook of his elbow and, with the horse trailing them on his far side, they walked back through the streets of Binché.

"May I ask what it is you were discussing with Mme Maçon?"

"Oh . . ." He wrinkled his nose in thought. "She is self-taught, and has some different ideas of colour and how it works in glamour. Nothing exciting, but a fresh perspective. I thought it might be useful."

"Is it?"

"Somewhat." He pointed with his chin. "Is that Madame Meynard?"

Jane wanted to shriek with vexation that he had changed the subject yet again, but she could hardly fault him for their acquaintance's decision to walk down their street.

Jane agreed that it was indeed Mme Meynard, and they crossed the street to greet her. Seeing Vincent shift his weight and check the height of the sun in the sky after a few moments of conversation, Jane took the opportunity offered to walk with Mme Meynard, thus releasing Vincent to ride on to Brussels. She longed to keep him, but it was clear that he wished to be away. And even if he stayed, he seemed to be finished with the topic of how he spent his days. Jane found that for every question answered, a dozen new ones clamoured.

Fourteen

Sunlight and Keys

Jane straightened her back, neck protesting from having been bent so long over her book. Signor Defendini's documentation of the Murano glassblowing techniques had been giving her less insight into what had gone wrong with their glamour than she had hoped. Brussels had a small circulating library for the British citizens who had flocked there as if it were Bath. Jane had applied to Vincent to search it for some useful text, and this had been the best he could offer. The slender volume had lavish illustrations to accompany the text and tantalizing hints that Murano glassblowers used glamour in their craft in ways that other glassmakers did not, but the methods themselves seemed to be secrets so closely guarded that the book read more as a sales catalogue extolling their virtues than an examination of techniques.

Sun streamed through the window of their apartments, in the first break from three days of spring rains. Steam rose off the paving stones in the courtyard below, and the smell of damp earth rose with it.

Putting her book to the side, Jane copied some notes into her sketchbook and then took up the glass ball they had made. She thought that she might try to draw it, hoping that setting the *Sphère* on the page would help her see it more clearly. When she was finished, she might ask Vincent to send the results to Herr Scholes to ask for his opinion.

Anne-Marie bustled around behind her, straightening the clothing which the laundress had sent up. "Madame, where shall I put this?" She held Vincent's riding coat in one hand and a small key in the other. Jane recognised it as the key to his writing desk. It was lucky that the laundress had not lost it, small as it was.

"I shall give it to my husband." Jane took the key, intending to put it somewhere safe until Vincent was next home. And yet, it would be simplicity itself to open the desk, take out his address book, and send Herr Scholes the drawing herself. She need not examine anything else inside, and after all, Vincent had said he was hiding things from M. Chastain's servants, not from her.

But even as she had that thought, she knew that, far beyond the impropriety of writing to a man to whom she had never been introduced, opening the desk would be a very real breach of Vincent's trust. Her curiosity begged her to use the key, but Jane set it resolutely in the drawer of the table and pushed the desk farther from her.

Even so, every time she lifted her head from the page to reference the glass *Sphère*, the writing desk beckoned as a tempting distraction from her purpose. What did Vincent keep so carefully concealed within it?

This would not do. Jane gathered up her drawing things and wrapped the sphere in a length of velvet to safeguard it. Going out of doors would remove her from temptation and offer her an opportunity for fresh air. Thus armed with a purpose she stood, aware of how much her back ached.

She must have moaned, for Anne-Marie came to her side quickly. "Madame, are you well?"

"I have been sitting for too long." To turn the conversation from her own frailty, Jane made comment on the first thing she noticed. A pretty pendant of a bumblebee, which hung from a slender chain at Anne-Marie's throat. "What a cunning bee. Where did you get it?"

Anne-Marie blushed deeply, and tucked the bee into her dress so it was out of sight. "A young man."

"Would this be a certain lieutenant I saw you walking with?"

Anne-Marie's flushed cheeks confirmed Jane's guess. "Please do not mention him." Anne-Marie patted her chest as if to make certain the bee were truly concealed. "I could lose my place."

"Over having a beau!" Jane shook her head. "Well, it is not unheard of for masters to have that rule, though I cannot say that I approve. You have my silence on the matter."

"Thank you, madame."

Jane went down to the courtyard with her bundle and headed for a stone bench which stood near the studio. With the sun shining on it, it made a pleasant place to sit for an afternoon. She unwrapped the *Sphère* and settled herself there, her sketchbook open on her lap. The sunlight illuminated all of the faults they had introduced into the otherwise flawless glass so they stood out with perfect clarity. The path the glamour should take almost glowed in the light, and she could see it even without adjusting her sight. What, then, had caused it to fail?

As she drew, she rotated the *Sphère* so that she could capture all sides of it in her drawings. It occurred to her to wonder if an imperceptible fracture could have marred the ball as it cooled. That would account for how it had stopped working.

Jane wished that she could test her theory by passing a strand of glamour, only a single fold, through the glass, but even the simplest ones were denied to her. Still, it was pleasant to be outside drawing. The courtyard bustled with activity as students came and went from the studio on various errands, and the relative calm of her bench was an oasis in the midst of activity. Through the windows of the studio, she could see Vincent talking with M. Archambault, and resolved to ask him to try passing glamour through it again, with an eye to discovering a possible crack in the glass.

She did not have long to wait before Vincent strode out of the studio and headed toward the stables. So focused was he that he did not notice her on the bench, for all that she was only fifteen feet from his path.

She called his name, to catch his attention. Vincent stopped and turned toward her voice, then looked past where she sat and, frowning, spun completely around.

"Vincent?" Jane raised her hand and waved.

Again he turned, and as before, his gaze passed through her. He faced the building, shading his eyes as though to spy her in a window. Breath quickening, Jane put her hand on the *Sphère* of glass, which practically glowed in the sunlight. "Vincent, can you not see me? I am sitting by the studio."

Rotating on his heel, Vincent faced her voice. "I cannot. Jane, you should not be practising glamour."

"It is the *Sphère*!" Only one thing had changed between here and their chambers. Jane pulled the velvet covering over the glass ball to mask it from the sun.

Vincent inhaled in shock, taking half a step back. She laughed, throwing her head back with delight and then, watching him, pulled the velvet from the *Sphère*. By the way his eyes widened and a slow smile grew to match hers, Jane knew that she had vanished from his sight.

Her husband ran forward, slowing as he met the boundary of the *Sphère*. Then he stood within its influence. "Hello, Muse. What have you done?"

"You will have to tell me. I can only tell that I have vanished" She traced a finger across the inclusion which lay closest to the surface of the glass. "It was sunny that day in the glass factory, but rained the next. Since then, the ball has been on your desk in shadow. My best guess is that sunlight is purer than any form of conjured glamour. What do you think?"

"I think that you are the cleverest woman in the world." Vincent knelt by her and let his gaze go distant. "It *is* bending the sunlight."

"If we can perfect our technique or make purer glass, then we might be able to use it to direct glamour yet." Jane tapped her chin, wishing that she could see what he was seeing. "I wonder if indirect sunlight will suffice?"

"Likely not." Vincent shaded his eyes and tilted his head up to the sky. He pointed. "There is a cloud coming, if you want to test your theory, but since the *Sphère* never vanished from our rooms, I would hazard a guess that the diffraction is too great."

As he began to rise, Jane caught his hand. "Wait. May I step out of the *Sphère* and watch?"

"Of course." He glanced past her to the studio. "They cannot see us, can they?"

"I do not believe——" Her words stopped as Vincent covered her mouth with his. Jane yielded to him, aware of the softness of his touch, the warmth of the sun, and the breeze which caressed her.

Vincent pulled back, cheeks ruddy and curving with his tender regard. "I quite like this thing you have invented, Muse."

"Mr. Vincent! You shock me." Try as she might, she could not keep her voice stern or hide her delight.

He compressed his lips into his private smile and nodded to the sky again. "The cloud is about to cover the sun."

Jane rose and hurried away from him until she felt certain she must be out of the *Sphère*'s influence. When she faced the direction whence she had come, the bench and Vincent were quite invisible, leaving only a view of the courtyard beyond. She held her breath, hardly knowing whether she wanted them to appear when the cloud masked the sun, thus proving her point, or to stay concealed.

The day greyed, and as if he were watercolour bleeding onto a page, Vincent faded into view, first as an ill-defined shape, then his colour becoming more vibrant until she could see him with unrestricted clarity. She had only time to say, "I see you," before the cloud passed from the sun and he vanished once more.

Gravel rattled close by and then Vincent appeared before her, walking with the *Sphère* held carefully before him. Jane knew that they had, at that moment, vanished from the view of those around them, and she could hardly contain her exuberance.

"Shall we show M. Chastain?"

Vincent bit the inside of his lip, tilting his head to the side to examine the *Sphère*. "Not yet, I think." Raising it, he peered into the interior. "I should like to have it written up, and run a few more trials first."

"But he might offer some suggestions."

"True." He paused, seemingly about to say something more, but then shook his head. "You know I prefer to present a finished work than to have someone observe my progress."

"Surely a colleague . . ."

"If you prefer." Some of his reserve had returned. Jane wondered what she had done to cause it, until he answered her unasked question. "The invention is yours."

Was it possible that Vincent was jealous that *she* had conceived the idea of using glass? Jane considered how long he had been striving to find a way to record a glamour so that it could be moved without effort. And she had leaped past his years of careful notes and theories with a child's plaything. "The invention is ours. Take the time you need."

Letting him put more time into understanding the glamour could do no harm.

Fifteen

Ribbons of White and Red

Jane woke the next morning and had an appetite for the first time since she could remember.
Sun streamed into their bedchamber, tiny motes
of dust dancing in the light. She stretched, feeling all the effects of good health that she had
not realized she had lost. Everything about the
day seemed as if it were made for wonder.

Vincent had already arisen, no doubt to make
his way to Brussels yet again. She could not
find it in herself to resent the trip. Her glamour in
glass had worked. What could be more perfect
than that? Jane threw off the counterpane, unable
to contemplate staying in bed. She felt the urge to
find an activity to match her spirits.

The doctor had advised her to take fresh air
and to go for gentle walks, so that is how she

would spend the morning. A hearty breakfast, and then a stroll into town. Perhaps she would even go so far as the old Roman walls. Dressing herself in her blue high-collared walking suit, Jane marvelled at what it was to be hungry again. It had been so long since the thought of food had not turned her stomach that she had not at first recognised the pricking in her middle as hunger.

Jane hurried downstairs to see if she could persuade the kitchen staff to provide her with an egg and some plum bread for breakfast. These acquired, she took herself to the parlour, hoping to find a cup of coffee. Mme Chastain was retying the sash on Miette's dress as Jane entered. "You seem to be in good spirits this morning."

They had recorded a glamour in glass. "Thank you! I am feeling well for the first time in ages." Jane pulled up her chair and took her place at the table.

"I am glad to hear it. The first is always the worst. You will not mind so much with your second." She brushed Miette's hair out of the little girl's face, smiling.

The notion of having a second child seemed utterly foreign at that juncture, but Jane did not care to dispute the claim. They had, after all, recorded a glamour. She poured a cup of coffee to distract herself. "I thought I might go for a walk today. Do you need anything from town?"

"I want a new ribbon!" Miette danced away from her mother, undoing her bow in an instant. "For my crystal."

"You shall have one." For that blessed, beautiful crystal which had delivered such elation that Jane could hardly contain herself. One ribbon? Why, the child should have a dozen, and still it would not be thanks enough.

Jane found that, though her appetite had returned, her excitement was too great to allow her to sit still for long. She took her leave with her errand in mind, and began the walk to the centre of town. Out of doors, the spicy scent of early geraniums mingled with the earthiness that marked the passage of carriages. Her feet rang against the cobblestones paving the street, and everything seemed scrubbed clean just for the purpose of giving her walk pleasure.

The town buzzed with life. Women in neat linen leaned out of their windows to converse with their neighbours on the street. A boy ran past with a wood hobby-horse, toy sword held over his head, shouting "Viva Napoleon!" For a moment she thought it was young Luc Chastain, but it was another child with similar colouring. A pack of boys chased him, so intent on their game that they bumped willy-nilly into the pedestrians.

As Jane approached the centre of town, she became sensible of a change in the knots of people lining the street. There was, in their general carriage, a tension that ignored the beauty of the day. Jane stepped into the notions store and found it astonishingly thronged with customers, but with a sharp line down the middle of the crowd. It took her a moment to comprehend the difference between the people standing on opposite sides of the divide. She noted that one group held red, blue, and white ribbons and the other held only white, but nothing else unified the sets, save for a clear animosity of each toward the opposite group. In all other ways, it was a cheerful space. The spools of ribbons lining the shelves caught the light from the street, and a glamour arched overhead to create the illusion of a ceiling full of fluttering ribbon and lace.

In the space between the groups, two women stood, pulling a single white ribbon between them. They shouted insults at each other, tugging the ribbon back and forth while the crowd jeered them on. The woman on the left had red and blue ribbons dangling from her grasp, while the one on the right had only the shared white ribbon.

"You are a traitor to your nation!" the one with white ribbon shouted.

"Ha! France is not my nation, you haughty bourgeois!" Red and blue jerked on the white ribbon.

Behind the counter, the gaunt shopkeeper tried to call for order, but was roundly ignored.

An older gentleman holding a white ribbon approached Jane with apparent trepidation. "Madame, you are British? You should return home."

"What has happened?"

"Napoleon has returned to France."

Jane's knees threatened to give way under her. Though she had understood the man perfectly, she felt the urge to ask him to repeat himself, as if that would make his words mean something different. Napoleon out of exile! How was that possible?

The import of the brigands who had accosted them on the road returned to her. She had thought that they had little to fear if Napoleon's only supporters were such ragged men as those. Around her, she saw the evidence that the Ogre had far more support than she had guessed possible.

On the outskirts of the crowd, a woman holding red and blue ribbons sneered at her. "She is British!" Her words brought silence to the room, and Jane felt the full weight of both groups' attention fall upon her. "What is she doing here?"

"She is here to buy ribbon. Are you not, madame?" The shopkeeper took advantage of the lull in fighting and drew himself erect. "In my shop, one only purchases ribbon or lace. Do I make myself understood, mesdames and messieurs?" When no one responded, he pointed to the ribbon held between the two women. "That piece of ribbon is spoiled, and I will not sell it to either of you. But I will gladly sell you both lace, which is also white. Will that suit?"

The women looked down at the white ribbon, stretched and spoiled by their struggles. As one, they let it drop to the floor.

Not willing to lose control, the shopkeeper rapped the counter. "Who is next, please?"

As the crowd began to sort out who had precedence, the gentleman with the white ribbon who had spoken to Jane first, gestured toward the door. She needed no further hint.

On her way out, one of the women with red, blue, and white ribbons shifted abruptly, driving her elbow into Jane's middle. "Go home, British."

The breath left Jane's body in a rush, and she struggled

to draw in the next. Pain, sharp and quick, drew a line from her toes to the base of her skull. Folded over, she wrapped her arms around herself and became more conscious of the child she carried than she had ever been previously. Heretofore, the inconvenience had taken precedence, but all she could think of now was that the child—her child—might be harmed.

Tears pricking her eyes, she forced herself erect and made her way out into the sunlit street. The day, so bright, so pleasant, seemed painfully at odds with the events, and yet there were those residents of Binché who were rejoicing at the news. The conversation from the dinner party when they first arrived came back to her, and she recalled Mme Meynard saying, *We have been passed back and forth between France and the Netherlands for almost as many years as there have been people living here.*

And here Jane saw the proof of that, for half the town rejoiced that their Emperor had returned, and half the town despaired. It was only with the greatest difficulty that Jane did not run back to the Chastains', where she knew at least *they* did not support Napoleon. She had no such faith about their neighbours.

Mme Chastain met Jane in the foyer of the home, her hand held to her breast. "Thank heavens. I have been so worried for you."

"You have heard, then." Jane tugged her gloves free.

"Yes. Colonel de Bodard just came with the news."

"I heard only that Napoleon was returned to France, nothing more."

"Come into the parlour." Mme Chastain took Jane by the arm. "You are as pale as death."

"I am only a little frightened."

They went to the parlour, where M. Chastain had gathered with his students and the household's senior staff. Colonel de Bodard stood at the mantel with the room's attention fixed upon him. Gone was the gentle chevalier who had comforted Jane at the dinner table. He stood now in the Belgian uniform, a dark blue jacket with red epaulettes at the shoulder. Jane scanned the room, growing cold as she realized that Vincent was not there. He had gone to Brussels, and would be on the road even now. He might not know that the Ogre was out of the box.

Jane put a hand on her middle, as if it would reassure their child.

Anne-Marie pressed a glass of Madeira on her, and offered Jane her seat. M. Chastain paced the room with one finger hooked over his nose and the other hand tucked behind his back. "Those of you who wish to go may, but I think the danger is not great."

"But I heard Napoleon was gone to Paris," M. Archambault said.

"Yes, but King Louis XVIII has sent General Ney to stop him. He will do so, and then we may all rest easy. Remember, Napoleon can have no great number of men, and those that he has are all deserters, not the steadiest sort in a fight." Colonel de Bodard left his place by the fire and came to Jane's side. "Mme Vincent, how are you taking it?"

"I am only piecing together what has happened, and

perhaps more frightened than I should be." The scent of the wine turned her stomach. Jane swallowed against bile and set the glass on the side table.

"Napoleon landed at the beginning of the month and is marching toward Paris. No shots have been fired, and garrison after garrison has surrendered to him. This sounds astonishing, but remember that King Louis is still in Paris, and has the army to back him. The Belgian army has been called up and we will join forces with the British to help oppose Napoleon."

"What if the French army surrenders?" Mme Chastain touched her husband's arm. "They might already have done so, and we will not know for another week, as slow as the mail service is."

"Do not alarm yourself over things that shall not happen. You might as well be alarmed that the sun will land in our courtyard." M. Chastain snorted. "I, myself, am not surprised to see him returned. He has never kept his bargains."

A small hand tugged at the corner of Jane's dress. Miette stood by her chair, prism held tightly in both hands the way another child might clutch a doll for comfort. "Did you fetch my ribbon?"

"No, dear. I am sorry, but I could not." Jane recollected the scene in the notions store and wondered how much worse it would be if more was at stake than a bit of frippery. Was Vincent safe? She took Miette by the hand and stood. "But you shall have your choice of ribbons from my collection."

It was not good to keep the little girl here amid so much worry and Jane was glad of an excuse to escape the atmosphere herself. She kept up a constant chatter as they went above stairs, trying to drive out any sense of unease from the both of them. Her mind, though, sought after Vincent at every minute.

In her apartment, she pulled out the bandbox which held her millinery supplies and settled down at the table with Miette. Without self-consciousness, the little girl climbed in her lap to see into the box better.

The weight and warmth of Miette's small form settled Jane, helping her focus past the concern for her husband. They sorted through the box, putting aside those ribbons too large to fit through the small brass ring at the top of the prism, until they settled on three: one red, one white, and one green. Jane could not help but see the symbols writ on the red and white ribbons, so she steered Miette toward the green one and helped her thread it through the ring. Then they stood at the window in the sun and admired the rainbows that Miette scattered about the room.

When that amusement faded, Miette tilted her head up, curls falling back from her cheeks. "Will you make me a glamour?"

"I am afraid I cannot, my dear." Jane cast about the room for some other activity which might suit to amuse a little girl. She had no toys, only books and art supplies. "Shall I read to you? Or we can do drawings."

"Why not?"

"Well . . ." Jane hesitated, uncertain as to the propriety

of explaining such things to a child. "The doctor told me that I should not. I listen to my doctor's advice. Would you not do the same?"

"No." Stoutly, she shook her head. "The doctor tells me to drink nasty tonics. I hate him."

Masking her smile, Jane crouched next to Miette in the window. "But you feel better after, yes? Sometimes we might not like what the doctor tells us to do, but it is only for a little time, and then we are well again."

"Are you sick?"

"No . . ." Jane rested her hand on her stomach. Though she had yet to begin to show, the changes were apparent to her. "I am increasing."

"A baby!" Miette's delight at this news was all too clear. "May I hold her when she comes?"

"Of course."

The sound of a horse trotting into the courtyard below pulled Jane to her feet. Vincent had returned, his mount lathered in sweat.

Sixteen

The Writing Desk

Jane took the marble stairs as quickly as the slick soles of her slippers would let her. Miette was not far behind, though the child could have no idea why Jane was in such a hurry. They reached the foyer just as Vincent strode inside, dust clinging to his coat and sweat making a map of the dirt on his face. Jane collided with him in an embrace in the centre of the hall. She cared not a whit for who saw them, only that he was safe and present.

"I take it you have heard the news."

Jane stepped back so she could see her beloved. "The town is uneasy."

"I am not surprised." Vincent wet his lips and rested his hand on Miette's shoulder, crouching down to be on eye level with her. "Will you fetch your father for me?"

As the little girl scampered away, Jane asked, "Did something happen on the road?"

Vincent shook his head, rising to his full height again. "Give me but a little time."

"Vincent—" Jane cut herself off as M. Chastain came hurrying down the hall. His face had as much worry on it as she felt.

Her husband pushed her gently toward the stairs. "I will be up in a moment."

Before she could protest further, Vincent had left her and gone down the hall to meet M. Chastain. They had a hurried and whispered conference, during which M. Chastain occasionally turned his gaze past Vincent to Jane. She shivered at the bleakness in his face.

After only a few minutes, Vincent returned to her, his long legs eating the space between them. The tails of his coat flapped as he walked. Without a word, Vincent took her by the arm and led her upstairs. She could feel him curtailing the length of his stride to match hers. No sooner had they set foot in their apartments than she said, "Will you tell me what happened to you today?"

"I was on the road to Brussels. It seemed to me as if the traffic were heavier than usual." He pulled aside the curtains by the window, looking first on one side then on the other. "I quickly learned that Napoleon had landed some two weeks ago, and was proceeding to Paris with no resistance."

"But General Ney . . ."

"Will not stop him." Vincent paced restlessly to their bedroom, peering into the room and then behind the door. "I have asked M. Chastain to arrange passage for you on the next ship to England."

"Passage for me? What of you?"

"I will stay and study with M. Chastain. There is no need for you to stay as well."

"Nor is there need for me to flee. We are in Belgium, not France, and we are perfectly safe here." She did not mention the incident at the notions shop nor remind him of the events on their trip to Binché. "M. Chastain is not sending his students away."

"None of his students are my wife, nor are they carrying my child."

Anger rose in Jane, and she knew it stood out like a red badge upon each of her cheeks. "I will not be sent away like I am an object. If you feel secure in staying here—"

"I do not!" Vincent stopped and wrapped both hands in his hair, pulling his head toward his chest. "I do *not* feel secure in staying here, but I must. Please, Jane, for the love you bear me, please go because I have asked."

Her breath was but shallow, and silence stood tense between them. "What are you not telling me, Vincent? Why must you stay?"

He groaned and paced in a circle away from her. "Why must I stay . . . why indeed?" Vincent stopped at the window and faced her, posture rigid with tension. "I am here as a spy for England. Somewhere in this town is a stronghold of the Bonapartist movement with plans to assassinate King Louis XVIII. With Napoleon on the move, it is all the more vital that I be here. Jane . . . any Briton who stays in Belgium is in danger, but if *we* were discovered, we would be shot. I can take that risk for myself, but cannot ask you to do the same."

Jane set her hands into fists so tight that her nails bit into the palms. She had to clench her jaw to keep the rage from spewing forth.

Vincent took a step back, and Jane had a moment to wonder what colour her face had turned. "Jane, I am sorry. I promised you a honeymoon and—"

"Do you think me so feebleminded that I am worried about a *honeymoon?* I am angry because you do not trust me. Do I not love King and country as much as you?"

"Yes, but—"

"What is more, you have lied to me. Methodically, since the day this charge was first laid upon you."

He shook his head. "I never spoke a word of falsehood to you."

"Lies of ambiguity and omission are every bit as great." Jane's entire body shook with anger. "What am I to think? That you have no confidence in my discretion? That you see me as weak, without the fortitude to even grasp that secrecy might be necessary? Tell me true: if I were a man, would you have had these thoughts?"

"No! It is not that at all. I was charged to tell no one."

"I am your wife!" Jane found she could say no more. She left him to go into their bedchamber. If he could not understand the very real breach of trust he had committed, then no words of hers, especially words spoken in anger and haste, would make him see it. Her hands shook so much that she had to cross her arms and clench her elbows to stop them from trembling. Jane paced back and forth in the room, trying to drive the fury from her body with activity.

On one of her returns, Vincent stood in the door. His broad shoulders drooped, and his hands twisted together in supplication. "Forgive me?"

"Why." She stopped her pacing.

"Because you are right. I should have either told you, or told the Prince that I could not accept the charge."

Jane waited.

"I thought only to protect you."

"By keeping me in the dark? How does that protect me? It is like not telling a child that a fire will burn, in order to protect him from the heat. What if I exposed you unknowingly?"

"And what if you exposed us both by an alteration in your behaviour?"

"Do you really think so little of me as that?" Jane took two furious strides closer. "You might recall that we ladies are trained from girlhood to give no hint of our feelings, lest we stray into an impropriety. That I am so open with you is only because of how deeply I trust you."

He had no response to that, and stood with his head bowed. When he spoke again, his voice was very low. "Is there no explanation I can offer to make it clear that I meant no harm?"

"I know that you intended no harm." Jane made an effort to calm herself so that she did not immediately refute her own assertion that she could govern her conduct. "That does not lessen the hurt I feel because you did not trust me. Vincent, I need you to understand the substance of my anger. Our marriage depends on mutual trust and respect, and at this moment I do not have any faith that you feel either for me."

Vincent grimaced and spread his arms to grip the doorway. He clung to it, veins standing out on the back of his hands, as a drowning man might cling to shipwreck. "On more than one occasion you have claimed that I do not trust you. First with glamours, now with this. What must I do to convince you that you are mistaken?"

"Act as though you trust me."

With an almost animal snarl, he released the door and stalked into the other room.

Jane closed her eyes, swaying. She had pushed him too far. Even if every word she uttered had been justified, a wife could not speak so to her husband.

"Actions." Vincent stood again in the doorway. He held his battered writing desk. "Sit with me, and I will explain all."

Now that she had won her point, Jane doubted the wisdom of her course. "What of the Prince Regent's command?"

"I am not married to him." Vincent tried for a smile and succeeded only in curling his lips. "Please, Muse. I have no gift with words."

Jane nodded and followed him into the sitting room, but she took no triumph from her victory, for she could not help but feel that she had used emotion as a weapon. Beneath that unease lay another, deeper fear: that Vincent had been right she would give him away by some change in her countenance, and her husband's life would be forfeit to her pride.

Seventeen

Retreat and Regard

Vincent sat Jane down at the table and put his writing desk in front of her. He pulled his pocket-book out from his coat and opened the slim leather folding-case to withdraw the keys to his writing desk. "Now, I have been taking notes and then passing them to Mr. Gilman in Brussels, so what I have here are only those which I have taken for my own benefit. They will require some explanation."

Frowning, Jane ran her gaze down the sheet of densely lined paper he had pulled out. "This is a recording of breeds of lambs."

"Yes." He drew up a chair and sat next to her. "Mrs. Gilman has no real interest in lambs gambolling. Her supposed requests were a code for Napoleon's movements."

"So you knew?" Jane lowered the sheet and stared at him in astonishment. "You knew he was in France."

"No. We knew that he had left Elba, but not where he had gone. The day that Mr. Gilman asked for the single lamb, he was passing on that message to the circle of spies in Brussels."

"That seems an awful lot of work, when you could just meet in private to discuss things."

Vincent nodded. "So we do. However . . ."

"However, you could not meet when I was present."

"Just so. Forgive me, Muse, for being so cross with you."

Jane raised his hand and kissed the back of his fingers. "Now that I know the reason, you are forgiven. But I still do not comprehend the purpose of the lambs."

"No one would take note of Mr. Gilman's meetings with a glamourist, so we were able to meet with relative ease. Mr. Gilman's chief benefit is that he is known to be a society man, absolutely disinterested in politics. If he were seen meeting privately with any of the political characters he would be suspect at once. A glamural in his drawing room can serve as a map which others may consult while at his home for parties. In much the same way, my benefit is that I am known to be a glamourist. It affords me entry into homes that would mistrust another Briton."

Jane remembered now the portrait of Napoleon over Mme Maçon's fireplace. "Such as discussing folk glamours with Mme Maçon."

"Exactly. That ostensible interest and a few small odd jobs took me to homes that our fellow countrymen do not have access to." He pointed at the Scottish Blackface section, which had a list of ewes and rams after it. "This is my most promising lead, given accidentally by you when you mentioned the tricolour cockade."

"Lieutenant Segal." That, coupled with the memory of the ribbon shop—which seemed so long ago now—came together in sudden understanding. She had been so used to the tricolours representing France during the long years that Napoleon reigned that she had not recognised the cockades as unusual, but with the Bourbons in power, the lieutenant should have been wearing a white cockade. Jane hastily told Vincent about the ribbon store, leaving out only the moment when the woman had struck her.

When she had finished, Vincent rubbed his jaw, a muscle tightening in the corner. "Are you certain you will not take ship? I would rest easier if you would."

She did not dignify that with a response, fixing her attention on the paper instead. "Should we visit Mme Meynard? I owe her a call, and the officers frequent her house."

"Not yet. Let us see how the week plays out. We may yet be taking ship."

"You have more breeds of lamb. Who are your other suspects?"

"The Awassi represent M. Archambault, M. Chastain's student who made the glamour *à la Chinoiserie*. Belgium Milk Sheep is M. Bertrand. Cotswold . . ." He sighed heavily and tapped the page with his finger. "Cotswold is the Chastain household."

Truly shocked, Jane could only stare for a moment. To

have accepted hospitality from a man and then to spy on him was beyond the pale. "You cannot believe that."

"Not willingly, no. And yet, Yves seems a likely choice, because of his youth and the influence that they might promise him for being a cousin of the Bonapartes."

"But he thinks that Napoleon is the wickedest man in Europe."

"That is what he told his youngest brother. But if he were a Bonapartist, and under his father's roof, what else could he say?" Vincent rested his hand on her shoulder and squeezed. "I do not like the thought any better than you, but I have been watching them. Your observation on our first day here was right: there is an unnatural tension between father and son."

"Surely though, were there cause enough for Yves to so betray his father's wishes, he would not remain under his roof."

"Yes . . . well." Vincent covered his eyes with his hand for a moment. When he drew it away, a shadow remained. "A young man might not always have his independence. I was fully an adult before I renounced my father."

"Love . . ." Jane stopped, unwilling to push him into a revelation he did not wish to disclose.

He drummed his fingers on the table, jaw working silently. "I have never related what caused the breach with my father, have I?"

"No, beyond that he did not want you to pursue glamour." She took his hand. "If it is too private, I do not wish to intrude."

He snorted. "No, I am learning that it is better to keep no secrets from you, though I would rather not burden you with my troubles."

"I trust you understand now that I do not think it a burden."

"I do." Vincent sighed heavily, then stood to pace around the room. "Forgive me. I am so in the habit of keeping this to myself that it may take me some time to order my thoughts."

Though she longed to comfort Vincent, Jane held still rather than risk frightening him into flight. He strode with the restless grace of a caged bear.

"My father, as I have implied, has strict ideas of propriety and exacting standards for what comprises the masculine ideal." He knit his hands together at the base of his neck and paced another moment before continuing. "He saw my interest in the 'womanly' art of glamour as being evidence of . . . partialities which alarmed him. When I refused to drop the interest, he whipped me. I was a stubborn child, and simply found ways around his injunction. He then devised a schedule and course of curriculum designed to turn me into the model of good breeding."

Vincent stopped his pacing and put his hands against the mantel, leaning forward and bracing himself there. Jane suppressed her own reaction, though she could feel nothing but horror. He blew out in a huff as if trying to dislodge some tension. "In a display of 'fairness,' my elder brothers were included in these lessons. If any of us performed with less than perfection, we were punished. The punishment ranged from whippings to privation of food. He once had me suspended from my arms for hours so that I might learn that my hands were not to be used for glamour. In defiance, I learned to work glamour with my toes. In fact, my ability to push past the physical limits many other glamourists face comes directly from my father's efforts to stop me, so for that I suppose I should thank him. I owe to him as well my command of French, Latin, and German, my abilities on horse-back, as a pugilist, and with a sword. Even my penmanship is borne of his desires."

Jane now understood the unexpected ability her husband had shown when they were accosted on the road to Binché. As much as those skills had saved them, the price still seemed too high.

"Where was your mother in all this?"

"My mother is very beautiful." That single phrase carried more condemnation than compliment. Bending his elbows, Vincent leaned forward until his head rested on the mantel. "As befitting a third son, my father sent me to Eton to study law. I studied, of course, because I did not know how to do anything else, but never before had I possessed unscheduled time. Every moment not spent in lessons was spent pursuing glamour. It represents the first unfettered freedom I ever experienced. You cannot know how glorious it is to *fail* with no consequences but one's education."

"This is why you feel that art must be free of constraints."

"Yes." He lifted his head from the mantel, rubbing the bridge of his nose. "I think this went on for two years.

And then, after my adventure with the clock tower, word reached His Lordship about what I had been doing with my free time.

"I thought I had seen my father angry before, but nothing matched this. What had changed was that he could no longer physically intimidate me. His own fault, of course." His smile was a cold and bitter one. "He threatened to cut me off entirely, but because I had spent my time studying law as carefully as I had studied any other task he set me to, I offered a counter-proposal. In exchange for a small living, I would give up my name and never trouble him again. If he refused, I would make public his displeasure with me and continue to practice glamour under his name. The threat of humiliation was quite enough."

Jane swallowed, remembering how Vincent had come to propose to her. He had brought his family's solicitor with him and had taken up his family name again. "You were ready to give up your art and return to that unfavourable circumstance to marry me?"

"Yes." Vincent sat in the chair next to her and took her hands. "Jane, I had nothing, and was afraid your father would decline my offer for your hand. That was not a risk I could take."

"And yet your father took you back?"

"Neither of my elder brothers have yet produced an heir." He placed a gentle hand on her middle. "That is why I have not written to him about our child. When you accepted me as I was, and we chose to continue working as glamourists, I had no reason to keep the Hamilton name.

If—when—my father learns that there is another potential Hamilton in the world, he will exert pressure to have an influence in the child's rearing."

Jane shrank from the thought of letting such an unfeeling man into their lives in any fashion. "He will have none."

"No, he will not." Vincent pointed to the papers on the desk. "So, you understand now when I tell you that it would be fully possible and even probable for Yves Chastain to have been seduced by the Bonapartists. If he is at all estranged from his father, they would be able to play upon that and appeal to his vanity through his relationship to Napoleon."

Jane grimaced with understanding. "He has run through his funds, and I believe that his father is not sympathetic to the situation."

"That alone could drive him to join the Bonapartists, and added with the rest . . . I hope that I am mistaken."

They went over the remaining papers, Vincent leaning over her chair to point out details. Though she was still greatly shaken from the disclosures which her husband had shared with her, Jane could not help but rejoice, for here was the camaraderie of their marriage, which had been replaced of late by a stiff and awkward reserve. To ask questions and have them answered without dissembling made her inexpressibly happy. The answers themselves disturbed her, but the fact that the behaviours which she had attributed to a diminishing regard lay instead in Vincent's secret duty gave her considerable relief. Jane reproached herself for the shallowness of her thought, and yet she returned to it again and again: Vincent loved her.

Though conspiracy was not the art to which they had pledged themselves, their thoughts fit together piece by piece over the course of the evening as they engaged in this new collaboration.

In the morning, all of Jane's nausea had returned. She was hard-pressed to tell if it were a result of her health or her anxiety. Vincent was still in their apartments when she arose. "Are you still having trouble?"

"I am quite well."

"You are green." Vincent narrowed his eyes. "I think more a Pomona green than a Hooker's. Certainly not emerald, but perhaps one that has been mixed with flake white."

"Continue that, and I shall wish you to Brussels."

He sobered. "It would look strange if I went. Anyone with sense will stay close to home today, in case there is further news."

They heard nothing new that day, nor the next, but as Jane went about her routines, she became aware of why Vincent feared that the knowledge of his charge from the Prince Regent would change her behaviour. She measured every action she took for what it might mean to an outsider. She weighed the words of every person who spoke with her as if they might be a spy themselves. She did not think any of these thoughts showed, as she put them in a compartment in the same manner as she had concealed her early regard for Mr. Dunkirk—hiding thoughts of spies and revolutions was not so very different from hiding a sensibility toward a gentleman—but she was constantly aware that they were there.

So Jane made no alterations in her plans, and the town settled back into an uneasy peace. Each passing day offered little news as the entire world waited to see what Napoleon would do. On the third day, they received word that Napoleon had reached Paris without a shot fired and that King Louis XVIII had fled to Brussels. The truth of it was impossible to deny, for the Bourbon retinue had travelled through Charleroi, the town next to Binché. Too many tradespeople had seen them for it to be a rumour.

But rumours abounded as the occupation of gossip was replaced with speculation about Napoleon. Napoleon would march to Brussels. No, he would march to Vienna. No, Queen Marie Louise was returning to him. No, he would abdicate again.

Many of the rumours Vincent was able to tell her were unfounded, but the one that would most directly impact them remained the likeliest. The chance of Napoleon marching on Brussels seemed almost certain if he continued his patterns from before his abdication. If he did go to Brussels, he would pass through Binché.

They sat at Vincent's writing desk, going over Mr. Gilman's questions about lambs and translating his ciphers into meaning. "Jane, I ask again: will you take ship to England?"

"Will *you*?"

He grimaced, seeming aware of his contradiction. "When we receive word that Napoleon is marching, I will retreat to Brussels. Wellington is there, and he means to hold the line at Quatre Bras."

"You think he can?"

"If any man among us can, it is the Duke of Wellington." Vincent tapped the paper with his forefinger. "I do not wish to paint a pleasant picture. Gilman says that we have 67,000 troops here. With the Prussians and the Dutch we nearly match Napoleon's numbers, but not his strength. Wellington is short of heavy cavalry, and though our men are better equipped than Napoleon's, his are all veterans of at least one war and are fiercely loyal to him."

He could offer her no better comfort than that he *thought* Wellington could hold the line. Jane tried to be content with that, but her fears often outpaced her rational mind. She tried to hide her concerns from Vincent, for she was sure that many of them derived from her situation: though she had only just begun to show, she was daily aware of the fact that she was increasing.

As the season began the turn into summer, Jane faced an interesting choice. Vincent had gone into town with M. Chastain that morning to prepare a glamour. The bourgmestre wanted elaborate festivities on the occasion of William of Orange's coronation as the monarch of the newly formed United Kingdom of the Netherlands. While M. Chastain likely needed little aid with his students in force, Vincent had hoped to get a sense of who held what beliefs while there.

To occupy her time, Jane sat in the parlour sewing a christening gown for her child, in the company of Mme

Chastain and some of the other ladies of town. Mme Meynard had been reading the novel *Amélie de Mansfield* by Sophie Ristaud Cottin to them. They had just reached the point when Amélie was contemplating throwing herself into the river when the reading was interrupted by Yves Chastain. Or, rather, Yves entered in an entirely decorous manner; his younger brother Luc followed him, protesting loudly about some ill.

"Luc, quiet yourself." Mme Chastain lowered the fringe she was working on and gave her son such a glare that he was silent in an instant. "Now. What is the trouble?"

"I want to go too, and Yves says I must stay home." His lower lip stuck out to an alarming degree.

Mme Chastain applied to her elder son. "Go where?"

"My chums and I are going to the celebration in town." He pointed at Luc. "He is too little to keep up."

"I am not." Luc stamped his foot.

"You are not impressing me with your maturity. Pray, do not stamp indoors." Mme Chastain tapped her finger against her crocheting needle. "As your father is doing the glamour, I will confess that your interest surprises me. You have shown little interest in his work before."

Yves winced. "But there will be fireworks."

Mme Meynard laughed. "You see how jaded one becomes living with a master glamourist. What are fireworks but colour and light?"

"They go boom!" Luc said, in all earnestness. "Please, Mama, please. Please."

Jane listened to all of this with great interest. Here

seemed an excellent opportunity to observe Yves Chastain and his friends to see if she might spy a clue, for if anything would betray their sentiments, then surely the celebration of the new kingdom would do exactly that. The difficulty she faced was in not knowing if her interest would be remarked upon. Left to her own devices, Jane would likely have chosen to stay in rather than venturing forth into the unrest that would surely surround such an event. On the other hand, did any here know her well enough to think it odd if she chose to go? She need only make her interest plausible.

Jane took another stitch and then dropped the gown with a sigh. "I will confess to being somewhat restless, and an excursion sounds appealing. Surely the city council would not have the celebration if there were any real danger from Napoleon."

Mme Chastain tapped her crochet hook again. "You may have something there. I will own that I am restless too. Mme Meynard, what do you think?"

"Even if Napoleon were to march straight toward us, it would be another two weeks before he could get here." She closed the novel with a snap. "I say we *all* go."

The dismay on Yves's face was not far from being matched by Jane's own feelings, though hers she kept admirably concealed. Having a contingent of women following him would surely curtail any potential exploits. Still, it afforded a better possibility for observing him and his compatriots than any opportunity that had yet arisen.

Mme Chastain tousled Luc's hair. "And as it is a historic occasion, you and Miette shall both come."

The boy expressed his delight with exuberance.

"I would say that historic is overrating the case." Mme Meynard pointed the novel at Mme Chastain. "It will only be historic if we remain the United Kingdom of the Netherlands for more than five years, of which I have my doubts."

"Fie. You always have your doubts about everything."

With events thus settled, by the evening, the party had grown from a small excursion to a quite a large group. They were joined on the streets by throngs of other denizens of Binché, who apparently all had the same sense of restlessness that had afflicted those in Jane's company. The royalists seemed to predominate, if one could judge by the profusion of white ribbons. Orange also fluttered everywhere in honour of William of Orange, so the evening seemed filled with a collection of small flames.

As they passed the A l'Aube d'un Hôtel, three boys on the verge of manhood tumbled out of the front room and crowded around Yves. His friends were so quickly introduced that Jane only caught the name of M. Giroux, a slight, bookish fellow who was the only one to pause long enough to acknowledge the introductions. The other boys were all for charging ahead into the centre of town.

Their enthusiasm was infectious, and the Chastain party quickened their pace, soon arriving in the square at town's centre. A stage had been erected and glamours hung from it, making it seem to glow in the night. Added to that were lanterns to light the speakers, and that, along with the orange banners, made a sort of pyre of spectacle. The bourgmestre approached the front of the stage with M. Chastain directly behind him, in position to amplify his words to the crowd. The substance of the speech was what one might expect at such an occasion, full of rhetoric about glorious history and unity and other empty phrases which politicians bring to any ceremony, stripping the meaning from even the most important events. Jane peered around, seeking Vincent, but he was not immediately obvious, so she fixed her attention on Yves.

One of the boys asked how long the speeches would last. Yves shrugged in response. "The old man only talked about the glamour. I found out about the fireworks from Giroux."

They spoke some more of wishing to see the fireworks, but their words carried no shocking disclosures. As the bourgmestre wrapped up his speech, Yves nudged M. Giroux with his elbow. "Fireworks now, eh?"

A shout rose from the crowd. Rather than fireworks, an enormous glamour blossomed almost directly above them. A massive French tricolour flag as it had appeared under Napoleon's reign waved over the crowd. Honeybees swarmed around it, dancing a beautiful fleur-de-lis in the air, and the French national anthem seemed to trumpet through the square, overpowering the last of the bourgmestre's words. Shocked into silence, the bourgmestre could only stare at the phenomenon. The glamourists on the platform were less sanguine. M. Chastain abandoned his place by the bourgmestre. Pointing, he shouted at his students to find the rogue glamourist and stop the display.

On a second-story balcony of the building in front of which Jane and her companions stood, a young woman leaned against the wall in a stance designed to mimic insouciance. From the stage, she must be obscured by the glamour, and even Jane's position offered little but the woman's chin and hands. Her fingers moved in familiar patterns, which made Jane certain that she was working the glamour, though to manage so large a display, she must surely have help.

All of M. Chastain's students, save the two women, leapt off the stage and forced their way through the crowd. Behind them, Vincent bounded onto the stage from the stairs at the rear and clapped M. Chastain on the shoulder. His mouth moved, but Jane could not make out the words. Then her husband spread his legs wide and inhaled deeply. Though she could not see the folds, by his movements, Jane could imagine that he was spinning out a fold of glamour to try to reach the other glamourist's strands from a distance. M. Chastain joined him in a similar stance.

The span across the square was very great, and even working together, Jane had doubts that the two men would be able to effect any change. All the while, the bees continued to buzz overhead and the anthem played on.

Jane almost let her sight slip into the ether to see whence the other folds came, but stopped herself. The crowd jostled around them, elbows and feet pushing against their neighbours in an effort to stay upright. Jane lost sight of Vincent as she staggered in the crush. Yves supported her arm and with a word, arranged his friends around her and the other ladies in a determined cordon. Though he still had the slight stature of a boy, in truth no taller or broader than Jane herself, he exuded a sense of being more than his size.

When Jane could see the stage again, M. Chastain was bent at the waist, hands on his knees. Even from where she stood, she could see his chest heaving. Of Vincent, there was no sign.

Had he been standing in Jane's spot beneath the balcony, he could have stopped the display as surely as he had worked the glamour on the clock tower in his university days. Jane thought that even she could break this one from where she stood.

If only she were able to perform glamour.

How much harm could it do to simply let her vision slip into the ether? Jane shook her head to clear it of the temptation. Even if she looked, what would she do with that information? It would tell her nothing that she did not already know. Above her head, the young woman worked glamour. Coming to a decision, Jane supported herself on Yves's shoulder and pulled off her slipper. Though she had no real hope, she threw it at the glamourist.

The shoe fell far short and landed in the crowd, provoking a renewed outcry. Mme Meynard gasped. "Mme Vincent, have you lost your mind?"

"I see one of the glamourists." Jane pointed at the young woman.

Before she had fairly finished speaking, Mme Chastain cried, "Your shoes, ladies. Yves?"

Grinning, he and his mates accepted the shoes and hurled them upwards. Catching their enthusiasm, if not their meaning, a display of shoe tossing spread through the crowd. Jane winced as a shoe went through a shop window, shattering a pane of glass. She hoped that the damage would be limited.

Then, one of the shoes—Jane knew not whose—smacked the young woman directly in the face. The glamour overhead stopped with an abruptness almost shocking to the senses.

The bourgmestre cleared his throat, his voice unnaturally loud in the silence. "Well. Now that the interruption is over, let us proceed to the fireworks for which you have all come. Long live King William the First! Long Live the United Kingdom of the Netherlands!"

The crowd, still confused by the exploit, responded with but a ragged cheer and threw more shoes into the air, but when the fireworks rose from the rooftops, they seemed more in homage to Napoleon than King William.

Jane stood on her toes trying to see her husband, but there was no sign of him or the students. She had little hope that he would be careful, so although it was contrary to his mission, she would rather the culprits escape than have Vincent discover them.

At every burst of light overhead and every crack of the fireworks, Jane flinched.

"I am certain they are well." Mme Meynard put her arm around Jane and patted her. "Poor thing, you are trembling."

She had not realized it until that moment. "It is nothing, just the excitement."

"What is the matter?" Mme Chastain peered at Jane. "Are you well? You are not, are you."

"Please do not concern yourself. I am only wondering where Vincent has gone."

"Is he not on stage with the others?"

Jane had been studying the crowd with such intensity that she had not seen him return to the stage. Indeed, he and the students were once more on the stage, working an enormous glamour in concert with one another. They rendered a silhouette of Gilles and the dragon, which fought in time with the fireworks. Much like the shadow plays after dinner, these figures had been simplified to be easier to manage. Jane could only presume by their actions that they were passing the threads from one student to the next in order to avoid being overcome by the effort of working such large folds at such a great distance. For though the base of the folds were firmly rooted to the stage, the tops of the figures reached nearly two stories over the audiences' heads.

It was a beautiful spectacle, but compared to the French flag and the bees, it seemed imperfectly rendered. The display was intentionally subtle to avoid distracting from the fireworks, but the effect compared poorly to Napoleon's grand showing.

A question occurred to her, and she applied to Mme Meynard. "Why were there bees with the flag?"

"Napoleon's emblem is the bee, the symbol of hard work. All the Bonapartists wear it." As Mme Meynard answered her, Jane felt as if a thousand slipknots of glamour had just shifted and revealed a new pattern.

Anne-Marie wore a pendant of a honeybee.

It had been given to her by Lieutenant Segal, who wore the tricolour cockade of Napoleon. Jane's breath caught in her throat. It did not seem possible that M. Chastain could have brought a Bonapartist into his house . . . but Jane remembered Anne-Marie's fear that she would lose her place.

Not for a beau, then, but for her politics.

Eighteen

The Honeybee Considered

Around Jane, her companions and the other townspeople continued their festivities unaware of the epiphany which Jane had suffered—and, in truth, "suffered" was the only word for what she now felt. She had trusted Anne-Marie; and yet, considering her actions, Jane could not but wonder at her own blindness. When taken with other details, Anne-Marie's interest in where the Vincents had been prior to Binché lost its friendly nature. Jane had been so relieved to have a confidant who spoke English that she had allowed her far more familiarity than any other servant. Added to Anne-Marie's curiosity, there was the bee pendant, which she had been so anxious to keep a secret. Her attraction to Lieutenant Segal came as no surprise when viewed in the light of her loyalty to Napoleon's France.

As their time together played through Jane's mind, a single image checked her recollections: Anne-Marie holding the key to Vincent's writing desk. A key which Jane had named, and then left in the apartment with Anne-Marie. She had not thought, or rather, Vincent had said that he was concerned about the servants, but Jane had discounted Anne-Marie from that equation, thinking he meant only the foreign servants. Anne-Marie was, after all, the daughter of an English woman.

But despite her mother's origins and her command of the language, she was French and described herself as a Parisian. For all that, Anne-Marie was less a foreigner than either Jane or Vincent. Jane bewailed her own blind naïveté and felt it urgent that she speak with Vincent at once.

But that she could not do, engaged as he was in working glamours on the stage. Jane chafed at the restraint she must display as the spectacle continued over their heads, but was grateful for the distraction, as it kept the others from paying her much heed.

Mme Chastain did glance at her once and inquire if she would not rather return to the house.

"No, thank you," Jane replied. "I had rather wait for Vincent."

"Oh!" Mme Chastain waved her hand in dismissal. "They will not be home until quite late. My husband always takes the students out after a successful endeavour.

He says a pint of ale rebuilds their strength after all this exertion."

Jane forced herself to be calm. Any urgency to find Vincent and speak with him would surely be remarked upon, and though much could be attributed to her situation, she did not think it wise to use that as an excuse more than necessary. She must also acknowledge that her revelation about Anne-Marie could wait. It needed to be communicated soon, but the few hours it would take Vincent to arrive home would mean no great delay.

Jane had abandoned books and music to instead pace in a wide circle around their apartment awaiting Vincent. Had he gone to seek the traitorous glamourist and her compatriots, or was he merely enjoying a pint of ale at an inn with M. Chastain and the students? The first provoked worry, the second, annoyance, and Jane wavered between the two states.

Finally the knob on their apartment door twisted slowly, and Vincent eased it open. He held his boots in one hand and jumped visibly when he saw her. "Muse! I thought you would be asleep."

Her concern vanished and left her with annoyance. "I have been so worried about you!"

"Worried?"

"I was at the celebration tonight."

"Ah." He set his boots by the fire. "Yes, that was less

surprising than I wish it had been. Unfortunately, all the culprits slipped away, and as a British glamourist, there was only so much I could do to insist that they be found and apprehended. There was a notable lack of concern, though the shoe throwing did hearten me somewhat that not all residents of Binché support Napoleon."

"They might well. I threw the first shoe, and I suspect that most of the crowd did it simply out of over-excitement." She tapped her thumbs together in thought. "I believe that Yves Chastain is not a Bonapartist. He rallied his friends to try to hit the woman, and unless he is a surpassingly shrewd actor, then I believe that he truly wanted to stop her."

"Muse, you are a wonder. Did you recognise the woman?"

"I am afraid I was not situated to see her clearly. Did you?"

Grim, he shook his head and settled into the chair with his writing desk. "I will need to write to Mr. Gilman to let him know that the unrest here is more serious than we thought."

"Before you do, I have something to tell you."

Vincent waited with the complete stillness that marked his deep attention as Jane recited her fears about Anne-Marie. When she had done, he worked his jaw, thinking. "You are likely right. I doubt that she was placed here to spy on us, but rather that Lieutenant Segal recruited her when he learned whom she served." Rubbing the back of his neck he scowled. "The one good thing is that all my papers on the Bonapartists are in code. Unless she has an interest in my more tedious observations on glamour, there is little in the writing desk to attract her notice."

"Vincent . . . Might she be the glamourist on the balcony?"

His eyes widened in alarm at that. "You said you did not recognise her."

"No, but all I could see was the bottom of the woman's chin."

He grunted. "Well. I will ride to Brussels tomorrow and confer with Mr. Gilman."

"And I will try to keep my behaviour unchanged toward her."

"I fear that you have the harder task. If you would like to accompany me so you do not have to face her, you may."

"No." Surely Jane could govern herself as far as that. "I would not want to alert her by a change in our routine."

"Very good." Vincent nodded. "And in the meantime, I feel that I should perform some form of absolution for doubting you."

"What could you mean?"

Vincent drew her onto his lap. "Clearly, I was wrong not to have told you straight away." He found one of the laces holding her night dress closed. "I should like to make an apology for that."

Jane's breath caught as he teased the lace free.

*   *   *

Vincent woke later in the morning than was his wont on days when Brussels was on his schedule. The sun was already streaming into their apartments. "Will you be all right today? I will likely be late tonight."

"I will be quite well, I assure you. After having survived Mme Meynard's parties, I feel equal to keeping my composure with Anne-Marie."

Vincent kissed her forehead. "I adore you."

Jane tilted her head up. "Perhaps you do not need to race off to Brussels?"

One corner of his mouth curled in a smile and he traced a hand down her shoulder to the bare skin on her arm. "I should like, above all things, to stay this morning."

"But duty calls." She sighed and raised her hand to her brow in mock remorse. "Woe."

Laughing, he caught her hand and kissed the inside of her wrist. His lips had barely touched her skin when the sound of horses entering the courtyard drew them both to the window.

Below, a company of men in the blue and white coats and breastplate of French *cuirassiers* positioned themselves around the courtyard. Jane's heart quickened with alarm. Though Lieutenant Segal might move in their social circle, it was too early to pay a call.

Vincent squeezed her arm. "Stay here. I will see what they are about."

"But—"

"I will only listen from the top of the stairs." Before Jane could object further, Vincent had left the room.

Jane, still in her dressing gown, could only stand at the door, listening to the muffled voices from below. She watched Vincent where he stood, just back from the top of the stairs. His shoulders tightened and he retreated slowly, then turned and ran down the hall toward her. Jane backed away from the door as he burst into the room.

Grabbing her by the arm so hard that it ached, Vincent hauled her to the window. "They want the technique of the *Sphère Obscurcie*." He snatched the glass globe off the desk and thrust it into Jane's hands, ripping the velvet free. "I do not think they know about the glass one. Keep it safe."

In the hall outside, boots clattered and Mme Chastain shouted.

Jane seized his arm in protest. "But, Vincent—"

"They will keep searching until they find me." Vincent shoved her into the sunlight. "I love you, Muse." With firm and erect bearing, he crossed the room so that he was standing in the middle of it when Lieutenant Segal flung the door open.

The sun coming through the window cast a square prison on the floor out of which Jane could not step without the glamour in the glass being interrupted.

Lieutenant Segal bowed to Vincent. "The Emperor Napoleon requires your services. Will you come quietly?"

"I am not a French citizen."

"No. As such, I am not compelled to ask you at all. You

will come. There is but the question of comfort." He gestured with his riding whip, and two of the soldiers came forward and took Vincent by the arms. "I hope this will teach you that you will only be *asked* once."

Segal struck Vincent across the cheek with the whip-stock. Her husband's head snapped to the side, and he gasped. Jane clapped her free hand to her mouth to prevent herself from crying out for him. Before Vincent could straighten, the Frenchmen hauled him forward. Stumbling, he lost his footing and they jerked him upright, shaking him. Jane could see Vincent's back tense as if he was about to throw them off, but he stayed resolutely still. By neither look nor action did he betray Jane's presence. "What do you want with me?"

"Such naïveté. But what else could we expect from a man who plays at the womanly arts?" Lieutenant Segal strode to the table where Vincent's writing desk sat. Jane moved to the far side of her small rectangle of light, praying that Lieutenant Segal would not step within the influence of the *Sphère Obscurcie*. Instead, he picked up the writing desk and slung it under his arm. "The Emperor is interested in your obscuring sphere. Let us go."

Jane pressed her hand against her mouth, biting down on the flesh of her thumb to stifle a sob so she would not give herself away by mere noise. She longed above all else to cast a glamour, covering the room in darkness to confound them. Under its cover, she and Vincent could flee. But to where? Into the waiting arms of the soldiers in the courtyard below, there delivering to them the glass *Sphère Obscurcie?* There was no choice, no action she could take beyond bearing witness.

Jane held still in the cold sunlight and watched them take her husband.

Nineteen

An Appeal to Sensibility

The door through which Vincent had been taken stood ajar. Jane waited in the sun, feeling trapped by the rectangle of light. So overrun were Jane's emotions that she had moved beyond feeling into an insensible state. She leaned her head against the window, the physical sensation of the warm glass replacing any deeper feeling, and stared down as Lieutenant Segal and his men brought Vincent outside. They loaded him in an enclosed carriage, locking the door once he was secured. Jane held her ground until they had ridden from the courtyard. She stood insensibly at the window, unable to think of anything beyond the fact that her husband was gone.

Footsteps in the hall awoke Jane to action as

Mme Chastain dashed into the room. The tendons in her neck stood out with strain, and her face had the pallor of a sheet. "Mme Vincent?"

For a moment, Jane thought that Mme Chastain could see through the glamour, but she crossed through the room to the inner bedchamber with an urgency that clearly said that she had not seen Jane. "Mme Vincent! Jane?" The tension in her voice was palpable.

Jane ran her hand over the glass *Sphère*, its core glowing with the light which hid her. The smooth surface was warm to the touch. *Keep it safe*, Vincent had said.

She tucked the glass ball behind the heavy curtains, which hung on either side of the window, masking it from the sun. "I am here."

Emerging from the bedchamber, Mme Chastain uttered a cry of relief. "Oh! I have been so worried. I will not ask if you are well, but are you unhurt?"

"Yes. Thank you."

Crossing the room with alacrity, Mme Chastain embraced Jane with all the emotion and display of sensibility which Jane felt herself lacking. "My dear. Oh, my dear. I am so sorry for you. Your husband—dear, dear David."

Jane stiffened, suddenly recollecting that while Mme Chastain offered her sympathy, there were other glamourists in the house, ones to whom Vincent had shown his technique for the *Sphère Obscurcie*. She should inquire if they were safe. It was the correct action to take. "And M. Chastain?"

Releasing her, Mme Chastain screwed her face up in a

scowl. "They would not dare touch him, due to his relation to Napoleon. Segal, that scoundrel, asked my husband to come. Bruno refused, of course, and thought that would be the end but—oh, it is too terrible." She faltered. "He did not think they would take your husband."

"And the students?" Jane pressed her hand to her middle, as if she could hold down the nausea now brewing.

"Bruno is sending them all home." She took Jane by the arm and led her to the stairs. "Come. We need to discuss your travel arrangements as well."

Unwillingly, Jane let herself be pulled along. "My travel arrangements? But you cannot think that I would leave while they have Vincent."

Mme Chastain patted her hand. "There, there. You have had quite the shock. Let Bruno explain it all, and I am certain it will help you think more clearly."

Jane was thinking quite clearly. She could do nothing *but* think. Her mind replayed the scene, searching for some different action she could have taken. Had she not delayed Vincent, he would have been well on his way to Brussels by now. Though she might fancy that he would still be at liberty if that were the case, the more likely scenario was that they would have captured him on the road, and then no one would know where he had gone. At least this way, she knew who had taken him.

Likewise, if she left Binché, then how would she find out where he was? No. The only sensible course of action was to stay in town until circumstances warranted her following Vincent somewhere else. Simply knowing where he was, of course, would not be enough, for there was nothing she could do on her own. She would need to apply to Mr. Gilman for assistance. Not knowing Vincent's codes well enough to write a letter, she would have to go to Mr. Gilman herself and alert him not only to Vincent's capture, but also to the involvement of Anne-Marie.

The scene downstairs was one of chaos barely contained. Servants sped through the halls, carrying items to store or pack out of sight. M. Archambault dashed past, hurrying upstairs with a text book tucked under his arm.

Mme Chastain led Jane down the hall to M. Chastain's study. He stood by his desk, sorting the pile of papers upon it. Over half of them he cast upon the fire burning in his grate. The rest he tucked into a wooden crate which already had books piled within. As they entered, he dropped those papers he still held into the box, heedless of their order.

Coming around the desk, he took Jane by the shoulders and kissed her on both cheeks. "Jane, I am deeply ashamed. I value David as my own brother and would have done anything to stop them if I could."

"Of course." Jane, distracted by the bustle around them, gestured to the box on the desk. "Are you going somewhere?"

"Brussels. It seems that Napoleon has discovered a late interest in the military potential of glamour. My relation to him, much though I despise it, was enough to keep his underlings from touching me, but he will not be so nice when he arrives." M. Chastain tucked his hands behind his back and began to pace. "I had thought that by denying my ability to work the *Sphère Obscurcie* and claiming it was too difficult, I would be able to convince them to leave us alone, but all I seem to have done is to make them take David in my stead. I cannot ask you to forgive me for that."

"But it is not your fault." They had thought that the danger would come from Vincent's spying, but Lieutenant Segal seemed unaware of that. She had not thought—neither of them had—that Vincent's glamour would place them in danger, but now, on the other side of his capture, she could see the intrinsic military potential of invisibility.

M. Chastain shook his head and frowned. "The fault must be mine. How else would they know about his abilities?"

Jane almost told him of Anne-Marie, but the caution which she had learned over the course of the last month stopped her tongue. It occurred to her that the Bonapartists *had* left M. Chastain alone. The possibility existed that he was a Bonapartist himself, but masked this fact with protestations of disdain for the man. Before she could rid herself of this foolish conjecture, M. Chastain had moved on to the next subject.

"We will head to Brussels tonight. Have one of the servants help you with your possessions—one small trunk only, I am afraid—and we will make arrangements for you to take ship back to England."

"I appreciate your concern, but if you have no objection to my continuing residence, I will remain here as long as Vincent is close by."

M. Chastain pulled up short at this. "You cannot. I mean, to the house, you are welcome, but it is by no measure safe, and David would never forgive me if I allowed you to stay."

"My husband knows me well enough to understand that should I choose to stay, the choice is mine."

"But it is not safe."

"Thank you. I have had ample proof of this, but I am firm in my determination on this point." Jane gestured to his packing. "I do not wish to detain you, but must ask if you know where they have taken him."

M. Chastain shook his head. "I only know that they were advance scouts. Napoleon himself will not be here for another week, perhaps two. Whether they have returned to the main body of the army or have remained here in town, I cannot tell you."

"Then I will have to learn it for myself." Though she had at first planned to go to Brussels and apply to Mr. Gilman in person, Jane decided to take advantage of the Chastains' departure. "Might I send a letter with you to one of Vincent's clients?"

"You cannot believe that anyone is worried about business now."

"No. But I can rely on him to get word back to my parents." This was close enough to the truth that Jane felt few qualms about dissembling. Even had she not felt so untrusting of everyone and everything at this moment, Mr. Gilman's secret was not hers to divulge.

M. Chastain acceded to this plan, though unwillingly.

Mme Chastain protested vehemently that Jane could not be allowed to stay, questioning whether her reason was intact. But the steadiness of manner which Jane had perfected to mask her feelings served well to make these arguments seem invalid. Her purpose, she explained, was to discover Vincent's whereabouts, then arrange to have him ransomed. She could not explain that he was a spy for the British Crown, but that fact gave her comfort that he would be ransomed, if she could but discover his location.

As soon as she could, Jane absented herself, returning to her rooms.

Her first order of business was to fulfil Vincent's last wish. No. She would not think of it as his *last* wish, for that implied that he could have no others in the future. Rather, this was a request he had made of her before departing for a time. His absence, though deeply troubling, was but temporary.

Keep this safe. Resolutely, she rewrapped the glass *Sphère* in velvet. Then, rather than returning it to its place on the table under the window, she opened her wardrobe and buried the ball in one of her bandboxes, beneath a hat. If the need arose, she could gather the bandbox and flee. For the moment, though, she must acquaint Mr. Gilman with the circumstances of the last day.

Jane pulled paper from the drawer and sharpened her pen, considering. While she could make an attempt at the code which Mr. Gilman and Vincent employed, she did not know it well, and to write that Anne-Marie was an inferior Cotswold ewe sired to a Scottish Blackface failed to capture the nuances of the situation. To get them across she must write in plain text, and while Jane might trust M. Chastain to deliver the letter directly to Mr. Gilman, she had no such discreet route to receive a reply.

Leaning back in her chair, Jane stared at the ceiling and chewed on her lower lip in thought. Even if she were to remain and find Vincent, she did not have sufficient funds to ransom him. For that, she must have the aid of a patron. Given his work for the Crown, she felt justified in asking for that very thing, though she knew Mr. Gilman hardly at all. Her fear, though, was that if she left Binché without discovering where Vincent had been taken, she would be unable to find him later. With no way to know when and where they might move him next, Jane was loath to venture too far from the town.

And yet, she absolutely must speak with Mr. Gilman.

Jane set down her pen and rose from the table. She would need help of a local sort and considered where she might turn for assistance. Mme Meynard was absolutely out of the question, given her relations with Lieutenant Segal. Even if she were not a Bonapartist, her discretion had proved notably lacking. Most of Jane's acquaintances were equally ill-suited for the task, but she thought of a few who might prove amenable.

Jane went first in search of M. Chastain, and acquainted him with her wish to accompany them so far as Brussels and then return to Binché. Though he was notably displeased by the latter part of her decision, he could offer little argument, save that he would be unable to send the carriage to carry her back to Binché. Jane rather suspected that he hoped she would remain in Brussels with no easy means of return, but she had no such intention.

She went next to find Yves Chastain. Though she was well aware that the boy would be accompanying his family to Brussels, she had hopes that his friends would remain behind. She had further hopes that these friends would be sympathetic to her plight, having seen the will with which they joined in throwing shoes at the glamourist the previous night. . . . Had it truly been only the night prior? Jane felt the weight of a lifetime between the two events, and yet not even a full day had passed.

When she explained what she wanted, Yves quickly supplied her with the direction of his friends. Jane began her visits with M. Giroux, the young bookish fellow who had accompanied them the previous night. She thought him the likeliest of the group to have some measure of discretion. Yves offered to run round to M. Giroux for her, but Jane declined on the grounds that his mother wanted him close at hand.

Instead, she called on M. Giroux in a modest house not many blocks from the Chastains' establishment. She was let into a bright parlour, well-appointed with furniture from fifty years ago, and waited there for M. Giroux. The worries that had been suppressed first by shock and then by a flurry of activity came upon her in a sudden rush as she waited. Dread knotted in her stomach, and she had to fight to breathe.

When the parlour door opened, Jane jumped in her seat

and then flushed quite red. A woman, likely M. Giroux's mother, entered the room with her chin held high. "You are the British woman?"

The coldness of her reception came as a shock. Jane could only nod.

"I do not know what business you think you have with my son, but I assure you, we have no interest in it." She inclined her head once. "Good day, madame."

"Please!" Jane gasped and held out her hand in supplication. "My husband has been taken by Napoleon's men. I only need help in finding him. I thought your son might know where they are encamped, boys being boys."

"You want my son to spy for you?" Mme Giroux's countenance darkened with anger.

"No. Certainly not. I only wanted to ask if he had heard any word of their whereabouts."

"I fail to see how that is in any way different from spying. We do not spy, and certainly not for the British." She pulled the door to the parlour open. "Good day, madame."

Jane searched her face for some hint of compassion, but was met only with cold disdain. Trembling, she left the parlour and went out to the street. She stood in the inexcusably beautiful day and stared at the cobblestones. Could she expect a different reception at the homes of Yves's other friends? Perhaps she should have asked him to run the errand for her, after all.

Grimacing, Jane trudged on to the next name on the list, passing through the town square on her way. The signs of the festivities from the night before had vanished, save for a few scattered shoes lying abandoned in odd corners. Under the balcony where the glamourist had been, a glazier worked to repair the window which had broken in the shoe-tossing fervour.

As he reached for a new pane of glass, Jane could not hold back a cry of surprise. The glazier was Mathieu La Pierre, the glassblower's son. Mind working quickly, Jane hurried over to him. "M. La Pierre! Might I trouble you for a moment?"

Raising his eyebrows, he set down the pane of glass he had been lifting. "Mme Vincent. Are you well?"

"I confess, I am not." Jane clenched her hands as she spoke and quickly acquainted him with the situation in which she found herself. "My hope is that on one of your deliveries you might have come across some information about where they are holding my husband. If you have, I do not ask you to do anything except to let me know."

When she had finished, he whistled, then resettled his cap. "If I do hear anything, you may be certain that I will tell you."

"Thank you. I go to Brussels tonight, but I hope to be back tomorrow."

He promised to meet her whether he had news or not. It was not much, but Jane forced herself to be content with this small bit of progress.

Twenty

To Brussels and Back Again

The journey to Brussels passed in tense and uncomfortable silence. Along the road on either side stretched encampments of British and Prussian soldiers, a grim reminder of the coming war. At first glance, the ranks of redcoats inspired a sense of confidence, but closer inspection revealed the soldiers as the motley crew they were. Alternately, the tall rye fields and the rows of stately orchards lent a sense of pastoral tranquillity which did not quite negate the military presence. Each rise in the road showed some new evidence to make them fret.

Having attempted to dissuade Jane from her course of action, the Chastains seemed bent on giving her no signs of approval. They did prevail upon her to at least stay over with them rather than applying to Mr. Gilman's residence so late at night. Road weary and dusty as she was, Jane had to acknowledge that it was the wisest course. There was nothing which Mr. Gilman might do that night, and, though she chafed at waiting even that long, the morning would come soon enough.

At the earliest practical hour, Jane made her way to the Gilman home carrying a small travelling case which contained a change of clothes and the glass *Sphère Obscurcie*. She was let in without delay and received by Mr. Gilman in his breakfast room. He set aside his serviette and rose as she entered. "My dear Mrs. Vincent!" Drawing out a chair, he beckoned her to sit. "Please, you are quite pale. What is the matter?"

His tone, so thoroughly alarmed on her behalf, undid half of Jane's resolve. Her hands trembled, and she had to clench them in her lap to keep the tremors from showing. With her eyes low to hide the incipient tears—Jane would not give way to them when there was so much to be done— she said, "My husband has been taken by the French army."

"Good God." He sat heavily in the chair next to hers. "When. How?"

Again, Jane relived those painful moments, relating them with as disinterested an account as she could. When she had finished, she added a piece of information she had told no other save Vincent. "We believe that my maid, Anne-Marie, has been acting as a spy and sharing information with a Lieutenant Segal. She certainly has an attachment to him, and has had ample opportunity to have access to Vincent's papers."

"That is bad news." Mr. Gilman slid his fork across his plate, as if compelled to some form of action, even a purposeless one.

"Vincent did say that none of his correspondence with you should be suspect, as it all pertains to lambs. He believed that Napoleon was more interested in his technique for quickly rendering things invisible."

"Possible." He let go of the fork and grimaced. "I am sorry to hear this, and I thank you for letting me know. We will arrange passage back to England for you, of course."

How could all these people assume that she would leave while her husband was in danger? "Thank you, but I will not return to England until Vincent is safe."

Mr. Gilman became quite still. "You do understand that there is a war coming? Napoleon is on the march and could cross into Belgium as early as next week. Mr. Vincent will not be safe until after he passes, and, forgive me, but a woman in your situation should not be here."

"My situation does not signify. It is still quite early, and my confinement is not for several months. Pardon me for the imposition, but I must ask your help in arranging a ransom."

"A ransom!" Mr. Gilman shook his head. "But that is not possible."

Pushing away the shame of asking for aid from someone so little known to her, Jane swallowed. "I know I have insufficient funds, but thought that surely you could draw from the Crown."

"It is not the funds that are at issue, I assure you. It is not possible to ransom your husband."

Appalled, Jane could only stare at him. "But I know officers who were ransomed back after capture. Why not my husband?"

"Because he is not an officer. If he were a nobleman or even a gentleman, then we might consider it, but he is— forgive me—only an artist. If I were to offer a ransom it would be so far beyond the pale as to draw unwanted attention to him. The ransom would surely be denied, at best. At worst, it would make them question our relationship and put the whole of our circle here at risk. No." He shook his head firmly. "Though I esteem your husband most highly, it is impossible for me to ransom him with any degree of impunity."

"You say 'if he were a nobleman.'" Jane took a breath, and asked forgiveness of Vincent for revealing his secret. "Then allow me to let you know that David Vincent is an assumed name. My husband is the Honourable Vincent Hamilton, third son of the Earl of Verbury."

Mr. Gilman's face twisted in sympathy. "Mrs. Vincent, that changes nothing. He is here as David Vincent. His papers say David Vincent. To suddenly treat him as Vincent Hamilton would, again, single him out for unwanted attention. If his father were to ransom him, then that would be different, but *I* can offer no direct aid. The best I might do is send a dispatch to the Earl on your behalf."

Given what she knew of the relations between Vincent and his father, she expected a chilly reception at best, but deemed any effort worthwhile, no matter how small the chance for reward. "Thank you."

He took her hands gently. "Take a ship for England. The best thing you can do for your husband is to reassure him that you are safe."

Jane could not do that. She would not abandon him. "I cannot. But if I might borrow paper and a pen, I will trouble you for but a short time longer before I return to Binché."

He leaned forward, placing one hand on the table before her in entreaty. "Please do not go back. Consider your child."

"I *am* considering my child, but I have a duty to my husband, and until I can find someone willing to help him, it falls to me." She derived a certain bitter satisfaction from seeing him wince.

"Can I say nothing to dissuade you?"

"No."

"Very well." He rang for a servant and gave instructions to show Jane to his study so she might write her letters in privacy. "Allow me to at least offer you some funds. Transportation to Binché will not be easy to come by. Everyone is fleeing to Antwerp."

Jane stood, brushing the folds out of her pelisse. "Thank you. That would be very kind."

With strained courtesy, they took their leave of each other.

As Jane was led to the study, they passed the open door of the parlour where Vincent had spent so many hours.

Begging leave, Jane stepped inside to see the glamural. Where once there had been a single lamb, the flocks she had suggested now gambolled. She could now conceive the expanse of hillside as a map, with the stream representing the border between France and the Netherlands. The whole of the hillside below the stream was covered with lambs, all moving with purpose toward the top of the hill. It was quite lovely. Even for something which served a practical purpose, Vincent had rendered each lamb with individual care.

Jane shuddered and returned to the hall, and thence to the study where she wrote two letters, one to the Right Honorable The Earl of Verbury, and the other to Skiffy.

Knowing full well that it could be weeks before she heard from either man, Jane left Mr. Gilman's home with an inexpressibly oppressed spirit.

Despite Mr. Gilman's prediction, Jane experienced no difficulty in arranging transportation back to Binché. This was due to the truth of his statement that everyone was fleeing town to Antwerp, Ghent, and Ostend, thus leaving the local carriages which travelled in the opposite direction quite vacant. Only two other people occupied the *diligence* that went to Binché: an old woman with a small pug on her lap, and a banker's assistant. It was obvious from their sideways glances that they knew that she was British by her clothes, and both sat on the opposite side of the *diligence* from her.

They chatted with each other with great animation, pointedly ignoring Jane. The one travelled to see to her daughter's lying in, the other to arrange to shut up his master's banking house in Binché.

Jane could not resist the opening. "Is there danger, then?"

"Madame!" He affected shock. "Have you not heard that Napoleon is on the march?"

"I had." Jane put her hand to her breast and let some of the strain she had felt show in her voice. "But you made me fear that there were troops close by."

"If you are fearful, then you ought to go home where you belong." The old woman snorted. "The British should let well enough alone, if you ask me."

Jane coloured deeply at this and had no reply to offer. She turned her face to the glass and sat in silence for the rest of the trip.

The *diligence* set her down in front of A l'Aube d'un Hôtel, whence she walked back to the Chastain household. Would that the walk cleared her head, but Jane's thoughts remained caught in a furious twirl of fruitless speculation. It seemed impossible that no one should know where the French troops were stationed. From what Mr. Gilman had said, they were not yet in Belgium, which made the question of where they had taken Vincent all the more perplexing.

Jane questioned her own judgement repeatedly as she walked. What could she do, alone, to rescue Vincent? Were she not better served to heed the advice of her friends and acquaintances and flee while there was a chance? Her nature, though, would not admit to that necessity without exhausting every other possibility. Once she saw Vincent and his situation, she would be better able to make a decision about what action to take.

When she arrived at the gates of the Chastain home, the building was dark and shut up. A solitary paper blew across the courtyard, which had so lately been full of life. Jane felt all the weight of the day press down against her, and she would have sunk where she stood were it not for the sight of Mathieu La Pierre seated on the front steps of the main house.

Jane hurried across the courtyard, breathless now as if she held the strands of a massive glamour in her hands. Mathieu rose as she came up the steps. "Pardon, madame. They said you had gone, but I was sure you were coming back."

"Oh, thank you, Mathieu. You are too good to wait for me."

"I wish I had better news."

Jane's knees gave way and she sat abruptly on the stairs. "Vincent?"

"They have left town. I *think* they have taken him to Charleroi, because that is the route that Napoleon will take to reach Brussels, but am uncertain about anything more precise than that."

"Thank you." Jane nodded, staring out the gates at the opposite side of the courtyard, her thoughts already focused on obtaining transportation to Charleroi.

"Please, madame. It is not good for you to sit outside. Let me help you indoors." Mathieu's face was so pinched with concern that Jane let him draw her upright solely to set his mind at ease. She offered him some of the funds which Mr. Gilman had so lately tendered to her, but Mathieu refused them. "I should be ashamed if I did. You and your husband are great artists and should not be so used."

Before she could protest, Mathieu La Pierre touched his cap and took his leave.

The housekeeper appeared not long after Mathieu had left and gave her a candle to carry upstairs, mouth bent down with disapprobation. Jane affected not to notice, treating the housekeeper with more courtesy than her ill temper warranted. If she were to be here alone, then she would need every aid she could garner.

The long, winding stairs to the upper floors seemed to have lengthened in her absence. Jane hauled herself up, one hand on the banister. The house echoed with ghosts, her every footstep bouncing back to her and making her aware of how empty it was. With more than a little relief, Jane pushed the door to her apartment open, ready to collapse in her bed without undressing.

By the window stood Anne-Marie.

Twenty-one

A Question of Innocence

Jane and Anne-Marie stared at each other, both sheet white. The pallor of Anne-Marie's face made the bruise under her right eye stand out in a livid purple. It was a bruise such as the heel of a shoe might make.

Anne-Marie ventured a smile. "Madame, I thought you had gone with the others."

"So I see." Upon further inspection of the room, it was clear that Anne-Marie had been making a thorough examination of its contents. "I had thought to pack your things and send them on to you."

Again, Jane said, "I see." She set the candle on the nearest table and shut the door, twisting the key set in the lock, then removing it. "Perhaps you might tell me where my husband is."

"It is horrible, madame. You must be so distraught."

"I am, and you would be well advised to remember that." Jane's fingers clenched the handle of the small travel case she carried. Anne-Marie's eyes locked on it. "Now, I ask again, where is my husband?"

In a mockery of innocence, Anne-Marie's hand rose to her chest. "How can you think that I should know?"

"Do you really require me to enumerate the reasons? Only look at yourself in the mirror and tell me how you acquired that bruise." Jane's ire was up. She stalked farther into the room. "I am well aware that you have been spying on us. All I require now is for you to tell me where Lieutenant Segal has taken my husband."

Anne-Marie gaped. "But, madame, you are mistaken. Spying? No. This is your distress speaking."

"That I am distressed does not lessen my ability to reason." She pointed at the clothes laid over the sofa. "Am I to suppose that you are here to pack my things without the aid of trunks? Am I to understand that the bumblebee pendant you wear represents something other than loyalty to Napoleon? Am I to believe that your relations with Lieutenant Segal mean nothing? No, no, and no. Understand me, Mademoiselle: I am with child, and you have taken my husband."

"But I did not. I did nothing!" Anne-Marie edged toward the door.

Jane stood her ground. "Do you think Napoleon will release Vincent when he is done with him? I think he will not. I think he will use him up. Tell me. How was it to grow up without a father? I wish to know, since *that* is the position you have placed my child in."

Crumbling, Anne-Marie sank into the chair by the desk. "I swear to you, I did not know they would take him when I told Etienne—Lieutenant Segal—about the *Sphère Obscurcie*. Had I known, I would never have done it."

"And now you do." Jane could feel no pity for the girl.

Anne-Marie stared at her hands as if wondering what to make of them. "I cannot weave the *Sphère*, not as M. Vincent describes it. I think that is why Lieutenant Segal took him."

Jane's neck throbbed with tension.

"They are at a farm just south of Quatre Bras. Gemioncourt."

"Thank you." Jane unlocked the door to the apartment and left it standing open. She gestured at the dresses strewn across the room. "You may put these away when you come in the morning."

Bewildered, Anne-Marie lifted her head, tears streaking her face.

"I shall need help, and you can take nothing else from me that you have not already." Setting her back to the girl, Jane took up her candle and went into the bedchamber.

She shut the door, locked it, and set the travelling case on the bedside table. With dry, dispassionate movements, she opened the case and pulled out the glass *Sphère* from where it lay swaddled in cloth. The clear glass cooled her fingers. Jane lay on the bed and curled around the ball.

In the other room, cabinets opened and shut. Clothes

snapped and rustled as they were folded. Jane lay awake until the outer apartment door clicked shut and then she lay still awake, wishing herself asleep.

Once, when she had longed for sleep, she had worked glamour to drive herself to exhaustion. This night, she lay dry-eyed and staring until the candle burned down. Then she watched the dark.

Twenty-two

Cravats and Easels

Jane had spent the night thinking about what she might do with the knowledge of where Vincent was. She had decided that the thing she must do before anything else was to see the location where the French held him. That would inform all her other decisions.

To that end, she left her room as the sun first lit the sky with pale, watery light. As if responding to her mood, clouds stretched from horizon to horizon with the promise of a grim and brooding day. She went to the wing of the house where the Chastains lived and let herself into Yves's room.

There she searched through the clothing that he had left behind and selected the plainest trousers, shirt and coat she could find. A battered pair of boots stood well back in the wardrobe, and Jane took those as well. With stockings, a cravat, and a waistcoat to complete her ensemble, Jane returned to her apartments.

Despite having worn men's garments at the glass factory, these felt strange and too confining. Where before the clothing had been too large and threatened to fall off of her, here she was aware of how the buckskin trousers clung to her legs and defined her thighs. The slight swell of her middle was not pronounced enough to show for what it was, but simply lent her a stouter figure. Tying the cravat seemed natural, given the number of times Jane had helped Vincent with his.

She had to pause, eyes closed, against the memory of the line of his jaw.

When she opened her eyes, Anne-Marie stood in the door.

"Good morning." Tucking the end of the cravat through its final knot, Jane finished tying it.

"Madame?" Anne-Marie had difficulty, it seemed, in reconciling Jane's appearance with her expectations.

"An Englishwoman would not be riding out to Gemioncourt, I think." Jane lowered her chin as she had seen Vincent do, to crease the cravat just so. "Come in. I may need your help in a moment." She picked up the blue coat from the arm of the chair. "Have you spoken with Lieutenant Segal?"

"No, madame." Anne-Marie slid into the room, staying on the edges, more like a wild animal than a young woman.

"Thank you for that." Jane had not been sure if Anne-Marie's about-face the previous night would last, and it might still break, but for the moment she would make use of the woman. As she slid the coat on, Anne-Marie came forward to help, as if unable to watch her dress without assisting.

With the coat in place, Jane had the tolerable appearance of a young man. For the first time, the severe features she had been born with served her well. Her long nose and sharp chin gave her the appearance of her father in his youth. Only her hair gave her away. Jane had tried one of Vincent's hats, but no amount of tucking her hair out of sight did anything to make it seem other than what it was.

She pulled it back into a tail as some gentlemen did, but it was not right. Her hair hung past the centre of her back, too long to be a man's, and the style was too old-fashioned to be a boy's. "I thought that might be the case." Jane pulled a pair of scissors from her sewing basket. "Can you cut my hair in the Grecian style?"

"No! No, you must not cut your hair." Anne-Marie waved her hands, and would not take the scissors.

"I think it curious that you find cutting my hair so much more horrible than betraying me." Jane grabbed the long tail of her hair and pulled it over her shoulder.

"I did not betray you. I am French, and I am loyal to my emperor. That loyalty must come first."

"Yes. I suppose so." Tightening her grasp, Jane lifted the scissors and hacked off the hair where it lay over her shoulder.

Anne-Marie shrieked as the hair came free. "Oh, madame!"

"It is not as if I am destroying my beauty." Jane gestured to the mirror and grimaced. At this length, her hair was closer to correct, but still out of keeping with what a young gentleman would wear. She had to hope it would pass. She dropped the hank she had cut off into the ash bin. If she were at all fair to Anne-Marie, Jane would acknowledge that Vincent had been here to spy as well. She could not, however, be fair in this. "Feel free to make an improvement if you think it possible."

Anne-Marie accepted the scissors and began the work of shaping Jane's hair into an approximation of a man's. Though her mouse-brown tresses usually hung limp unless she exerted great effort with an iron, once her hair was freed of its own weight, it had some life to it.

When Anne-Marie had done, Jane ran her hands through it and rumpled her hair as she had seen Vincent do. This simple action, coupled with the physical sensation of her abbreviated locks, dealt Jane's sensibility a hard blow. She sat with her fingers pressed against her scalp for some moments, trying to press the fear back into her skull so that she might continue at her tasks.

Jane sighed. "Well. That was the simple part. Now, Anne-Marie, would you please ask the stable master to saddle a horse for me."

"I do not know if there are any horses left. They might have taken them all."

She had not considered this possibility before, but once

stated, it made sense, for if M. Chastain had been earnest in his desire to send all the students away, he might well have lent them horses to aid in that. And with servants travelling with them, it would be only natural for the horses to be in use. "Well. See what you might do. If I need to buy one, then I shall do that."

With a curtsy, Anne-Marie left. Jane could not rely on her to stay cowed long, and wished she had some other, more reliable ally, but she suspected that even if Anne-Marie turned on her again, she would continue to help simply to remain close to Jane and know her movements. So long as Jane was careful to let her know no greater part of her plans than strict necessity required, she could make tolerable use of Anne-Marie.

In the meantime, with Anne-Marie out of the room, Jane packed Vincent's travel easel, slipping the glass *Sphère* into his satchel of art supplies while she was at it. From the vials of ground pigment, she shook out a small quantity of vermilion crimson and mixed enough oil with it to create a thin paint. She applied this to the centre of one of Vincent's pocket handkerchiefs. She folded the oil carefully into the centre of the cloth so that it was not showing, and tucked it in her breast pocket. Jane wished she might have a pocketbook such as her husband's, but trusted that no one would note the lack.

Anne-Marie returned within the half hour. "We are in luck. One of the horses had thrown a shoe and M. Chastain had not wanted to wait for it. They are readying it for you now."

"Thank you." Jane shouldered the easel, grunting under the weight. Anne-Marie reached for the satchel to help her, and Jane snapped. "Leave it."

Startled, Anne-Marie jerked her hand back. Jane winced, for she had not wished to draw attention to the satchel nor its contents, and now she surely had done so.

"If I am dressed as a man, it will appear strange if I let you carry a burden for me." Jane bent down and swung the satchel to her other shoulder, careful to keep the end with the glass *Sphère* well away from the easel. "I will, however, ask you to introduce me to the stable-master, who I am rather hoping will not recognise me."

"Of course, madame—or should I rather say 'monsieur'?" She waited until Jane nodded before continuing. "And how shall I introduce you?"

"I am Henri Villeneuve, come to study with M. Chastain but arrived too late." Jane strode to the door, her trousers clinging to her legs. She would be grateful to return to her dresses when this was over.

"But . . . your French. It is much improved, but you still have an English accent."

"My parents were émigrées. I am, of course, deeply embarrassed by my accent and long to return to my motherland." In truth, Jane would endeavour not to speak at all, for even if her accent would pass, her voice was too high to be a man's.

At the stable, Jane encountered an unexpected problem. The stable master had saddled the bay gelding with a sidesaddle.

Jane cleared her throat and then realized that she did not know the word for a gentlemen's saddle in French. She leaned close to Anne-Marie. "What did you tell him?"

"That I needed a horse for Mme Vincent."

"Then tell him you meant Mme Vincent's friend. I cannot ride a side-saddle in these garments without remark."

Anne-Marie twisted the corner of her apron. "I will not."

"You confuse me."

"You cannot ride astride in your situation."

"I am not going for a gallop. We will walk there and back. Having ridden astride before, it is easier to keep one's seat."

"You have said that I have taken everything I could from you. There is yet one more thing, and I will not be blamed for the loss of your child." Anne-Marie crossed her arms and backed up a step. "No, *sir*, I know it must surprise you but there are things to which even I will not be a party. I will not put a woman who is increasing astride a horse. All of your actions today are a mark of nervous disorder, and I well know that the fault is mine, but this is wildest folly."

Jane inhaled through her nose, jaw clenched. She recognised the truth of what Anne-Marie said, and though she did not want to admit it, she should not attempt riding. Yet she must get to Quatre Bras, and the distance was too great to cover on foot, particularly with the easel and satchel. "Is there a cart or phaeton of some sort?"

"I will ask."

As Anne-Marie did so, Jane set the easel down, but not the satchel, and began to pace. The cloud cover meant that she would not be able to use the glass *Sphère Obscurcie*, but she had no intention today of doing more than seeing how Vincent fared and how he was held.

After much grumbling, the stable master harnessed the horse to a dogcart phaeton, complaining the whole time about how it was a saddle horse, not a cart horse. Jane ignored his complaints and drove out of the Chastain estate as soon as she feasibly could.

When Jane was growing up, her father had let her take the reins on occasion, but she had never driven for any distance on her own. By the time she arrived at the farm at Quatre Bras, her shoulders ached. She stopped the wagon at the base of a low hill overlooking the farm and tied the horse to a tree. Taking up the easel and satchel, Jane climbed to the top of the hill and set up her paints.

She quickly sketched in the scene in pencil, always seeking signs of Vincent. The farm was spread across a rising countryside, rich with tall fields of rye, which stood nearly as high as a man's head. Thick stone walls surrounded scattered out buildings, a remnant of the days when every settlement was fortified against the armies that had rampaged across the region. French soldiers dotted the grounds, mostly in idle activities such as smoking and dicing. The only show of any real discipline came in the form of a soldier who marched on the far side of one of the out buildings, mostly out of sight save for the close end of his circuit.

Since that was the only military activity evident on the farm, it seemed likely that Vincent was being held there.

Beyond the walls of the farm on that side rose a small prominence which might afford a prospect on the front of that building. Jane packed away her paints, satisfied that the rough sketch she had done showed enough of this side of the farm to serve for planning purposes. She had, as yet, no idea what she would do, but trusted that the solution would become apparent with enough study.

The second rise she tried offered less visibility, as it was thickly wooded. This gave Jane the opportunity to abandon her pretence of painting, but also meant there were sections of the yard that she could not see. The guard continued to march back and forth, and after some consideration, Jane realized that he was not guarding the door to the out building, but rather a trellis in front of it. The troops' wash had been thrown over the trellis to dry, though from the grime visible even from her distant aspect, it appeared as though none of it had been washed.

The wash shifted and Jane dropped to her knees, breath rushing out of her. What she had taken for stained clothing was Vincent.

Twenty-three

Champagne and Rope

Jane stood on the hill, watching, for hours. She could not see him well, but she would know Vincent anywhere, by the line of his shoulder, by the shape of his head, by the movement of his arms. Toward evening, Lieutenant Segal arrived and, by his gestures, ordered Vincent to be untied from the trellis.

Two soldiers grabbed him by the arms and hauled him to his feet. When they let go, he staggered and fell heavily to his knees. Through a break in the branches, she now had a clear line of sight to him. His shirt hung in tatters, and his back bore lines of burnt umber crossed in a welter of dried blood.

Jane moaned, and had to press her hand to

her mouth to keep more sound than that from escaping.

They jerked him to his feet again and Segal shoved a paper in front of Vincent. He bent his head over it, scarcely moving otherwise, and nodded.

Segal beckoned another officer forward. When that man stood in front of Vincent, her husband lifted his hands and the group of them vanished.

Curses carried up the hill. Moments later, the group reappeared. Vincent had fallen to his hands and knees and was retching on the ground. Lieutenant Segal drew back his boot and kicked Vincent hard in the side.

Jane shouted.

As her voice echoed down the hill, the officers lifted their heads as one toward the woods where she stood. Segal sent two of them racing toward the hill, and Jane's hiding place. She grabbed the easel and satchel, spinning and carrying them a few feet down the slope.

There was no chance she would outrun the men, and if she could not risk riding a horse, she could risk a fall still less. Jane knocked the easel over and grabbed the paint closest to hand, smearing it on the canvas. She dropped to her knees, hoping first that they would not see her, and second, that if they did, her subterfuge would be convincing. Cursing those few French oaths she knew, Jane mopped ineffectually at the paint with a rag as the soldiers came crashing through the brush.

"You there! What are you about?"

Jane sat back on her heels with a cry of surprise, keeping

the timbre of her voice as low as she could. Then she coughed.

Still coughing, she gestured at the spoiled painting and endeavoured to appear annoyed.

"Did you shout?"

Jane nodded and transformed the cough into wheezing. Fumbling at her breast pocket, she drew forth her pocket handkerchief and pressed it to her mouth. The smell of the oil paint tickled the back of her throat and Jane bent double, coughing in earnest now, until her throat was raw. Straightening, she pulled the handkerchief from her mouth and let it fall open to show the spot of red paint. "Pardon," she whispered.

The soldiers took a step back, the soiled handkerchief and her blotched face evidently painting a clear portrait of disease. One of them said, "You cannot paint here."

Jane nodded to show she understood and pressed her other hand to her chest as if trying to gather the resolve to speak. Her heart thudded against her palm. They stood over her but did not press her to speak, nor did they come too close as she gathered her supplies and started down the hill. Not until she was at the bottom did they leave their station. Without further incident, Jane reached the phaeton and clambered onto the bench seat. There she began to shake.

If they had not believed her to be a consumptive painter and she had been captured, there would be no one to speak for Vincent. Only the two letters to Skiffy and Vincent's father gave any hint of their circumstances, and none at all of their whereabouts. She was a fool, and more than a fool, to attempt a rescue of her husband alone, but neither could she leave him. Jane saw little alternative but to make an attempt.

She would first, however, write to Mr. Gilman and apprise him of what she had learned so that there might be at least one person who knew where they were. As she drove back to Binché, Jane pondered what she had seen. It would not do to leave Vincent there for long, and yet she must wait for a sunny day. It served her then to lay her plans carefully so that they might have a chance of escape.

Thanks to Mr. Gilman, Jane had funds, but had few other resources beyond that. The man's dress she had adopted allowed her to walk through the streets of Binché without comment, which made her errands easier, but she was hampered by her voice, and being a consumptive artist only afforded her so much latitude in avoiding conversation. In the week following Vincent's capture, Jane had done her best to make Henri Villeneuve a fixture in the environs. She purchased a second easel, some sailcloth, three blankets, a Claude glass, and two of the Gilles masks. The evenings she spent locked in her bedchamber at the Chastain home, working on her handicrafts.

Every morning weather permitted, she drove out to paint in the environs of Gemioncourt. Though she never ventured quite so close to the farm, she did her best to be seen by the soldiers so that her presence became unremarkable.

They soon paid little heed to the consumptive artist she tried to portray.

She became familiar with the ebb and flow of life in the camp, watching as she did. With the Claude glass, she pretended to sketch the landscape through the obscured glass in the manner which had swept the more romantic painters. Though she disdained the use of such artifice in paintings, it served her as a mirror so that she might stand with her back to the farm, and yet observe as the camp followers arrived to meet their lovers. Their forms were obscured and muted in the glass, but Jane needed only to learn the rhythms of the camp, not the identity of the people. In that flow she hoped to find a path to freeing Vincent.

Besides her innocuous appearance, the one fold she had to ply in this affair was that no one, save Vincent, knew that the glamour in glass existed. No one in the entire world had the notion that it was possible to travel unseen, and on that she was forming her plans. For if one did not know it was possible, one would not guard against it.

This meant, however, that she must wait for a sunny day, without chance of clouds, before attempting a rescue of her husband. The week preceding had been overcast or with scattered clouds, but showed promise of clearing on the morrow. The fact that he was tied in the open worked to her advantage, in that she would not have to risk passages where the glamour would not work, but it also meant that his absence would be noted more quickly. To delay that moment, Jane needed a distraction.

Anne-Marie had been arriving every morning as had

become custom, and helping Jane into her gentlemen's habit. At moments, the absurdity of a lady's maid appearing to dress a man reduced them both into fits of giggles, not so much from how amusing it was, but from the enormous tension both women were under. Jane made no pretence of having forgiven Anne-Marie, but they had achieved a sort of peace. Though Anne-Marie's loyalty remained to Napoleon, her remorse at having been party to Vincent's capture seemed genuine.

Jane sorted through her options repeatedly, yet she found little recourse. She would need help to rescue Vincent. She would not be so foolish as to trust Anne-Marie entirely, but had hopes that her guilt might induce her to offer some aid.

Jane rested a hand on one of the trunks which Anne-Marie had packed for her. "I should like to ask you for help, but I shall understand if you do not wish to be involved."

Anne-Marie brushed out her apron and straightened her shoulders. "What would you like me to do?"

"Would you arrange to have my things returned to England?"

"Might I ask why?"

Jane settled in a chair and leaned forward, resting her elbows on her knees. "Because you are correct. There is no way to free Vincent from Gemioncourt."

"Oh, madame . . . I am so sorry."

"Are you?" Jane threaded her fingers together and kept a studied gaze on the heavy carpet covering the floor.

"Though you have no cause to believe it, I am." A

silence passed between them before Anne-Marie continued. "I have seen you at Gemioncourt, when I go in the evenings."

Jane lifted her head and met Anne-Marie's eyes, surprised that the woman had not made use of the information. "And you have not said anything?"

"No."

"Thank you." With that much understood between them, they spent the rest of the morning packing, until Jane left to run her errands.

She carried with her, as always, Vincent's satchel with the glass *Sphère* within it. Jane had made the plan as simple as possible, believing that—as with glamour—the fewer threads there were to tangle, the more robust the illusion. Her first stop was M. La Pierre's glass factory.

The gruff man met her at the door of his shop, showing no signs of recognising her, save from her previous visit as Henri Villeneuve. "I was wondering when you were coming. It is been done these last two days."

"The weather." Jane wheezed and gestured out of doors as if to imply that she could not chance the rain in her state. She coughed, holding the handkerchief to her lips.

He took a step back, caution guarding his face. Jane felt a small burst of relief that he had clearly already heard that M. Villeneuve was consumptive. It gave her more latitude in her movements if no one wanted to approach her.

M. La Pierre shook his head and hauled a wooden crate up onto his counter. Removing the top, he pulled out a glass lamb, a Scottish Blackface, to be precise. "Is this to your liking?"

It was exquisitely crafted, with the hooves and wool cleverly rendered so that it seemed ready to gambol with its brethren. Jane nodded, and as he replaced it in the crate, tucking straw around the lamb, she pulled an envelope from the satchel. When he had done, she tucked it into the crate on top of the lamb.

She waited until he had nailed the crate shut, and then, still in a whisper asked, "Your son?"

"Will deliver it, yes. I will send him out tomorrow."

"It must be tonight."

The old man frowned as though he would balk at that, but Jane opened her satchel and pulled out some additional guldens, over and beyond what she had already paid for the commission. He rubbed his whiskers and then opened the door to the furnace room. "Mathieu!"

A few moments later, Mathieu appeared, face still ruddy from the fires within. He stripped off his gloves as he came through the door. Though she had requested that he make the lamb, this was the first time he had seen her in this guise, and she quailed at the trial it now faced.

Mathieu searched Jane's face, as if finding her familiar, but unable to place her. "Sir?"

Though she trusted Mathieu, she had no wish to involve him directly in her troubles and so felt the greatest relief that he failed to recognise her.

"You are off to Brussels tonight on delivery," M. La Pierre said.

Jane gave him Mr. Gilman's direction, written on a card. "Into his hands directly, if you please."

Mathieu touched his forelock in reply and Jane left the shop, tolerably satisfied that the lamb and her message would reach Mr. Gilman without incident. Even if Mathieu were stopped, the letter within was as innocuous as she could make it. It stated her honest plans to leave Binché, and told of a fine herd of Scottish Blackface sheep—the code for Lieutenant Segal—which waited at Gemioncourt. If the letter were removed and opened, Jane had hopes that at least the glass lamb would be delivered and serve as a partial message.

She hoped that it would arrive in time to be of use, but not so early that Mr. Gilman might attempt to stop her.

Jane stopped at the grocers for a luncheon, and purchased a basket in which to pack it. She also bought a bottle of champagne, a length of rope, and a sharp knife. With her purchases, Jane returned to the Chastain estate and locked herself into her bedchamber. She might not be able to work glamour, but there were other illusions which she hoped would serve as well.

In the morning, Jane rose with the sun. Though it took several trips, she carried her basket downstairs, with the results of her evenings' handicrafts rolled in one of the blankets. The stable master, good man, was waiting for her when she entered the stable, and had the horse already harnessed. Jane thanked him and loaded her provisions into the cart, covering them with a blanket.

She had spied a pasture within an easy walk of one of the back gates to Gemioncourt, its chief feature being that when the sun was directly overhead, there were no shadows along the path between the two.

She drove there and set up Vincent's travel easel and her paints. She put the picnic basket and the champagne conspicuously on the bench of the cart as set dressing for her tableau, then began to paint. Despite the pastoral setting, she had difficulty focusing her attention on the canvas. As little interest as she had in painting, it was important that the canvas show signs of work. She painted for some two hours until the sun was well overhead. After checking the road to make certain it was clear of traffic, she lifted the blanket. In the bed of the cart she had two manikins, one clothed from Yves Chastain's wardrobe.

Yves's manikin, she had built around the second easel she had purchased. She now propped it in front of the canvas to create the appearance that Henri still stood there contemplating his work. It would not suffice at close range, but she hoped that her days of tramping around the countryside would suffice to dissuade anyone from approaching.

The other manikin, she had crafted to bear as much resemblance to her husband as she could, remaking the Gilles mask for the face. She had dressed it in his clothes, then shredded them and saturated the remnants with paint to resemble dried blood. It would fool no one for long, but filled her with intense disquiet nevertheless.

Taking a deep breath, Jane opened the satchel and pulled out the glass *Sphère*. The sun entered the ball, lighting all the inclusions and tracing a path of invisibility around her. Jane slipped her free hand into the loop of rope she had affixed around the manikin and lifted it to her shoulder. She had built it in a curled posture, but even so, it hampered her movements considerably.

Holding the glass *Sphère* with care, Jane walked across the field, following the tracks that her phaeton had made through the rye. She crossed the road without incident and began walking down the path to Gemioncourt. Her every footfall sounded loud in her ears. When the manikin bumped against a bush or a twig cracked underfoot, Jane cringed.

As she neared the farm, a solitary shadow lay across the path, cast by a tree. Jane stood at the edge of it, chewing on the inside of her lip. It would clearly betray her when she returned along the path, but for the moment. Jane would have to hope that no one was watching this part of the small orchard. Holding the glass *Sphère* above her head, Jane tried to keep it as much in the light as she could and crossed the cool shadow in two strides.

On the other side, her heart sounded as loud in her ears as gunfire.

She reached the gate and paused outside it. The scene within was much as she had last seen it. Vincent lay with his hands tied to the trellis. She hazarded a guess that they were afraid he would attempt to vanish, and so wanted him in plain sight at all times. A single sentinel patrolled in front of the trellis. Around the farmyard, other French soldiers lounged and diced.

Steeling herself, Jane waited until the sentinel faced

away from her, then undid the latch and let it swing open. She slipped through quickly, and stood within the yard of Gemioncourt.

Her path to the trellis could not follow a straight line, as she had to avoid the shadows of out buildings and trees at intervals throughout the property. Instead, she followed a circuitous route which reminded her of the shrubbery maze at her parents' home. By creeping along and pausing to let soldiers pass before her, Jane managed to reach the trellis without incident.

She went to the back side of it rather than the front, and knelt in the sun by the lattice. So close to her husband, Jane caught her breath at the sight of him. Vincent's head lolled against the upright post of the trellis. Bruises mottled his exposed skin. The flesh above his right eye had split open, and a fly buzzed around the dried blood that caked there. His hair lay matted against his scalp. Jane had thought she had taken the wounds on her manikin too far, but none of it matched the horror of what they had done to her husband.

The emotions which she had struggled to govern during the course of the past week now threatened to overwhelm her. Though she longed to let Vincent know she was there, she dared not risk the sound of her voice carrying. She could not even approach too closely without the *Sphère* obscuring him too soon. Lowering her bag from her shoulder, Jane settled as quietly as she could in the sunlit space by the trellis. She placed the *Sphère Obscurcie* on the ground next to her, careful not to let her own shadow fall upon it.

Positioned close to the wall as it was, she was in no danger of a soldier walking through the spot she occupied. Jane withdrew a leather case, unfolding it to reveal the slender glass rod she had commissioned. The rod had been ground down to dull its sheen, and bent at an angle a few inches from the end.

She slid the rod forward until its tip was in the loose dirt under the trellis in what she hoped was Vincent's line of sight. As black and swollen as his eye was, she was not entirely certain that he could open it.

Carefully, she wrote in the dirt:

VINCENT. IT IS JANE.

A long minute passed before Vincent saw her writing. She recognised the moment by the way his head jerked as though he were going to lift it, and only just stopped himself. The sentinel marched, his feet grinding against the dirt of the yard. Dice rattled together and a soldier shouted with laughter. In the distance a rooster crowed.

When the sentinel's back was once more to them, Jane wiped her words clear and wrote, I WILL CUT YOUR ROPES. DO NOT MOVE.

He coughed and adjusted his head in a nod masked as a lolling movement. Jane let out a breath she had been unaware she was holding and waited until the sentinel faced away again. She stretched her hand out, keeping within the limits of the *Sphère*'s glamour, and put the knife against the rope on Vincent's right hand. His eyes widened at the touch of the blade, and he held very still.

It was but the work of moments to cut through the ropes

binding Vincent. His hands freed, Jane looked again to the guard. His steady pace took him past Vincent again, ennui clear in each step.

She wrote: WHEN CAMP FOLLOWERS COME. I COUGH 2, YOU ROLL LEFT.

He grunted to show he understood.

While they waited for the followers, Jane adjusted the manikin she had so carefully built, and composed it in Vincent's sprawling posture. Each scrape of her boots on the gravel sounded as thunder in her ears, making her freeze in terror, but it seemed that the sounds blended into the general hubbub of camp life.

As the sun crept on its path, Jane eased her way around the trellis, moving the *Sphère* and the manikin in a slow, careful progression, until she was standing by the side of the trellis, ready to spring forward. Until the camp followers arrived to provide a distraction, Jane could do nothing but wait.

She thanked the heavens for the glass *Sphère*, without which she would have had no way to reach her husband. Even were she not with child, walking any distance while controlling the glamour of a *Sphère Obscurcie* would have been too great an effort to have been successful.

A bead of sweat tickled past her ear. One of the flies on Vincent found her and buzzed around her head, tempted by the salt on her skin. Jane's apprehension grew with each passing moment, yet she could do nothing but sit and count each breath Vincent took.

The laugh of a woman echoed over the wall. Jane lifted

her head and stared at the gates as the first of the camp followers arrived. Still, she did not move, waiting for more to come so that they might distract the guards. As the women arrived in twos and threes, there came an unexpected but hoped for sound: the clop of horse hooves and the rolling grind of wagon wheels against gravel filtered through the orchards to the east of Gemioncourt. Anne-Marie and an aged driver pulled up to the gate of the farm. Piled in the back of their wagon were the crates and trunks holding Jane and Vincent's possessions.

She had not been sure if Anne-Marie's guilt would exceed the opportunity offered by Jane's supposed departure from Binché. It is a grim situation when one finds oneself hoping to be betrayed, and yet that is exactly what Jane had wished for. She could not ask for a greater distraction than that which Anne-Marie unwittingly provided.

Laughing gaily, Anne-Marie hallooed the farm. Lieutenant Segal swung her down from the wagon, greeting her with a kiss on the cheek. From across the courtyard came fragments of Anne-Marie's merry chatter as she talked of how she had fooled Mme Vincent and assured her of sending her things on to her in England. How she was certain that the secrets Lieutenant Segal sought would be in one of these trunks.

Jane coughed once. Before she could draw her breath to cough again, Lieutenant Segal turned to the trellis. He strode across the yard, beckoning a soldier to accompany him. His intent was clear. He wished to question Vincent about the contents of the trunks. This, Jane had not considered.

When he arrived, Segal would find Vincent unbound. With his attention fixed on the trellis, there was no time for Jane to swap the manikin for her husband. Her mind raced, seeking some answer, but Lieutenant Segal was upon them too swiftly for any to present itself.

Segal's soldier bent down to untie Vincent's bonds. The moment the soldier's hand touched Vincent's wrist, he moved with a speed that belied his wounds, grabbing the man's leg and toppling him.

With a single motion, Vincent pummelled the soldier and forced himself to his feet. Lieutenant Segal drew his pistol, aiming it at Vincent.

Jane leaped forward with the *Sphère Obscurcie* held firmly in her grasp and pushed Vincent out of the way. Lieutenant Segal cursed as Vincent came within the influence of the *Sphère* and vanished from view.

"What good will it do you to be invisible, Vincent?" Lieutenant Segal shouted. "You cannot run from us."

As he kept his gaze on the spot where Vincent had last stood, Jane and Vincent crept away from the trellis. It was apparent to Jane that the cost of his flurry of movement was great. Vincent leaned much of his weight on her. She transferred the glass *Sphère* to her left hand and wrapped her right around his waist to help support him. Her hand brushed something rough and sticky as Vincent gave a muffled cough and tensed under her arm.

She had touched the mass of wheals on his back. Moving her hand lower, she braced herself as he put his arm around her shoulders.

Jane risked a glance behind them.

Lieutenant Segal had his men surround the area where Vincent had been and tighten the circle. This gambit would have worked well, had Vincent still been there. As it was, their attention was drawn away from the Vincents' careful progress. Locked in step, Jane led her husband through the maze of sunlight.

The manikin tangled their footsteps, slowing them. Jane squeezed Vincent's waist as they passed a supply wagon, bringing their progress to a halt. She eased the manikin off her shoulder and tucked it into a nook in the supplies. Though it would not serve her intended purpose, she hoped it would still act as a distraction.

The progress was slower than her route in, as Vincent needed to stop every few feet. His breath was ragged and hot against her skin. She feared what would happen if he fainted while they were in the middle of the courtyard.

Lieutenant Segal shouted in rage, drawing Jane's attention back to the trellis. He and the soldiers patted the ground where Vincent had been, clearly bewildered about where he could have gone. Crossing the yard in great strides, Segal bore down on Anne-Marie where she stood by the wagon. "Where is he?"

"I do not know!" She held up her hands in protest.

Segal slapped her. "Liar. You brought us the news of his technique. Tell me how he can walk with it."

Anne-Marie's hand went to her cheek and her voice caught before she answered him. "He cannot. It is impossible."

Snorting in disgust, Segal looked at the items on the wagon. "I am not insensible to the fact that he made his escape only after you arrived with the Vincents' effects. Do you think me such a fool as to believe that this is a coincidence?"

The astonishment on Anne-Marie's face was unmistakable. "I tell you, it is not possible to walk any distance and support a glamour."

"And yet, he is gone." He gestured to the wagon, directing soldiers to it. "Unload it. I will find the answer even if I have to throw sticks instead of arrows."

Jane watched this activity, wincing. The carter had stopped the wagon in the sun.

It lay directly across the path where Jane and Vincent must walk. She pulled to a halt and surveyed the farm. Unable to speak for fear of drawing attention, she could not explain the trouble. If they retraced their steps, there was a route that passed through only one shadow, but it was farther away, and she had her doubts about how much longer Vincent could remain standing. Another option would be to pass behind the wagon and try to hold the *Sphère* in the sun. The third choice was to walk toward the front gates, which she could reach without shadow, but which opened onto a tree-lined drive.

As the soldiers worked to unload the wagon, she realized that their activity would, of necessity, take them inside the farmhouse. There would be very few people in the courtyard, and perhaps the carter might pull the wagon out of the way.

Jane watched as the last trunk came off. Anne-Marie, rather than moving the wagon, stayed in the courtyard, hand pressed against her bruised cheek. She alone stood near their path, and Jane judged that they would not have a better opportunity.

Tightening her grip around Vincent's waist, she started them forward again, conscious of how much weight he leaned upon her. They reached the wagon and moved as close to its bed as she could. Jane stretched her left hand out to keep the *Sphère* in the sun as they crossed the cool shadow.

On the far side of the shadow, Vincent stumbled.

Jane threw her hip under him trying to slow his fall, but he outmassed her by a considerable percent and dragged them both down. The glass *Sphère* tumbled from her grasp.

She and Vincent tangled together, trying to catch it, but it shattered against the ground. The crack of breaking glass bounced off the buildings around them. All other sound in the courtyard stopped.

Anne-Marie turned, spying them. Her eyes widened.

They were, for the moment, blocked from view by the bulk of the wagon to everyone save Anne-Marie, but other footsteps ran toward them. Vincent lay nearly insensible on the ground.

Jane could not let them take him again, and if discovered, they would take her as well, which would put their child in danger. Where before one life had been at risk, she had now imperilled all three of them.

Desperately, Jane reached into the ether and drew out a

fold of glamour. She twisted it, and with a speed she had
not known she possessed, blew a *Sphère Obscurcie* around
them. Spots swam in front of her eyes and the courtyard
pitched beneath her. Jane dragged air into her lungs.

Anne-Marie shrieked. Flinging her hands in the air she
raced toward the house and away from Jane and Vincent.
"If they have broken Mme Vincent's looking glass, I shall
have words with them. I had my heart set on it."

At the end of the wagon, Lieutenant Segal stood staring in their direction, but did not come any closer. He
tilted his head as if it would change the view. "You think
of looking glasses when our prisoner has escaped?"

"Has it escaped your notice that I am a French woman?"
Anne-Marie walked next to him and pressed her body
against his. Her voice softened. "I am sorry you are angry
with me. Is there nothing I can do to make it up to you?"

He traced the back of his hand down her face, pausing to
caress the bruise beneath her eye. "Perhaps." He lifted her
hand to his lips and kissed it, eyes never leaving her face.
"Napoleon will be so interested to meet you, tomorrow."

"Will you see to my looking glass?"

"No. I must find our prisoner before the Emperor arrives." He kissed her again. "The mirror will not be any
less broken if I attend it now." Turning from her, Lieutenant Segal shouted for his horse, and made arrangements
to begin the search for Vincent.

When he had gone, Anne-Marie stood with her hand at
her breast, fingering the bumblebee pendant which hung

there. Spinning so that her skirts flared around her, Anne-Marie took up one of the blankets and shook it out. Then she lay it over the rails of the wagon so it formed a tented space large enough to cover two people.

She patted the bare wood bed of the wagon the way one might beckon a dog. "Before I change my mind."

Jane got to her knees and pulled Vincent up to his. Helping each other, they clambered to their feet. Jane reached again for the folds of the *Sphère Obscurcie* but Vincent stopped her with a hand on hers. He shook his head once.

Untying the threads, he managed them for two steps and then swayed. Jane caught the fold from his hand and played it out two steps more. Passing it back and forth between them, they reached the end of the wagon. Anne-Marie stood in the bed with her back to them, holding a blanket outstretched and shaking it occasionally. With the cover in place, they could safely drop the glamour long enough to clamber on board.

The wagon creaked and groaned under their weight. The driver shifted in his seat. "What are you doing back there?"

"Just arranging the blankets." Anne-Marie lowered the cloth and tossed it behind her, keeping her attention focused away from the wagon, as if she wanted to be able to say in truth that she had not seen them.

Jane caught the blanket as it fell and pulled it over them. A hand pressed her shoulder and the wagon creaked as Anne-Marie crouched beside her. In a low voice, she whispered. "I do not want you to think that I betrayed you again. I had thought to endear myself to the camp to tend M. Vincent in your absence. God speed, madame."

Her hand lifted, and the wagon shook as Anne-Marie hopped down. Muffled in the dark, Jane lay scarcely breathing, moved beyond all measure by Anne-Marie's words. Then the tail-board latched shut and they rolled into motion.

Twenty-four

Into the Rye

Through the blanket, sun and shadow alternated in dappled patterns that gave hints of their whereabouts. When the sun predominated, Jane pushed the blanket off and peeked out. They were on the road to Binché, but to Binché they must not go. The soldiers would almost certainly think to look for them in the wagon and the Chastain house. Though Jane had thought that possibility was a natural misdirection, it had only been desirable when the plan had them travelling to Brussels.

She was not sure how long Anne-Marie's change of heart would last, but was grateful for it. Nor did she wish to chance what the driver would do upon seeing them, and for both reasons thought it prudent to take their leave. Jane pressed her mouth to Vincent's ear. "We need to get off the wagon."

He wiped his hand over his face and nodded. Moving with as much care as they could, they unhitched the tailboard and let it lower. The driver sat with his shoulders bowed and his head bent to his chest, as if trusting the horse to find its way back to town.

They swung their feet over the tail of the wagon and jumped down to the dirt road. Jane staggered and nearly fell as she landed, and had she been in skirts, she surely would have. Catching Vincent's hand, she pulled him to the side of the road and into the tall field of rye.

He stopped her when they were well into the field. "Muse, I do not think I can go much farther." His voice cracked with weariness.

Jane squeezed his hand with compassion. It was possible that Vincent might be able to remain where they stood until she fetched him. The rye was close to harvest, and stood nearly a man's height. If one crouched down, it would be enough to hide him or her from the road, for which Jane was grateful, because she doubted her ability to handle another glamour. Jane ran her hand across her middle as if she could reassure their child that this trial would be over soon. "Would you stay here, then? I have a dogcart phaeton waiting for us not too far away. Let me fetch that and then we can be on our way to Brussels."

"How did you come to have a cart?"

Jane flourished a bow. "I am Henri Villeneuve, the

consumptive artist. The locals know me for my love of painting their fields *en plein air*. I had planned for us to—"

She stopped as Vincent held up his hand. "Jane, do you know that until this moment I had not noticed that you were in men's clothing?"

Colouring, Jane ran her hands down the breeches which left her legs so indecorously exposed. She had quite forgotten her state of dress as well. "I hope you do not mind."

"Mind? Muse, you are a marvel to me." He sat down heavily in the rye. "Please. Go and fetch this famed dogcart phaeton."

Jane hurried through the field as fast as she could. Though her heart rejoiced to have freed her husband, she would not rest easy until they were in Brussels. The sun, which had been so necessary to reach Vincent, had now become oppressive. Jane did not understand how men suffered through the summers wearing thick coats and buckskin breeches. Her shirt clung to her back.

In the distance, she heard dogs barking.

Likely a hunter, but if they had decided to use hounds to track Vincent . . . Jane quickened her pace to a run, pressing her hand to a stitch that formed in her side. The tableau she had created had been left quite undisturbed, and for that she thanked providence. She hid the manikin behind a small bush, tossed the easel and paints heedlessly into the back of the phaeton, and untethered the horse, which had cropped a wide circle in the grass.

Jane returned the champagne, now quite warm, to the basket. As she did, the ripe scent of the cheese which she had procured caught her nose, inducing a wave of revulsion. Barely backing away from the phaeton in time, Jane retched in the grass. Gasping, she wiped her mouth with her red-stained pocket handkerchief and dropped it, no longer needing that part of her costume.

The cramp in her side seemed only to have worsened with her upset stomach. Jane gritted her teeth against the pain, set herself in the seat, and directed the horse toward Vincent. She drove west a few minutes before she reached the crossing that led to Brussels.

A heavy tramping sound pulled her attention toward Binché. At the edge of her sight, row upon row of men in blue and white uniforms marched toward her under the tricolour flag of Napoleon's France. Jane groaned and steered the phaeton toward Brussels.

What had seemed to take so long on foot passed in only a few moments by phaeton, and she quickly lost sight of the French army as the road bent behind her. She urged the horse to more of a trot until she was close to where she thought they had stopped. The rye grasses showed no signs of their mad dash, so Jane pulled the horse to a halt and stood on the bench of the phaeton spying for Vincent. The rye rustled and parted like the Red Sea as he limped out. She pushed aside the easel and helped him clamber into the cavity in the rear.

He lay down with a groan.

She did not want him to worry about the soldiers on the

march, and there was little either of them could do, save flee. Jane kissed the split skin above his eye and the rank scent of his unwashed flesh sent another wave of nausea through her. Staggering back, Jane again was sick in the field.

Vincent raised himself on his elbow. "Muse?"

"I will be well shortly. The stress has made the nausea worse. I am sorry it alarms you." She straightened and pushed him back into the compartment of the dogcart phaeton. "Now lie still." Jane arranged one of the blankets around him and climbed back into the bench seat.

She urged the horse into motion. Though she wanted nothing more than to push him to a gallop and race toward Brussels, that would draw unwanted attention to them, so she kept him to a slow and leisurely walk. By necessity, the road took them past Gemioncourt. Jane tensed, waiting for someone to come out and stop them, but they passed by unnoticed. Were it not for the dread twisting knots in her stomach, Jane might have been out for a Sunday ride.

Once past Gemioncourt, she urged the horse into a trot, which also had the benefit of smoothing out his gait and making the ride gentler for Vincent. Jane's chief concern though, was to put as much distance between themselves and the camp as possible before the French army arrived, increasing the number of men that might be employed for pursuit.

They had gone nearly an hour down the road when she heard horses thundering toward them. Jane glanced over her shoulder, heart rising into her throat.

Three French officers galloped toward them. The one

in front saw her take notice of them and shouted, drawing his sabre.

If Jane were an innocent, she would stop and see what he had to say, but if Jane were an innocent she would not have the escaped prisoner they sought in the back of her phaeton. "Vincent. They have spotted me. Can you hide yourself if I stop?"

"I am not certain I have the strength."

"Then I think we had better make a run for it." Matching words with action, Jane snapped the reins across the horse's back. It sprang forward, and Jane let the reins out like long strands of glamour, conjuring the horse to speed.

At first they pulled away from the officers, as their horse was fresher than theirs, and eager to run. The phaeton rattled down the road. But as they went, the cart began to wear on their horse and the gap between them narrowed. Fire raced up Jane's arms as she strained to hold on.

They overtook a carriage travelling toward Brussels and Jane fought to steer their phaeton around it. The coachman looked astonished as they came round.

Jane shouted, "Napoleon is behind us!"

With a glance over his shoulder, the coachman cursed and whipped his horses so they lumbered into a gallop behind Jane and Vincent. One of the French officers got past and drew alongside.

Vincent roared, rising to his knees, and flung Jane's canvas at the soldier. His horse shied and reared, tossing his rider under the hooves of his comrades. Cursing, one of the other riders drew his pistol and took aim.

The retort alarmed Jane's horse. He sprang forward with a new burst of speed, but they did not have long before one of the other riders gained on them. Vincent lifted the easel and swung it at the man. The officer caught it on his sabre, splintering the wood. With the shattered remnant, Vincent aimed next at the horse's head and neck.

Jane split her attention between the view over her shoulder and the road before her. Though the latter demanded her attention, her greatest interest lay with her husband as he tried to fend off the Frenchmen. As they began to climb one of the rolling hills that marked the Belgian countryside, her horse flagged. Taking advantage of the slower pace, the coachman's outrider levelled a long carbine and aimed it at the soldier in the rear. The shot went wide but caused him to drop back nevertheless.

Mounting the top of the hill, Jane surveyed the road ahead. A peasant woman drove her flock of geese along the road, and beyond her, a carriage rode toward them from Brussels with riders before and behind. Jane doubted of her ability to steer clear of the woman and still miss the approaching carriage.

Gaining speed as they charged down the hill, Jane shouted, "Alarm! Alarm! Napoleon is behind us."

The woman shrieked and tossed her apron over her head. She and the geese scattered, she to the side of the road, the geese rising into the air. Jane's horse liked this not at all, and broke from the road, galloping into the rye fields.

The carriage bounced and slowed as the rye caught in the wheels and bound around the axle. The French soldier closest to them followed, and his horse having fewer encumbrances, soon caught them. Passing the cart, he snatched the traces of their horse and pulled the lathered beast to a stop.

Breathing heavily, he railed at them from his saddle, cursing their parentage and their persons until his tirade broke off abruptly.

Jane became aware of the rustle and clop of more horses approaching through the rye. She dared look behind her to see what had produced such a look of alarm in the Frenchman.

Mr. Gilman rode through the rye, a group of redcoats at his back. "I should unhand them, were I you." He looked Vincent up and down, lifting his brows at his sorry state. "Well, Vincent, I am glad your wife cannot see you now. She would have my hide for abandoning you to the French army's attentions."

Vincent cleared his throat and clapped a hand on Jane's shoulder. "This *is* my wife."

Mr. Gilman's eyes widened to a gratifying degree. He sketched a bow from the back of his horse. "Mrs. Vincent. Then I must thank you for your most uncommon gift of a glass lamb."

On the ride back to Brussels, Mr. Gilman explained that Jane's letter, which had accompanied the glass lamb, had been sufficient to spur the Duke of Wellington into action. Though Vincent was clearly in sore need of a physician and rest, he insisted on being taken at once to the British military headquarters. Under an elm, which cast a welcome shade upon a neat white military tent, His Grace, the Duke of Wellington received them and had his personal surgeon attend to Vincent's wounds while he delivered his report. Around them, officers and aides-de-camp took notes as he spoke.

Jane sat on a camp chair next to him, still feeling the effects of her exertions. Her shoulders ached and her arms felt leaden. Both palms were raw from where the reins had cut into her hands. The cramp which had plagued her earlier came and went, coupled with nausea.

Vincent winced as the surgeon cleaned the wounds on his back, but did not stop his recital. "From what I was able to gather, your Grace, the French are planning on establishing their defences at Quatre Bras, then driving through into Waterloo and then Brussels. Lieutenant Segal had hoped to use the *Sphère Obscurcie* to lay in an ambush for your troops."

"We could have used this technique of yours sooner." Wellington gestured to the map of the battle, which one of his tactical glamourists had sketched in the centre of the tent. "The glamourists in the Royal Engineers are restricted to creating the illusion of groves of trees, which is useful at the beginning of an engagement, but not so once forces start moving. In battle, they are largely limited to attempts at breaking the enemy's attention with flashes of light and blasts of noise. You should have told Mr. Gilman of this *Sphère Obscurcie* at once. "

"I am not a military man and did not conceive of its potential in war. Once I became aware . . ." Vincent rubbed his head, showering dirt onto his shoulders. "I demonstrated the wrong technique for the *Sphère* to the French and claimed that it must be worked quickly or it would collapse. I do not think they ever mastered even that. But if they do, their efforts will render them invisible, but sitting in a dark sphere and reliant only on their hearing. The true *Sphère* is transparent both within and without."

"So your wife's letter stated." Wellington beckoned his tactical glamourist forward. "Can you teach Major Curry here?"

Vincent assented, and with Major Curry watching, slowly worked the fold necessary to create the glamour. When they vanished, Wellington exclaimed. "Good God! Is it as fast as that?"

From her seat, Jane offered a weary smile at his astonishment. "Faster, once you have the trick of it."

Vincent and Major Curry reappeared as her husband untied the fold. His face was paler than she liked, and he shook his head. "I fear my strength might be at an end."

"I think I have it, sir." Major Curry pulled a fold of glamour from the ether. "With permission?"

"Granted." Wellington leaned back against a table and watched them.

Major Curry stretched and twisted the glamour, vanishing from view. He cursed. "Beg pardon, ma'am."

"Not at all, Major." Jane smiled at him as he reappeared. "Was it black or silver inside?"

"Silver." Red lit his cheeks, but she suspected it was embarrassment at cursing rather than exertion.

"Then you nearly have it. Do the same fold, but twist it widdershins."

He glanced at Vincent, who nodded. "My wife is an extremely accomplished glamourist."

The Major attempted it again and disappeared from view. "Thank you, ma'am. That did the trick."

Wellington had him cast the glamour a few more times, watching from within and without. "Very good. I want you to train the rest of your team to do this, but tell them that they are under orders not to share the knowledge with anyone. This is a state secret."

Vincent shifted in his seat, uncomfortably. "I beg your pardon, your Grace—"

"Mr. Vincent. I can anticipate what you are about to say. Allow me to stop you from a conflict neither one of us wishes. Your technique has won the war for us. I have no wish to quarrel with you about my desire to keep it a military secret. I trust you can see the importance of keeping this ability quiet."

"Yes, sir. However, I should let you know that I taught it to M. Chastain and some of his students while in Binché. None of them are Bonapartists, but this particular fold of glamour is out of the box."

Wellington narrowed his eyes and Jane could see him adding that information to his calculations. "Well. Let us hope that Napoleon does not find that out."

The mention of the Ogre's name recalled to Jane's mind what Lieutenant Segal had said to Anne-Marie. "There is one thing more to relate, and I am sorry not to have told you sooner. I heard Lieutenant Segal say that Napoleon will be here tomorrow."

Startled exclamations sprang from the lips of every man in the tent. Wellington clapped his hands for silence. "Are you certain?" When Jane asserted that she was, and recounted spying the first troops on the road, he scowled and narrowed his eyes into an expression of fixed determination. "Then, if you will excuse me, this changes my preparation significantly. One of my aides-de-camp will see you back to Brussels."

The Vincents rose. Jane could not stifle a groan as she did so, and another cramp wracked her stomach. Wellington exclaimed, staring in astonishment at the seat from which she had just risen. "Madam! Why did you not tell us you were wounded?"

Her cushion was covered in blood.

Twenty-five

Glamour and Rue

You must not imagine the horror which engulfed Jane as she stared at the seat she had so recently vacated, and at the blood which stained it, and as she became aware of how her trousers clung to her skin with more of that same blood. Nor should you imagine the guilt that overcame her sensibilities, or the heartbreak as Jane recognised that she had lost her child.

The activity around her buried these sensations in a whirl of confusion that left Jane all too aware of her own culpability. It overwhelmed her senses to the point of numbness. She could not look to Vincent. He was at once the source and the victim of her guilt.

The surgeon carried her away into the hospital tent as if there might yet be something that could be done, but Jane knew the damage had already occurred. She only lacked the knowledge of which of her actions had caused it. Had it been the glamour? The run through the fields? Their precipitous flight in the carriage and the jolt as they went off the road? Or was it woven from some combination of these threads? There was even the possibility that she, like her mother, was prone to trouble and might have lost the child regardless of circumstances, but Jane thought it unlikely that she could escape reproach so easily.

Beneath all of this guilt lay another, deeper layer of shame, for one of the first thoughts to go through Jane's mind after apprehending that she had miscarried was that she could, at last, work glamour again.

The surgeon hastily erected an enclosure around her to protect her from the prying eyes of the men who worked in the tented hospital. Vincent was denied entry as the surgeon went about his business. For that, Jane was thankful, as it saved her from his disappointment.

The surgeon, used to dealing with soldiers, was perfunctory in his manner, but thorough for all that. There was nothing to be done for her child, and yet Jane submitted to his ministrations with her eyes closed while around her began the sounds of war.

Jane lay on a camp bed, curled on her side in the borrowed dress of a captain's wife. Where had once been life, a dull ache filled her from hip to bosom. Vincent pushed his way past the curtain that they had shielded her with. The deep sadness in his face was in no way masked by the evidence of his ill-treatment. Even bruised, the way his brows bent down and the corners of his mouth dipped broke the last reserve of Jane's strength.

Her eyes burned and her throat knotted. She squeezed her eyes shut and buried her face in her hands rather than confront him.

"Oh, Muse." The chair by the side of her bed creaked with Vincent's weight. "Jane, I—" His voice broke and he rested a hand on her shoulder.

Jane could not bear his touch, but neither could she speak past the palpable guilt that clogged her throat. His ragged breaths told her all she needed to know of how he bore the news.

Vincent stroked her shoulder. "Jane, please forgive me."

This plea opened her eyes. "Forgive you? This is none of your doing. Every person of sense implored me to take ship for England, but I would not. The guilt in this is entirely mine." She rolled on her back, away from his hand, and put her arm over her eyes.

"If we had left when Napoleon first marched . . ." The seat creaked as Vincent shifted. "Reason told me to go then, but my pride kept me here."

Outside the tent, a company marched past, feet tramping the earth in perfect rhythm. A horse whinnied in the distance.

Vincent cleared his throat. "You had no choice, in any event. We would have been discovered had you not masked us. I wish I had been equal to it, but your quick action saved us both."

"I know!" Jane dropped her arm and the empty bitterness inside made her wish to expose all her flaws so that he truly understood her culpability. "I know I had no choice, but what does it say of my sensibility that my first sensation upon realizing the miscarriage was one of *relief*? What woman can see such gruesome evidence and think, 'Thank god?' Yes, husband, know that your wife values *glamour* more than our child." Jane dug her nails into the flesh of her brow and groaned.

Vincent pulled her hands away and held them tight. "Jane, look at me." She would have counted every fibre in the cotton ticking rather than obey that request, but he said her name again, with more force. "Jane. Do not torture yourself this way. To have had this passing thought is not unnatural and does not mean it is the whole of your reaction. That it repulses you tells me clearly that the greater part of your emotion is grief."

Jane searched his face, beneath the bruises and the dark stitches over his right eye, for any sign of insincerity. Instead, she saw love.

The guilt, which she had held within her and cradled to her bosom like that lost child, broke into grief. As the first sob took her, Vincent pulled her to his chest, stroking her hair. "Jane, Jane . . . You will always be my muse, whether you are doing glamour, or a mother, or solely my wife. I shall honour you and keep you all the days of my life."

Jane clung to him and wept until her lungs ached.

Vincent held her until exhaustion took them both, and they slept, leaning against each other for support.

In the days that followed, the love which Vincent bore for her, and she for him, sustained them both. As Wellington clashed with Napoleon, the Vincents retreated to Mr. Gilman's home in Brussels until recovery from their trials was sufficient to allow them to sail for England. Jane's parents received them at Long Parkmead, and though Vincent had feared reproach for his part in Jane's miscarriage, Mrs. Ellsworth showed rare compassion and tenderness, mourning for them without a word or implication of censure.

Thanks in no small part to their contribution to the war effort, Wellington defeated Napoleon soundly in the Battle of Quatre Bras. The war, so long trumpeted and feared, was over almost before it began, with little loss of English life. Though the specific reason was kept a secret from the general public, the Prince Regent made Vincent a Knight Commander of the Royal Guelphic Order for his service to the Crown, and would have raised him to a peer had the newly made Sir David Vincent not implored him otherwise. The Prince did, however, insist upon giving a dinner in honour of Sir David and Lady Vincent.

Jane suffered through the dinner, filled as it was with conversation which seemed commonplace and insipid after the erudite dinners at the Chastains. At the end of the meal, the Prince Regent excused the ladies. Jane resigned herself to the cliquish gossip that would follow and the near certainty of questions about her cropped hair. As she reached the door, the Prince Regent clapped his hands in anticipation. "Now, Sir David, what we all really want is to hear every bloody detail of the war."

Vincent cleared his throat. "One moment, sir. Jane?"

She stopped in the door, all surprise. The gentlemen at the table had already begun to pull out their cigars, and fiddled with them impatiently.

"Yes, my love?"

"Would you care to stay?" Vincent held his hand out to her and inclined his head in a seated bow to the Prince Regent. "With your permission, sir, I have learned that it is to my folly to do anything without my wife."

With pleasure, Jane took her place by her husband's side. Together they related their story to the astonished gentlemen, who were forced to admit that Lady Vincent was a formidable woman and more than an equal partner for her husband.

Of this, Vincent and Jane had no doubt. And Jane? Jane discovered that a formal English dinner party was not a cause for dismay, but for delight—so long as she had her husband by her side.

Author's Afterword

The morning after I won the Campbell Award for Best New Writer, I met David Brin at Strolling with the Stars at WorldCon. It's a lovely thing where established authors, artists, and editors walk along and chat with anyone who wants to do so. I've been a fan of David's since the first book of his I picked up. He was very gracious to a baffled writer and asked me about *Shades of Milk and Honey* which was, at the time, unsold. After I told him about it, he asked, "What happens in your magic system if a woman is pregnant?"

What a good question. What a very, very good question. I hadn't thought about it, but I started to do so. From that simple question came the basic idea for *Glamour in Glass*. It is a subject that Jane Austen did not touch on directly in her books, but you can see the effects that children have on a woman of her period by looking around the edges of her stories. Those attitudes had as strong an influence on Jane Vincent's feelings about her "situation" as Mr. Brin's question. I am indebted to them both for the kernel of the novel.

The errors are mine alone, but I had some useful assistance in reducing the number of those errors and would like to take a moment to acknowledge the people who helped me avoid the worst of the anachronisms.

Thanks to the Oregon Regency Society, who helped me get a better understanding of the period, as well as having lovely excursions and balls. I need to particularly thank Charlotte Cunningham and Nora Fosberg Azevedo for their friendship and support. Also thanks to Tara Ryan and Christian Valois for looking at the French details of the Empire and to Madeleine Robins, who gave the whole thing a last minute going over for period details. Mr. David Koch, a New York City carriage driver, took considerable time to talk to me about carriages and how the gait of a horse affects the ride.

Of course, I would be remiss if I did not thank my editor, Liz Gorinsky, who suggested the closing scene. My agent, Jennifer Jackson, is amazing and spots plot problems before I even start writing. The erstwhile Michael Curry, who turns up as Major Curry, is a perceptive reader and gives me very clear feedback, without coddling. Thanks as well to all those who make the book look good: the inimitable Irene Gallo, Tor's art director; Cassandra Ammerman, my always able publicist; my copyeditor, Susan Andrew; production editor Elizabeth Curione; the wonderful cover artist Larry Rostant; and the cover designer, Jamie Stafford-Hill, as well as the book designer, Nicola Ferguson.

Writing a historical, even an alternate history, is always fraught with the pitfall of What Really Happened. The most difficult scene in this regard was when Jane rescues Vincent, because I had originally had Vincent held in a chicken coop. You see, I needed a way for him to be contained, yet able to be reached without going into shadow, and also plausibly somewhat obscured. The problem is that the book is set in 1815 and chicken wire wasn't invented until 1847. There are times when I can fudge history, but this gap was too large, because if they had chicken wire, then there was a whole host of other technologies that they would have had as well. Attempting to come up with a different way to secure him, which met my constraints, drove me to distraction.

On the train to the 2009 World Fantasy Convention in San Jose, I had a conversation with Jim Fiscus, who helped me come up with the way in which Vincent could be held, as well as useful information about period military torture. Disturbing, useful conversations, and yet a relief in that it allowed me to continue on and use a trellis in place of my chicken coop. Then I discovered that this containment was too good.

I couldn't come up with a way for Jane to plausibly save Vincent.

While chatting with then Science Fiction and Fantasy Writers of America President Russell Davis about SFWA business, we were both venting about writing. I explained my problem and he said, "You need to look at the environment and see what she could use as a distraction instead of having her try to create her own." He suggested camp followers, who would certainly have been present. La! That got me out of the giant trap that chicken wire had laid for me.

Other thanks are due to Aliette de Bodard, who translated my English sentences into French for M. and Mme Chastain. After much consideration, I decided to use classic French rather than the dialect that would have been spoken in the region, so that more English readers would be likely to understand those passages. Also . . . well . . . I know Aliette, and I don't know a Flemish French speaker. She also helped me find idioms for Jane to misunderstand. My lack of French was further aided by Lucie Le Blanc, who heard my plea on Twitter for a French idiom that meant "if it kills me" and came up with "même si je dois faire flèche de tout bois," which means "if I have to throw sticks instead of arrows." I quite adore that.

Thanks to all the folks who beta read this on my website, but particular thanks are owed to: Emily De Cola, Kate Baker, Kelvin Kao, Patty Bigelow, Jamie Todd Rubin, Chris Billet, Laurel Amberdine, Ami Chopine, John Chu, Jim Stewart, Jessica Wick, and Michael Livingston.

Beth Wodzinski and Sean Markey are heroes of the revolution for letting us stay with them when our moving truck broke down in their town. I wrote the last two chapters of the novel in their guest room. While I was in the throes of revisions, Merrie Haskell let me sit on the porch of her cottage at the lake and patiently listened to me try to explain how glamour worked. She also kept me sane during the last day of my copyedit.

A special thanks to Alex McVey, Julia Rios, John Rhea-Hendrick, Daniel Rice, Tracy Erickson, and Katie Dunneback, who listened to me read the entire novel aloud on Google+ and were better than any SF artificial intelligence in spotting continuity errors or suggesting alternatives to anachronisms in language.

Finally, I could not have written this without my husband, Rob, who was endlessly patient as I was trying to finish the novel while we were moving across-country.

A Note on History and Alternatives
Historians will note that Wellington beat Napoleon a day early in this version of history, at Quatre Bras instead of at Waterloo. I am very much indebted to Nick Foulkes's wonderful book *Dancing into Battle: A Social History of the Battle of Waterloo* for an understanding of what life in Brussels and the surrounding area was like during the Hundred Days. I highly recommend it to anyone interested in the period. I also employed Edith Saunders's *The Hundred Days: Napoleon's Final Wager for Victory* and *Arms and the Woman: The Intimate Journal of an Amorous Baltic Nobleman in the Napoleonic Wars* by Boris Uxkull for some details of camp life.

The town of Binché does, indeed, have a Gilles Day parade, but without dragons, alas. The rest of the festival is true to our history. Mostly.

The very astute reader will note that in *Shades of Milk and Honey*, Vincent's father was a Count. This was a bizarre error, which I'm still not sure how I managed to commit, since there are no Counts in England, not even in my alternate history. He is an Earl and we will assume that Vincent was so overcome during his interview with Jane that he misspoke. Please do me that favour?

In *Glamour in Glass*, I tried to be somewhat more exacting. Because I am something of a geek, I wanted to eliminate as much language as possible from the book that would have been an anachronism. To that end, I created a word list from the complete works of Jane Austen and used that as a spell-check dictionary. It flagged any word that she didn't use, which allowed me to look it up to see if it existed in 1815 or if the meaning had changed. I then either selected an alternate word, or, in a few cases, opted to keep the word because it was clearer than the other options, and I am writing for a modern audience.

Some of the anachronisms that surprised me were words such as: bandstand, belongings, blink, condone, harrumph, knowledgeable, needlepoint, and utilitarian. If you are interested in reading more about the words that I removed from the novel, visit www.maryrobinettekowal.com/deleted-words

By the way, these words did not exist in the Regency

but I decided to keep them anyway: windswept, scissored, and outmass.

There are other anachronisms. There always will be. If you spot one, please let me know by emailing anachronisms @maryrobinettekowal.com. They vex me and I would like to avoid them in future novels.

If you are so inclined, I thought I would mention that I have extras for my readers, including short stories, a game, and behind-the-scene peeks. Simply drop by www.ShadesOf MilkAndHoney.com.

Thank you for reading.

Glamour Glossary

GLAMOUR. This basically means magic. According to the Oxford English Dictionary, the original meaning was "Magic, enchantment, spell" or "A magical or fictitious beauty attaching to any person or object; a delusive or alluring charm." It was strongly associated with fairies in early England. In this alternate history of the Regency, glamour is a magic that can be worked by either men or women. It allows them to create illusions of light, scent, and sound. Glamour requires physical energy in much the same way running up a hill does.

GLAMURAL. A mural that is created using magic.

GLAMOURIST.   A person who works with glamour.

CHASTAIN DAMASK.   A technique which allows a glamourist to create two different images in one location. The effect would be similar to our holographic cards which show first one image, then another depending on the angle at which it is viewed. Invented by M. Chastain in 1814, he originally called this technique a jacquard after the new looms invented by M. Jacquard in 1801. The technique was renamed by Mrs. Vincent as a Chastain Damask in honor of its creator.

ETHER.   Where the magic comes from. Early physicists believed that the world was broken into elements with ether being the highest element. Although this theory is discredited now, the original definition meant "A substance of great elasticity and subtlety, formerly believed to permeate the whole of planetary and stellar space, not only filling the interplanetary spaces, but also the interstices between the particles of air and other matter on the earth; the medium through which the waves of light are propagated. Formerly also thought to be the medium through which radio waves and electromagnetic radiations generally are propagated." (OED). Today you'll more commonly see it as the root of "ethereal," and its meaning is similar.

FOLDS.   The bits of magic pulled out of the ether. Because this is a woman's art, the metaphors to describe it reflect other womanly arts, such as the textiles.

LOINTAINE VISION. French for "distance seeing." It is a tube of glamour that allows one to see things at a distance. The threads must be constantly managed or the image becomes static.

OMBRÉ. A fold of glamour that shades from one colour to another over its length. This technique was later emulated in textile by dip-dying.

NŒUD MARIN. A robust knot used for tying glamour threads. This was originally used by sailors for joining two lines, but adapted by glamourists for similar purposes. In English, this is known as a Carrick Bend.

PETITE RÉPÉTITION. French for "small repetition." This is a way of having a fold of glamour repeat itself in what we would now call a fractal pattern. These occur in nature in the patterns of fern fronds and pinecones.

SPHÈRE OBSCURCIE. French for "invisible bubble." It is literally a bubble of magic to make the person inside it invisible.

Reading Group Guide

- Did you learn any new historical facts from *Glamour in Glass*? If so, what?
- *Glamour in Glass* is set in 1815, after Napoleon's return from exile. What role did this setting play in the story?
- How did you feel when Jane miscarried? Do you think she and Vincent will have children at some point?
- At several points in the book, the narrator directly addresses the reader, a technique which is unusual today. How did this affect your disposition toward the narrator?
- How would you react if someone in the real world created a glamour in front of you?
- How did you feel about Vincent's lies of

omission to Jane? Would you be angry at your own partner if you were placed in a similar situation?

- Jane defines herself as a glamourist, and struggles when she is forced to stop performing glamour due to her pregnancy. What real-world situations does this parallel? Does it remind you of any events in your own life?

- During Jane's rescue of Vincent, she made the choice to work a glamour to hide them, even though this put their child at risk. What would you have done in her place?

- Did you read *Shades of Milk and Honey* before this? How did that affect your reactions to this book?

- *Shades of Milk and Honey* has often been described as being like "Jane Austen with magic." Do you think that *Glamour in Glass* also fits in the Austen mold?

- Kowal addresses both marriage and career in this novel. Do you think either of these is the major theme of the book? If not, what is?